WHERE HE ENDS AND I BEGIN

(2ND EDITION)

Aggressive, physical, and brave, Jake Owens is a small town football hero turned big city cop who passes his time with meaningless encounters believing he can't have who he really wants: Nate Richardson, his best friend since before forever. Thoughtful, quiet, and kind, Nate is a brilliant doctor who has always known who he is and has never been able to shake his crush on loyal, courageous, *straight* Jake.

After a passionate night together, Nate realizes Jake isn't as straight as he assumed, but he worries that what they shared was a fluke, a result of too much closeness for too long. For Jake, the question isn't how they ended up in bed together because he has always known that Nate holds his heart, it's how he'll convince Nate that he wants and needs to stay there.

Word Count: 82,569

COPYRIGHT

REVIEWS

He Completes Me by Cardeno C.: Cardeno C. has written a beautiful and compelling story about the power of love.

— *Fallen Angel Reviews*

Home Again by Cardeno C.: A beautiful story of two men who meet at an early age and depend on each other when they have no one else. It's a fourteen-year journey through Noah and Clark's lives. ...There is just not enough good things to say about Home Again. It is a book that I've read more than once and will probably read again. In fact the series is one of my all-time favorites. I highly recommend Home Again by Cardeno C.

— *Joyfully Jay*

Just What the Truth Is by Cardeno C.: This was, truly, one of the best coming out journeys I've read and I loved taking it with Ben. I adored him and Micah, with the added benefit of seeing Ben grow closer to Noah and Clark. This was an excellent addition to the series and I'm so very glad the author wrote a story for Ben.

— *Rainbow Book Reviews*

Love at First Sight by Cardeno C.: Love at First Sight is a sweet story about finding love at first sight, then trying to actually locate the person, coming home, getting a second chance, and all that happens in between and after. I thoroughly enjoyed reading the book.

— *Night Owl Reviews (Top Pick)*

The One Who Saves Me by Cardeno C.: Ahhh, Cardeno C. always writes an incredible story and this one is no different. The story of Andrew and Caleb is very sweet and touching and at times frustrating.... The sex between them is very hot and sexy and it was wonderful to see that over so many they still fancied each other rotten. I recommend this to those who love a friend to lovers story, deep abiding love, hot sex, heartache, frustration and a belated happy ending.

— *MM Good Book Reviews*

Walk With Me by Cardeno C.: Beans: Walk with Me is the best book Cardeno C has written in the Home series. It was everything I look for in a good book. The characters felt real. The story drew me in from the first page to the last. It was sweet, funny, lovely, and sexy as all hell. ... I laughed so hard my stomach hurt. I laughed even harder the second time I read the book. Yes I have read it four times already...it's that good. And the the sex? Wowza. Hold on to your hats ladies and gentlemen. Cardeno C takes off the brakes and kicks it into high gear. ...This story is a must read.

— *Gay Listed Book Reviews*

DEDICATION

To L.A. Borgaard and Dennis Milholland, who were with
me at the beginning. I appreciate all of your help.
And to the kind readers who took the time to e-mail me and
encourage me to publish my work. I wouldn't have had the
courage to do this without your support. Thank you.

CHAPTER ONE

Jake

I **LOOKED** over at the body next to me—long legs, flat stomach, smooth chest—and closed my eyes, wondering how the fuck I got here. Not literally, of course, because "here" is the bed in my hotel room. I know damn well how I got here. But "here" as in how did I get to a place where I want—no, where I need to touch another man; to feel that stomach, that chest under my fingers and those long legs wrapped around me. And not just any man— Nate. My best friend since the day I was born. And that I mean literally.

OUR MOTHERS had grown up together in a small Southern town. Next door to each other, in fact. My mom was the fifth child in her family—four older brothers. Nate's mom was third in a family of eight, also the only girl. Both wanting to get away from all that testosterone, they'd been inseparable since childhood. Same classes, same Girl Scout troop, same church group. Same everything. So it was no surprise that, when my mom got engaged to her high school sweetheart, Nate's mom followed a month later. They had their weddings two weeks apart, the summer after graduation, bought houses next door to each other in that same town, and then decided together a few years later that it was time to start a family. They announced it to their husbands only *after* they came to the agreement with each other. And yes, I mean "a family." That was how we grew up—like we were one family.

Luckily, my father was very easygoing and Nate's dad? Well, he just wanted to please his wife. Besides, they each knew what they were getting into when they started dating our moms. It was a package deal. You couldn't have one without the other. So it was no surprise to anyone that as soon as Nate's mom went into labor, my mom's contractions started. Several hours later, Nate and I were lying side by side in one hospital bassinet, right in between the two hospital beds occupied respectively by each of our mothers.

The doctor told Nate's mom that something had happened during her labor, fuck if I know what, but the bottom line was she couldn't have more kids. So that was it for my mom too. When I asked her if she ever regretted not having more children because her best friend couldn't, or if she ever wished she had a bigger family, she laughed and said we were a family of six (including Nate and his parents) and she didn't want a family any bigger than that.

So you see: Nate and I were destined to be best friends. I don't even think I had a choice in the matter. Not that I minded, of course. How could anyone mind being friends with Nate? He was always so fucking likable. As long as I can remember, Nate's had nothing but kind words for everyone around him. He's one of those people that everyone is drawn to. And when he's talking to you, you always feel like you're the only person in the room, like you have all of his attention. Well, almost always, that is. When I happen to be in that same room, you have to fucking share Nate's attention with me. Tough shit, I had him first.

Anyway, he always seems to know when I walk into a room. Even if I'm not saying anything and his back is turned. He somehow knows and he stops whatever he's doing (coloring with crayons when we were in preschool, learning how to write his letters in kindergarten, standing at the front of the room in the ninth grade writing the answer to a calculus problem), turns around, flashes me that Nate smile, and then gets back to work.

Of course, that road goes both ways. I can always sense when he's walking into a room too. It's almost like things are empty until that moment and then suddenly they aren't. Suddenly, things seem right. That's when I look up from whatever I'm doing (breaking some fucking toy when we were in preschool, learning how to spell "fuck" when we were in kindergarten, fucking some cheerleader in the corner of a basement full of drunken teenagers when we were in the ninth grade), and I see him walking into the room and, of course, flashing me that Nate smile. That might seem weird, I guess, but no one thought anything of it in our town. Not even that cheerleader when I stopped mid-pump to turn around, catch his eye, and return his smile, before I could focus on her again and finish the deed. After all, we were our mothers' children and everyone knew they were inseparable. Besides, that's just the way it'd always been between us, since the day we were born.

Other than that deep connection, the connection that I can't even put into words, we've always been completely different. And I mean completely fucking different. Where Nate is fair, with blond hair and piercing blue eyes, I have an olive complexion, black hair, and green eyes. He's always been very slender, a swimmer's build, whereas I'm more muscular, big biceps, six-pack even when I'm not in the middle of a sports season. So even though we're about the same height (his six-one to my six-four), I outweigh him by a good fifty pounds.

But the differences aren't only in our appearance. Like I said, Nate has always been Mister Kind, Mister Nice to everyone. I swear he actually rescued a kitten from a tree branch once. A fucking kitten from a tree branch. I'm not all that nice. In fact, I can be a real prick. I have a violent temper and sometimes I just want to hit something or someone, feel the adrenaline running though my body.

After I got into a few fights in high school, some people in our town started thinking I was a little crazy— fuck, maybe they thought I was a lot crazy. The thing is: I didn't care. I've never given a fuck about what most people think, and unless someone is a good friend, and that's just Nate, I don't think about them at all. I've always been too busy with practice (in high school it was football in the fall, basketball in the winter, then baseball in the spring), trying to get into some girl's pants, and, of course, hanging out with Nate. The rest of it, well, it never mattered to me.

The other thing about Nate is that he's a fucking genius. Seriously, even as a kid, he was scary smart. Our small town never had anyone like him go through that school. They didn't know what do with him, how to teach him. Shit, that's why he was always at the front of that room, doing calculus problems on the board—even the teachers couldn't figure that shit out, but to Nate, it all made sense somehow. He once told me he could see the numbers and how they worked together in his head. I never understood what the fuck that meant. I'm surprised they didn't graduate him early, especially when he took the SATs during our sophomore year and got a perfect score. He didn't miss one fucking question. That's how he got offered a full ride to so many colleges.

Now I'm not stupid but I'm no Nate, not even close. Thankfully, I'm not too bad at sports and my rough side turns into an asset on the football field, so I, too, had my choice of a few schools. Senior year, Nate and I looked over our lists of schools, found the ones that matched, and picked a school with a good football team and a great science program. That's how we ended up moving to New York when we were eighteen.

I **STARTED** thinking back to that first day in New York, ten years ago, but I snapped back to the present when Nate sighed and moved a little. It was enough, though. Enough to move the sheet over his leg, enough to have the moonlight shine across his waist, his hips, his cock. It's perfect—pink, smooth, long, and thick when it's hard. Until last night, I had never seen it hard.

All those years of friendship, all those nights sleeping over at each other's house, in each other's bed. Somehow, I had never seen it hard and I sure as hell never thought it would happen like it did last night. Last night—fuck! We've always been almost like one person. I've never known where he ends and where I begin. But that was never truer than last night, when I licked him, sucked him, heard him moan.

My entire body shuddered with that memory when I looked over at Nate. I worried the movement would wake him, but he was still breathing heavily, fast asleep. I closed my eyes, draped my arm over them, and thought about last night. His slender, almost concave stomach, his smooth chest, both heaving as I ran my hand up and felt his skin. I had to run it up because I was on my knees in front of him, opening the buttons on his jeans, pulling them down to his ankles. I could see his excitement as he bulged to get free from his boxer briefs, and I was more than willing to help. First though, I let my face rub over the bulge. Let myself feel him through that fabric that was becoming more and more wet by the minute from his leaking dick. I wanted to taste it. To taste him.

My hands shook with anticipation, with lust for him, as I slowly pulled the briefs down and saw him in the flesh. God, I wanted him so much I couldn't stop shaking, and then it wasn't just my hands. My whole body trembled with anticipation, need, and desire. I tried to calm down. I looked toward the ground, closed my eyes, hoping I could regulate my breathing, but he was so close to me. I could smell him; I could feel his heat against my face. Fuck calming down!

I opened my eyes, took his cock into my mouth, and swallowed him to the root. I don't know how I did that; it was the first time I'd ever touched another man's cock, let alone sucked a man off. But it was Nate, my Nate. My desire to consume him was so desperate, my need to have him be a part of me physically so overwhelming that I think any gag reflex I might have had just shut down, went to hide, knew it had no fucking place in my throat. Not when Nate was there. I bobbed, twirled my tongue around his skin, and then he moaned.

I hadn't ever heard him make that sound, hadn't ever seen him experience that kind of pleasure until that moment, and realizing I had evoked his reaction was almost too much. I almost came right there. I took a moment to calm myself again—thinking, I was twenty-eight fucking years old and that was way too old to be losing my load in my pants.

I pushed the orgasm back and kept going. I took

just the head of his cock into my mouth and sucked hard. Again he moaned, and he put his hand on my head, combed his fingers through my hair, and started crying out my name, over and over again as his hips bucked forward and he pushed himself into me. Slowly at first, then more quickly, still moaning my name, pulling my hair toward him until he was completely buried in my mouth, and then he released.

I could feel his warm liquid in the back of my throat and I swallowed furiously. I didn't want to spill a drop. This was part of Nate in me and I was going to keep all of it. When he stopped pumping into my mouth, I looked up at him with my lips still wrapped around his cock. I didn't want to move. I wanted to keep him in me forever. But then his knees buckled, his eyes closed, and he crumpled to the floor.

I caught him in my arms, and at first I was petrified, but his breathing was regular. I guess he'd had more to drink than I realized, and that, combined with the orgasm, knocked him out. I carried him to the bed. Then I sat and watched him sleep, made sure his breathing remained even and he was okay.

After I was certain he was just tired and sleeping it off, I noticed the wetness in my pants. Fuck, I came from sucking him off. Hopelessly pathetic, I know, but then, he's Nate, my Nate. No one else does it for me like him. No one else ever has, no one else ever will. I just hope, when he wakes up, he'll forgive me for sucking him off while he was so drunk. I just hope he'll understand. Fuck, what a mess.

CHAPTER TWO

Nate

I LEANED my head back in my seat and listened to the plane's engine rumble as it started to taxi down the runway and prepare for takeoff. A week away from the lab, lying on the beach, relaxing, and having a good time. That was what Jake told me as he packed my bags, explaining that he had already cleared it with my boss and that it was ridiculous that I hadn't taken a vacation in a year, especially after all those fourteen-hour days in the lab. And even though there was way too much work for me to take off for a week, I couldn't say no to Jake. No one could ever say no to Jake. He's a force, an incredible, powerful force. I made it through middle school and high school intact solely because of the force that is Jake Owens.

I WAS short and skinny then. Didn't have my biggest growth spurt until I was seventeen—late bloomer, I guess. So I was one of the smaller guys in the class all those years we lived in our small town. I also spent most of my time with my nose in a book or writing formulas, trying to understand the mysteries of science. And if that nerdy picture I'm drawing for you isn't enough to get most guys a few good ass-kickings in high school, the fact that I came out in the eighth grade sure as hell would have.

When I came out, Jake was the first person I told. Seemed only fair, seeing as how he was the reason I knew I was gay—not that I told him that, of course. When puberty hit and the other guys started talking about girls, all I could think about was Jake. They'd look at pictures in magazines of this actress, that singer, and talk about how hot they looked, how they wanted to fuck them, and I could only see Jake. When I'd sit alone in my bed at night, he occupied all my fantasies. Even when I tried to think of someone else, anyone else, when I masturbated, my mind always came back to Jake before I could get off.

So that was how I figured out I was gay. The realization terrified me. I didn't know what to do. So, of course, I had to talk to Jake. It would only be real after I said it out loud to him and I could only figure out what to do by talking with him. Math, science, things I found in books, those things I could do on my own, understand all by myself. But life, people, my own fucking feelings, those things required my whole person, and I wasn't whole without him.

I'd been trying to get the nerve up to tell him all night. We were out with a bunch of kids from school. Everyone was drinking, hooking up. Jake was on the couch with some girl—hard to remember which one because he spent time on some couch or some bed or some corner with every cute girl at our school, and the neighboring schools, at some point or another before we moved away. Anyway, she was laughing at everything he said, twirling her fingers through her hair, basically working straight off the "I want you to fuck me right now" playbook, and then Jake looked up at me sitting across the room and told her that he had to take off. She was stunned, but he just got up, adjusted his obvious boner (guess that flirting was working), walked over to me, squatted down so that we were eye to eye, and said, "Let's get out of here. You look like you need to talk."

I was quiet as we walked home, trying to find the words, trying to gather the courage. We were spending the night at my house that night—we did that every weekend, either slept at my house or his. We had been doing that as long as I could remember, so it really didn't seem weird when we walked into my room and he immediately started taking off his clothes. Of course, I chose the moment that he had his underwear down and was standing fully naked in front of me, rummaging through the drawer where he kept some clothes, looking for sweats or pajamas, to blurt out, "Jake, I think I'm gay."

Now, you announce that to almost any other thirteen-year-old boy in a small Southern town and you're likely to get a beat-down. Make that double when the guy you're announcing it to is nude and standing in your bedroom. Not Jake, though. He just stopped rummaging through the drawer, walked over, and sat down next to me on the bed, wearing nothing but a smile.

"Gay? Cool. Hey, do you have any sweats or something that'll fit me? I think I wore my last clean pajamas last time I was here and it's too fucking cold to sleep naked."

And just like that, all my fears went away. Jake didn't mind, didn't seem to think anything was wrong with me, so I decided nothing was wrong with me.

The next day I told my parents (of course by "my parents" I mean both sets—Jake's and mine). They were surprised but not too upset, except for their fear that I'd have a hard time at school. Our moms started telling me that maybe I should keep it to myself. Jake had been sitting on the couch next to me while I was telling our parents, but he was reading a magazine and I didn't think he was listening until that moment.

He put down his magazine, looked up at our parents, and said, "No one will hurt Nate, no one will tease him. He outshines every kid at that school and he has no reason to be ashamed of who he is because he is fucking incredible." Then he picked his magazine back up and kept reading. That was it.

At school, I stopped pretending I was interested in girls. It didn't take long before everyone knew I was gay, and I didn't deny it, but like Jake promised, they never hurt me, never even teased me. Not once. That was because of Jake. He was the most popular kid in school, best athlete, best-looking, and he had a mean left hook— even then. People knew better than to mess with him, and I was his best friend, so I was safe by association.

THE PLANE landed with a bit of a shake, waking me up.

"We're here, sleepyhead. Get ready for a fan-fucking-tastic week."

That deep voice poured over me as his hand gently patted my thigh.

"Wake up, Nathaniel."

I was already awake but I didn't want to let him know. I hoped that he'd keep his hand on my thigh a bit longer. Eventually, I looked up and saw him smile.

"I'll get our bags. You look beat."

And he did—he took both suitcases and walked us through the crowd, always making sure I was still beside him. Then he hailed us a cab and opened my door for me before putting the suitcases in the trunk.

"I saw online that there's a great sushi place right by our hotel. I thought we'd check it out tonight. I mean, if you're up to it. Shit, Nate, you look so tired."

Now you tell me, how can I not love him? I mean, the guy doesn't even like fish, for fuck's sake, but he's looking up sushi restaurants because it's my favorite. He holds my door open, carries my luggage, feels genuine concern over my well-being. Is it any surprise that, at twenty-eight years old, I've never been able to maintain a relationship for longer than a few weeks?

No one can hold a candle to Jake and it doesn't take long for them to realize that. And I could never pretend otherwise. I would always rather be with him, sitting on the couch watching a movie, than out at some bar getting a blow job in a back room. Even when I was getting those blow jobs, I'd always close my eyes and see his face. That's still the only way I can finally get off. And when that's done, I want to go home, always hoping he's still up so we can talk about our day.

I think most gay guys at some point or another have a thing for some straight guy, a hopeless crush that eventually ends in heartbreak or at least extreme frustration. Now imagine if that straight-guy crush had been going on as long as you could remember. Imagine if that was the only man you'd ever loved, ever cared about, ever really wanted.

It was hopeless. I always knew that. Jake likes girls. He'd slept with enough of them to fill one of those football stadiums he played in all through college. Well, slept isn't the right word. He'd fuck them, then always come back to our apartment to sleep afterward. The point is, though, Jake likes girls and I have a dick. So the situation is, was, and always would be hopeless.

I always knew that and I'd resigned myself to it. I had decided long ago that I could live my life with him as my best friend. That it was enough somehow. I'm not sure what changed in that cab as we pulled away from the airport, but something did. Something in me snapped and I was mad as hell.

He could tell something was up all through dinner at the sushi restaurant. If my foul mood and dirty looks weren't enough, the fact that I was drinking more sake than I was eating sushi surely tipped him off.

"Hey, man, slow down on that liquor a bit, okay? I don't want you to get sick."

He was speaking softly, looking across the table with concern in his eyes. I almost felt guilty, until he reached over and stroked my arm.

"Talk to me, Nate. What's wrong?"

My skin felt like it was on fire. It always felt that way when he touched me. His fingers on my arm turned me on in a way that nothing else ever had, and I mean nothing—not even a tight ass wrapped around my cock. Nothing.

"Don't fucking touch me, Jake!" I pulled my arm away and stood up too quickly, knocking the chair down. "Don't you ever fucking touch me again!"

I stormed out of the restaurant and back up to our hotel room, slammed the door to the room behind me, kicked my shoes off against the wall, and marched to the closet. He'd unpacked all of our clothes when we'd gotten to the room, giving me time to rest. As I flipped my suitcase open and started ripping my clothes from the hangers, his kindness just pissed me off more.

It was just like him—always taking care of me, always protecting me. He loved me, I knew that, but not like I needed him to love me. He loved me just enough to keep me from ever being able to love anyone else. I was stuffing the last of my things into the suitcase when I heard him come in and sit down on the bed behind me.

"What did I do, Nate? I'm so sorry. Please forgive me. What did I do?"

His voice was so soft, almost trembling. I had

never heard him sound so vulnerable, but I was too tired, too mad, too drunk to calm down.

I turned to him with rage in my eyes and yelled, "I'll always be alone because of you!"

Pain and confusion crossed his face.

"You're not alone, Nate. I'm here. I'll always be here with you. You know that. I'll never leave you."

I was sobbing by then.

"Yes, you're here, you've always been here, but it's not enough, Jake. I need more."

And I knew it was true. I *did* need more. I needed a complete relationship. I needed someone to hold me and touch me and love me. And I needed to love that someone back. The problem was…I couldn't love anyone but him.

"More? What do you mean, Nate? I'll give you anything you need, buddy. Please, just talk to me."

If I had been sober and calm, I probably would've explained it to him. I would've said that I was in love with him, that I'd always been in love with him. But I wasn't sober and I sure as hell wasn't calm, so instead I just said, "I need a blow job, Jake. Still think you can give me anything I need?"

I started to turn back toward my suitcase when he got up from the bed and dropped to his knees in front of me. It was such a shock that, at first, I couldn't process what he was doing, but then his hand reached under my shirt and rubbed across my stomach and chest, leaving a trail of heat so powerful I started to sweat.

I ripped off my shirt to cool down, then realized he must have been using his other hand to unbutton my jeans because they were down on the floor. I gasped as his hand caressed my cock through my briefs, and then his face rubbed across me before he pulled my briefs to the floor. My naked cock grazed his face and I almost exploded, but then he stopped.

I saw him lower his head and close his eyes, and I thought, *he can't do it. I disgust him. What the fuck was I thinking?*

Then he opened his eyes, looked up at me, and swallowed my cock whole. All my senses came alive. It was like I could feel his tongue and his mouth all over my body. I moaned, and he stopped moving.

I realized then, at some level, that he couldn't be enjoying it. He was just doing what he'd always done—he was taking care of me. I should've stopped him. I should've told him a blow job was way beyond the bounds of any friendship, even ours. But I couldn't. I needed him so desperately, and the thought that he'd stop was more than I could handle. So when he kept licking, kept sucking, I decided to accept his token of friendship.

Knowing I'd never get the chance again, I let go completely and lost myself in the feelings. I stroked his hair and pulled him toward me as I pushed into his mouth. I remember hearing moans and then realizing they were mine.

"Jake, Jake, oh God, Jake."

I came hard. It was the most powerful orgasm I'd ever had and I felt myself falling into the warm, safe darkness.

CHAPTER THREE

Nate

I **WOKE** up and looked around, trying to remember where I was and why I had that dull, thumping feeling in my head. I rubbed my eyes and it hit me like a slap in the face. I'd been so mean, so childish, so damn selfish. Oh my God, what did I make him do? How could I have pushed him to suck me off when all he was trying to do was talk to me, help me, be my friend?

I got up, surprised my head didn't hurt more than just the faint throbbing I was feeling. Looking around the room, I noticed the clothes I had worn the previous night were no longer in a crumpled pile on the floor. My suitcase wasn't on the other bed anymore either, and all the clothes I'd stuffed into it during my rage were back neatly on the hangers in the closet. For a moment, I wondered whether none of it'd actually happened or if it was all just a nightmare. But I wasn't that drunk and I knew the previous night wasn't a nightmare, or should I say dream? Well, whatever it was, I knew it'd happened.

I got into the shower. The warm water felt good running over my head and body, and I rubbed the soap all over, pausing a little over the scar on my stomach from the accident.

The time after that accident was the worst time of our lives. Neither of us was hurt too badly, physically. Jake mostly had bumps and bruises, and I was fine once they stitched me up and gave me some blood.

Jake's parents weren't so lucky though. They both died on impact. I was sad, of course. It was almost like losing my own parents. But mostly, I was worried for Jake.

He didn't sleep well for a long time after that. I would hear him crying out during the night, so I'd run into his room and see him flipping around on the bed, trapped in some nightmare. Then I'd crawl into bed next to him, wrap my arms around him, and whisper in his ear.

"It's okay, Jake. I'm here. It's all going to be okay."

He'd calm down after that, press his head into my chest, and sleep peacefully. Neither of us said anything after those nights when we'd wake up in bed together, holding each other. We just got up, got ready for school, and went about our days.

I had a hard time concentrating, though, after spending all night pressed against him. It all made me want him even more, and then I'd be angry at myself for getting off on his pain. That was what it was, after all. He was in pain and needed a friend after losing his parents, and I couldn't take care of him without sporting a painful boner the entire time. The whole thing put me on edge.

I tried asking him about the nightmares and about

the accident—I was unconscious from the moment the
truck hit us until after my surgery, so I don't remember
any of it—but he looked uncomfortable and said he'd
rather not talk about it. I didn't want to press him, so I
let it go. After all, what was there to say? A truck driver
fell asleep, hit our car, and killed his parents on impact.
Anyone would have nightmares after that.

I shut off the water and toweled myself. I'd just
finished getting dressed and was starting to wonder
where Jake had gone when the door opened, and he
walked in, holding a paper bag and a huge cup of coffee.
He set the bag and the coffee on the table, tossed me
a bottle of aspirin, and said, "You don't look so bad,
considering how much you had to drink last night. Still,
I thought a couple of aspirin, a cup of coffee, and some
food in your stomach would help."

I looked into his eyes and tried to read his
emotions. He seemed nervous, guilty. Well, I guess that
was what happened when you forced a straight guy to
suck your cock.

"Look, Jake, about last night..."

I was going to apologize, blame it all on the alcohol
and the long nights in the lab over the past few weeks. I
wasn't ready to tell him the truth: that my feelings for
him had somehow grown to the point where I could no
longer focus on anything but him. That my desperation
for him was so all-consuming I couldn't function without
some physical release, some way to let my body express
what my heart felt. But he cut me off.

"I'm so sorry, Nate. Really, I feel like shit about

it. Let me grab a shower and then we can talk. I feel disgusting and I just need to get cleaned up."

He walked into the bathroom and closed the door. His words sliced through me. Disgusting. I made him feel disgusting. I felt tears stinging my eyes.

Jake

I MUST'VE fallen asleep for a few hours, because when I opened my eyes, the sun had started to stream in through the sheer balcony curtains. Nate was lying next to me, still asleep and still naked.

I remembered how good his skin had felt the previous night when I touched him and I wanted desperately to reach out and run my fingers over his chest again, but I didn't want to wake him. Instead, I got up, picked up his clothes, lying in a pile by the closet, and unpacked his suitcase. I hoped, when he woke up, we'd talk and make up. Then I threw on some clothes and quietly left the room.

The morning air was still cool and there was a light breeze that felt good across my face. I remembered seeing a coffee shop not too far from the hotel as we were driving in, so I figured I'd go there to get us some breakfast and coffee. Lots of coffee. I'd always tried to take it easy on the stuff, because it's not really good for athletic performance and I'd spent so much of my life on a football field, but Nate was a caffeine addict. I actually considered having an intervention when he seemed to be living off the stuff, but settled for a vacation, thinking he just needed to get away from the lab and relax.

He'd been wound so tight. He was so edgy. I'd never seen him like that. Not even after our parents died. Well, technically they were my parents, but then, we'd always been one family.

IT WAS the summer after our sophomore year in college, and we both came home to visit for a few weeks. Nate's dad had had a business dinner one night and his mom went with him. My parents thought it would be fun to take us to a new restaurant that'd opened in the next town over. It was pretty rural where we grew up, so a new restaurant in the next town was kind of a big thing.

We had a great night, laughing and catching up. Nate and I told my folks all about school, New York, our apartment, everything. We finished eating and started the drive home. It was pretty late by then and the road home was deserted. Suddenly, I saw a bright flash and we were flying through the air. I felt steel across my body and heard crunching so loud I couldn't figure out what was going on; then everything was silent.

I looked around and realized our car had been thrown off the road. The next thing I noticed was blood.

Lots of blood. My parents were in the front seat of the car, and their doors were so crumpled that they were wedged in with no way to get out. My mom was cut up and unconscious. My dad was in the driver's seat, moaning. And then there was Nate. He was slumped next to me with a piece of metal through his stomach and blood gushing out.

I threw off my seatbelt, pressed on his wound, and desperately tried to stop the bleeding. I knew we weren't too far from town. I could open my door and run to get help. I told my dad I'd go just as soon as I stopped Nate's bleeding. He wouldn't make it otherwise. He had lost so much blood. My father turned his head and assessed the situation. Then in a voice tired and weak, he spoke.

"You're not going to be able to stop the bleeding with anything I have in this car, Jake. That gash is too big, too deep. I don't have anything to close it, and without your hands putting pressure on him, the ambulance won't make it back here in time to save him. Not in time to save *him*."

I looked at the front seat and understood what my father meant. My mom was still unconscious and breathing, but very slowly. My dad had his hand across his stomach and I could tell he was in a lot of pain. They were hurt too, really hurt, and if I left and ran into town, help might arrive in time to save my parents. But not in time to save Nate.

I knew what I had to do. I told my father I loved him but he couldn't hear me because he'd passed out. Then I gently picked Nate up, squeezed us out of the car, and ran, all the while keeping my hands pressed firmly over his wound in order to curb the bleeding.

I'd always been a fast runner, but I'm not usually running at night while carrying a man in my arms. It slowed me down, but I didn't stop until I got to the hospital. When I came through the door, I screamed for help and they came running. I put Nate on a gurney, told them his blood type, and only removed the pressure I was putting on him to curb the bleeding when they started wheeling him down the hall. Then I told them where to find my parents and explained they needed help right away. Even though I knew it'd be too late.

I just hadn't been able to make good time, because I was carrying Nate and focusing on putting pressure on his wound. I knew by the time the ambulance got to my parents, they'd be dead. But I also knew that Nate would make it. Nate, my Nate. I knew he'd be all right.

I'D BEEN wearing the same clothes since the previous morning, and I knew I smelled pretty ripe. I couldn't sit and talk to Nate, couldn't apologize for taking advantage of him while I still had the cum stuck to my body reminding me of just how pathetic I was—taking advantage of my best friend while he was clearly going through a hard time and after he'd had way too much to drink.

I gave Nate the food and coffee and took a quick shower, then wrapped a towel around my waist, and opened the door.

"Hey, man. Can we talk?"

Nate was sitting on a chair, drinking his coffee and eating the plain bagel I'd brought him. He wasn't yelling at me anymore or shooting daggers with his eyes, so I thought maybe everything would be okay. I even let myself hope he'd liked it, that he'd want to do it again, that he'd want me. But then he looked up, raked his eyes over my body, and I saw anger again.

"Damn it, Jake, put some clothes on! How can I talk to you when you look like that?"

My heart sank into my stomach.

"I get it, Nate. You're not attracted to me. You've never been attracted to me. But I'm not such a monster that seeing me with my clothes off should repulse you to the point of losing the power of speech."

Shaking, I turned toward the closet.

"Not attracted to you?"

His voice was quieter; he was no longer shouting at me.

"What are you talking about, Jake? How could anyone *not* be attracted to you? You're perfect."

Was that sarcasm? Was he fucking with me? I didn't think so. He sounded sincere.

"Look, Nate, it's okay. We can't choose who we're attracted to. But let's not pretend, okay? I've been in love with you since we were kids, and you know it. You've never given me a second look. Hell, when you told me you were gay, I was so happy. I thought maybe you felt about me the way that I felt about you. But then when I

sat down next to you—completely naked, by the way—
you didn't touch me, you didn't even look at me. So I got
the message loud and clear—we're just friends. And I've
lived with that for the last fifteen years. I've never gotten
in your way, even when you left those bars with every
Tony, Bill, and Tom that walked in the door. And I never
touched you. But last night—"

He interrupted me.

"How do you know about Tony? I told you about
Bill and I dated Tom for a few weeks, but how do you
know about Tony?"

Shit. Shit. Shit. He hadn't ever told me about Tony
and now I was caught. Oh well, I was already waving the
"how could you be more hopelessly pathetic" flag so I
may as well raise it to full mast.

"I know about Tony because I saw you with him
at the bar. I was following you, making sure you were
okay. It wasn't that long after the accident and that bar
is in a sketchy part of town. Frankly, you should thank
me, because if I hadn't been there, you might have had
an unwelcome introduction to some homophobic pricks
that were scoping out the place."

I hadn't meant to tell him about those guys outside
the bar. I was frustrated and being defensive, so I'd said
too much. I needed to calm down. I sat on the bed and put
my head in my hands. He was quiet for a long time, then
he sat down next to me and put his hand on my shoulder.

"How can you think I've never been attracted to
you?"

We were sitting right next to each other on the

bed and I was still wearing nothing but that towel. I could smell his hair and feel his body heat radiating against my skin. And his eyes, the look in his eyes. I couldn't control my body, couldn't stop it from reacting to him, and it was pretty clear to both of us what he does to me because my cock was rock-hard and pushing up against the towel, making a very obvious tent.

He looked down at my lap and I thought he'd laugh at me or yell at me to get dressed again, but instead, he reached his hand over and untied my towel, letting it drape on the bed, and exposed my erection. Then he looked back into my eyes, stroked my face, leaned in, and kissed me.

CHAPTER FOUR

Nate

I COULD hear the water running in the shower and I tried to fight back the tears. Why was I crying anyway? Did I expect him to think sucking my cock was anything other than disgusting? I'd never even kissed a girl, and believe me, if someone forced me to take part in some below-the-belt mouth-to-vagina action, I'd probably vomit.

I put a few aspirin in my mouth and swallowed them down with the coffee. Then I took a bagel out of the bag and munched. I started feeling more calm and even somewhat at peace with what'd happened the previous night.

I'd been a complete jerk, but in my gut I knew Jake would accept my apology and we'd move forward. We'd been friends too long for one drunken mistake to permanently damage our friendship. I knew that.

The bathroom door opened and I heard Jake asking me if we could talk. I looked up, ready to start into my apology, and then caught sight of him. His hair was damp and tousled, he had a towel wrapped lightly around his hipbones, and there were drops of water sliding down his lean, muscled chest. He looked like a walking wet dream.

My mouth went dry and I told him to get dressed. I mean, seriously, how could we have a conversation when all I could think about was bending him over the first flat surface I could find? All of a sudden, he started shouting.

"I get it, Nate. You're not attracted to me. You've never been attracted to me. But I'm not such a monster that seeing me with my clothes off should repulse you to the point of losing the power of speech."

I didn't understand what had made him so angry, and I certainly didn't understand why he said I wasn't attracted to him. I'd been nothing *but* attracted to him for as long as I could remember. That was why I wanted him to put his clothes on.

"Not attracted to you? What are you talking about, Jake? How could anyone *not* be attracted to you? You're perfect."

"Look, Nate, it's okay. We can't choose who we're attracted to. But let's not pretend, okay? I've been in love with you since we were kids, and you know it. You've never given me a second look. Hell, when you told me you were gay, I was so happy. I thought maybe you felt about me the way that I felt about you. But then when I sat down next to you—completely naked, by the way—you didn't touch me, you didn't even look at me. So I got the message loud and clear—we're just friends. And I've lived with that for the last fifteen years. I've never gotten in your way, even when you left those bars with every

Tony, Bill, and Tom that walked in the door. And I never touched you. But last night...."

My mind was reeling. Did he just say that he's in love with me? That I'm the one not interested in *him*? I had so many questions. He's straight, how could he be in love with me? And how on earth could he think I'm not interested in him? My God, I practically needed full-body restraints to keep from jumping all over him.

I actually felt dizzy from all the thoughts and emotions bouncing through me. I didn't know how to formulate my questions, so I started with an easy one.

"How do you know about Tony? I told you about Bill and I dated Tom for a few weeks, but how do you know about Tony?"

Tony was the first guy I let fuck me. I didn't really like him all that much, but it was during the time when Jake was having all those post-accident nightmares, so I was spending my nights in his bed and my days with near-constant erections. I was so damn horny I couldn't see straight, and Tony was there. I know that wasn't a great reason to have sex with someone, but I figured waiting for true love would mean dying a virgin, because I'd never love anyone other than Jake.

"I know about Tony because I saw you with him at the bar. I was following you, making sure you were okay. It wasn't that long after the accident and that bar is in a sketchy part of town. Frankly, you should thank me, because if I hadn't been there, you might've had an unwelcome introduction to some homophobic pricks that were scoping out the place."

I froze as I remembered the night Tony and I had met. We'd been inside, drinking and flirting. He asked me if I wanted to go back to his place and I agreed. I'm really not a complete slut, I don't usually go home with random guys, but like I explained, there were extenuating circumstances, namely my extreme and uncontrollable horniness.

When we stepped out of the bar, I noticed three guys lurking around across the street. I started getting nervous when they crossed over to our side, but then we walked around the corner and didn't see them again. When I got home that night, I went into Jake's room to check on him, and he was lying awake in his bed. His knuckles were scraped and bloody, he had a split lip, and the side of his face was all bruised. I could tell he'd also taken some hits to his body from the way he was moving, and I just hoped he hadn't broken a rib. I went into the kitchen and brought him a bag of frozen peas.

"Put these on your face. Did the Incredible Hulk catch you fucking his girlfriend or something? I think this is the first time you've ever lost a fight."

He sort of smirked at me.

"What makes you think I lost this time? You should see the other guys. You want to watch a movie or something? I don't feel like going to sleep yet."

So he'd been following me, saw me leaving the bar with Tony, noticed the group of guys following us, and stepped in. I remembered those guys. All three of them were big and mean-looking.

I wasn't surprised Jake would defend me, even if it

meant taking a beating from three big guys all by himself. It was actually just like him. Maybe he really *was* in love with me. Was it actually possible that the only thing standing in our way was his incomprehensible belief that I wasn't interested in him?

He was sitting on the bed, holding his head in his hands. I sat down next to him, put my hand on his shoulder so he'd look up, and peered into his eyes.

"How can you think I've never been attracted to you?"

There was love and longing in his eyes, and then I looked down and noticed his dick straining against his towel. I wanted to see it, to prove to myself that his body was actually reacting to me the way mine had always reacted to him, so I reached over and untied his towel, leaving him completely naked.

My God, he was so beautiful; so unbelievably beautiful. I looked back into his eyes, stroked his face in the spot those thugs had bruised all those years ago, and leaned in, letting my lips brush lightly over his. I half expected him to pull away, but instead he whimpered and leaned into me. So I kept going, kissing him softly a few times and letting my tongue slowly wander over his lips until he opened his mouth to let me in.

He tasted so good, minty and manly all at once. I pressed him back on the bed, so he was lying down with his legs and feet hanging over the edge of the mattress with me leaning over him, straddling him. I had fantasized about making out with Jake so many times in so many ways, but none of my fantasies were like that. He was being so gentle, so soft. It was a strange juxtaposition to the tough guy who was always cussing, looking for a fight, and knocking people around on the field. There was nothing rough about Jake on that bed. He was lying back, still whimpering, giving me soft kisses and reaching his tongue out of his mouth to lick mine. His arms were wrapped around me and his fingers were gently combing through my hair.

We stayed like that for a long time, tasting each other, then I pulled away from his mouth and looked deep into his eyes. There were so many emotions flowing through me, and I realized I was trembling a little. He noticed and looked concerned.

"What's wrong, Nate? Are you okay? You're shaking."

I still had a lot of questions. I couldn't understand why my straight best friend was all of a sudden lying naked beneath me with a very large erection pressing against me. But those questions would have to wait.

"I'm fine. No, better than fine. I'm shaking because I'm happy. Really happy."

I leaned back in and gently kissed his lips, his nose, his forehead, his cheeks, his eyelids; I covered his face with gentle kisses and little licks. I moved around to his ears and sucked on his lobes. His whimpering got louder and more frequent. Encouraged, I moved down and licked his neck, letting my hand start wandering over his body, exploring him.

The whimpers turned into moans when I reached his chest and took his nipples into my mouth, sucking on one and then the other. He arched his body up against me and breathed heavily. I kept sucking for a while and then started licking his nipples, his stomach, all the way down the trail. When I reached his dick, I dragged my face against it, letting it caress my cheek. Then I scooted down off the bed, kneeled between his legs and licked up and down the length of his cock. It was long and thick, just like Jake. Probably the biggest I'd ever seen in real life, but it wasn't porno-size, thank God.

His near constant moans and thrusting hips told me more than words that he was enjoying my ministrations. I put his legs over my shoulders and raised myself so his ass was off the bed, then leaned in and ran my tongue down his crack. He tasted soapy and clean. I could tell he liked my tongue in his ass, because he gasped, and his hands were tightly grasping the sheets. I kept licking up and down the length of his ass, and then stopped at his hole and jabbed my tongue in, slowly at first, and then more quickly, until I was pushing the length of my tongue inside him.

Jake's whimpers and moans were loud and uneven. He was gasping for air.

"Nate, oh God, Nate, that feels so good. Oh God, I can't hold back, ugh!"

He came, shot after shot, all over his stomach and chest. I put his legs back down, stood up, and bent over him to lick up all of his release. His face was a mixture of amazement and arousal, his breathing still heavy as I made sure that I got all of his seed, leaving him completely clean. Then I stood up, looked down at him, and smiled.

"Let me get these clothes off. They're not so clean anymore."

That action had been so arousing to me, that I had come somewhere along the way.

"Besides, I want to feel my body against yours."

I stripped off my clothes and we both got under the covers. We were lying on our sides facing each other, our hands caressing each other's back and arms. We stayed that way for a long time, quietly touching, looking, and thinking.

Eventually, I started talking.

"I'm really confused here, Jake. You've always been interested in girls. Seriously, man, do you even have a count of how many girls you've dated over the years? When did you become attracted to guys?"

He didn't even hesitate before answering me.

"I never dated anyone, Nathaniel, not anyone. But if you mean how many girls I've fucked, I lost count after I ran out of fingers and toes. And I'm not attracted to guys. Well, other than you, that is."

Well, he managed to answer my questions, but I was no closer to understanding what was going on. If anything, I was even more confused.

"I don't understand what that means. I never thought you could want me because you were always all over every cute girl in sight. And I don't understand how you could be attracted to me if you're not into guys. I really need you to fill in the pieces for me."

He sat up, slid back, and rested on the pillows leaning on the headboard, and then he looked down at me and smiled.

"Come here."

I scooted up so my head was resting on his stomach, and he moved his fingers through my hair again.

"I was really into you when we were kids. I mean, as soon as puberty hit, sleeping over at each other's house took on a whole new level of excitement for me. I didn't know whether you felt the same way, and I wasn't sure how to figure it out. Then when you told me you were into guys, but you didn't seem into me at all, I figured that was it. You didn't want me.

"I'd never even kissed a girl before then. But, I don't know, I have a high sex drive, I guess, and after the day you came out, I figured there was no reason to hold back waiting for you. I mean, you made it pretty clear that you weren't interested in me, so I figured I'd look for release somewhere else. And as far as why I chose girls instead of guys... Well, other guys just don't do it for me. They remind me too much of what I don't have."

I was trying to wrap my mind around what he was saying.

"What you don't have? What, like some sort of competition? I've seen your equipment now, and I doubt very much there are many guys who have anything close to what you have."

I let my hand graze over his dick as I spoke, and he hardened up a little in my hand, immediately causing the same reaction in my groin. Jake laughed.

"I don't mean what I don't have physically. I mean having sex with another guy would just remind me of you. *You* are what I didn't have. I honestly don't think I could even get it up for another guy. I think I'd be too depressed thinking about you, wishing I was with you. My mind would never relax enough to let my body get into it. You're all I've ever wanted, Nate, and if I couldn't have you, there was no point in being with other men. Girls are different. They don't make me think of you, so I can fuck them. But that's all it ever was with any of them—just sex. I never loved them or even really liked them all that much. You know that, right?"

It was true. Jake was never particularly nice to any of the girls that streamed in and out of his life. I don't remember him ever meeting their parents or cooking them dinner or doing whatever other romantic gestures guys do with their girlfriends. In fact, I don't think he ever even let them into his bed.

Years earlier, we'd had a big New Year's Eve party at our place. I was dating Tom back then, and he was at the party, hanging all over me all night. It was super-crowded and everyone was pretty drunk. I'd lost track of Jake sometime before midnight, and when the clock struck twelve, Tom leaned over and gave me a big kiss. I caught Jake's eye across the room and he made his way through the crowd. He came right up to me and whispered into my ear.

"Happy new year, old friend. We made it through another one together. Here's to many more."

Then he kissed me lightly on the cheek and walked away.

The next morning Tom and I woke up a little

hungover, and I smelled coffee and breakfast. We stumbled out of the room, and Jake was in the kitchen, flipping pancakes.

"Morning, guys. I thought you might be hungry after all that energy you exerted last night."

I guess we'd been pretty loud. And by "we" I meant Tom. That man was a major screamer in bed.

"Sorry, Jake. Did we keep you up?"

I blushed. Then Tom jumped in.

"I'm sure Jake was having his own fun last night, Nate. That cute blonde girl wouldn't leave his side all night. Where is she, still asleep in your bed?"

Jake seemed upset and he clenched his jaw. Then he glared at Tom.

"I don't do sleepovers, man. The only person I like to see in the morning is Nate."

He flipped the last few pancakes onto a plate, slid it over to us, and headed back to his room.

"See you guys later. I need to grab a shower and head out."

That entire exchange, the New Year's kiss, the conversation over breakfast, all of it, suddenly took on a new meaning in my head. Had Jake been jealous that entire time? Had he been into me while I was keeping him up, listening to me having sex with other guys, making him feed them breakfast? How could I have missed that all those years?

"You said you're in love with me, that you've been in love with me since we were kids. But why didn't you ever let me know how you felt about me?"

He seemed genuinely surprised by my question, maybe even a little hurt. He put his hand gently on my chin and raised my face so we were looking into each other's eyes.

"You don't know how I feel about you? I try to show you how much I care about you every day. How can you not see that?"

I thought back to how much Jake took care of me. How he'd always taken care of me, stood up for me. How he'd been there for me every step of the way throughout our lives. I'd always known he cared about me; that much was true. I guess I just hadn't realized his feelings toward me were romantic. I'd thought it was a deep friendship, brotherly love. But I surely didn't know he was *in* love with me.

"Of course I know you care about me. I just thought you were being a friend. I guess what I mean is, why didn't you tell me you love me, Jake?"

"I can't believe you didn't know. And I have told you that I love you. I've told you more than once. Do you want a rundown?"

I didn't respond. I just looked at him and stayed quiet, so he kept talking.

"Okay, there was the time you and that dickwad Tom broke up. I never understood what you saw in that fucker, anyway. So you had gotten home from your date with him and you seemed pretty upset, talking about how you screwed up another relationship, how you couldn't manage to keep anything going for longer than a few weeks, asking me what was wrong with you. I told you there's nothing wrong with you, you're fucking perfect, and you're great at relationships, with the proof being that you managed to tolerate my pathetic ass all these years. And then I told you that I love you, that I'd always love you."

He scooted back down on the bed while he was talking so he was lying flat on his back and I was propped up on his chest, looking into his eyes.

"I remember that night. I just didn't understand what you meant, Jake. I'm sorry. I'm so sorry."

And I *was* sorry. I was sorry for obviously hurting him all those years and I was sorry for hurting myself. But mostly, I was sorry for the time we'd lost. My eyes got misty and I could feel a few tears slide down my face. He kissed my cheeks and wiped my tears away with his tongue.

"It's okay, Nathaniel. Hey, they say friendship is the best foundation for a relationship. With the years of friendship we have under our belts, we're bound to have the best relationship ever. That is, if you want to have a relationship with me. What do you say, Nate?"

Was he actually asking me, like there could be any doubt?

"I say yes, Jake."

I snuggled into his chest, closed my eyes, and fell asleep with his arms wrapped around me.

CHAPTER FIVE

Jake

I HADN'T slept much the previous night because I'd been so worried about Nate and everything that happened at dinner...and after dinner. So in the morning, after we talked and then some, I fell into a deep sleep with Nate cuddled up in my arms.

I had never been happier. Having Nate respond to me the way he had—kissing me, licking me—I finally felt like I understood what the big deal was about sex. Kind of a weird thing for me to say, seeing as how I'd had a lot of sex. Seriously, a lot of sex. But it had always been just a physical release for me. None of my sexual experiences were particularly gratifying or memorable. And as soon as I'd finished, I'd always wanted to get away as quickly as possible. But that morning, the last thing I wanted to do was get away. I wanted to melt into Nate, have him melt into me, so we could combine somehow and I'd never be apart from him for even a second.

As amazing as Nate is—incredibly smart, handsome, kind, fun—he's somewhat insecure. I think it stems from the fact that he was a small guy growing up and spent so much time in his books. Our hometown was kind of machoville. Guys were into sports and cars and physical labor. Nate never fit that mold, and I suspect it made him feel like he was somehow less than other people. The truth is, he was fucking hot.

Nate would get into some book or scientific theory and then he'd talk to me about it, try to explain the details. It was such a turn-on when he did that, because his unbelievable intelligence would shine through. I was in awe of him. And his eyes always had such depth; they look like crystal-blue pools I wanted to jump into and drown in.

I'd always thought Nate knew how I felt about him. I mean, he sure as hell had a way of knowing how I felt about everything else, and I hadn't exactly been hiding the fact that I was in love with him. But that morning in the hotel, I really put my feelings out there, told him I was in love with him, that I'd always been in love with him. Although he didn't exactly reciprocate, at least not verbally, his actions and the look in his eyes showed his love and desire. At least, I thought that was what it was.

I wasn't sure whether it was wishful thinking on my part, but really, the way he'd made me feel, the way he'd made love to me, it was so passionate. I'd never experienced anything like it and it made me believe he shared my feelings, at least on some level, even if he hadn't said so. Maybe his insecurities were keeping him from telling me his feelings. I'd been waiting for Nate to want me my entire life, and now that we are finally heading down that path, I'd do everything and anything

I could to show him how I felt about him—how much I wanted him, needed him, loved him. Maybe if I showed him what he meant to me, how much I cared for him, he'd want me too. Those thoughts were running through my mind as I opened my eyes to find Nate watching me.

He was sitting cross-legged on the bed, clutching a sheet that was draped around his back and over his shoulders. I immediately flashed back to Halloween, when we were six.

I'd insisted we were too old to wear the costumes our moms normally picked—generally some sort of cute animal—and said we should be something scary, like a zombie, goblin, or ghost. So I dressed like the undead, with scary face paint and torn, bloody clothing. Nate had a white sheet draped over his head with holes cut out for eyes. He told me he was Casper the friendly ghost. I cracked up. Even on Halloween the kid couldn't be anything but nice and friendly.

We had lots of fun that night, going to every house in our neighborhood with our dads following behind us and chatting with the neighbors. It was really hard for Nate to eat his candy under the sheet, though, so when we got home, he pulled it off and wrapped it around his shoulders before he sat cross-legged on the living room floor and dug in; not so ghost-like that way, but he had much better access to the treats.

Flash forward twenty-two years, and Nate was sitting in front of me in the same pose, with a sheet draped around him the same way. Only difference was, I knew there was nothing under that sheet and, of course, that immediately turned me on.

"Good morning, Casper. Or should I say, good afternoon? What time is it?"

As I was talking, I reached my hand over, slid it under the sheet wrapped around him, and rubbed his leg. Nate smiled and shuddered.

"It's two thirty. We slept most of the day away. Mmmm, that feels so good, Jake. It feels so good to have you touch me. God, I still can't believe you want to touch me like this."

I kept petting his leg softly as I raised my body so I was sitting in front of him.

"I guess I'll just have to keep touching you, to make sure you believe it."

I pulled him over until we were sitting face-to-face with our legs wrapped around each other. He had let go of the sheet, so I was able to look up and down his naked body.

I'd always loved Nate's body. His perfect skin glowed. I kept my hand on his thigh and trailed my other hand up his smooth, flat stomach and chest. Then I caressed his throat, under his chin, reached around behind his head, and pulled him over to me for a kiss.

We sat there, wrapped around each other, caressing and kissing for several long minutes before my hand found its way to his dick. Nate must have had the same thought, because I felt his hand on my cock at almost the same time. We kept kissing as we stroked each other slowly, both of us moaning.

When I felt the wetness on the head of Nate's cock,

my need became more urgent. I rubbed his precum into him, with my thumb sliding over the head of his cock, then increased the speed of my strokes. We were still kissing and moaning, and our hands were moving up and down at a feverish pace.

Nate eventually broke our kiss, leaned his forehead against mine, and grunted as he came, shot after shot, on our chests and stomachs. His loud moans and grunts, combined with the smell and feel of his cum on my body, sent me over the edge, and I let go, letting my juice combine with his. We were both panting, still leaning into each other with our foreheads touching.

"I've always liked seeing you when I wake up, Nathaniel, but man, this really adds to the experience."

He was smiling broadly and he gave an out-of-breath chuckle.

"Unless you dragged me here just to seduce me and then keep me in bed the whole time, maybe we should try to venture out of this room for a little bit. How do you feel about going to the beach for a couple of hours?"

I groaned at him and rolled my eyes.

"You're a real spoilsport, you know? Fine, we can go out, but if you're just wearing your trunks at the beach, I can't promise to keep my hands off you."

I looked down at our cum-covered bodies.

"And I think we need to wash off first. There's room for two in that big shower."

I waggled my eyebrows at him and he laughed. We got out of bed and into the shower, shared the hotel's shower gel, and quietly cleaned ourselves and each other.

It felt so good being with Nate in the silence, the water cascading over us, our hands moving from body to body. I once again had that content feeling of not knowing where he ended and I began; like we really were just one person.

After a few minutes, we rinsed away the soap and Nate turned off the water. We'd both taken showers earlier in the morning, so there was only one dry towel left in the bathroom. I took it and used it on Nate's body. He stood quietly and looked at me as I gently dried his arms, torso, and legs. By the time I was done with him, a lot of the water had already dripped off my body, so it just took me a couple of seconds to dry myself.

We stepped out of the bathroom, put on our swim trunks and T-shirts, picked up a couple of beach towels, water bottles, and sunscreen, and headed out the door. Our hotel was right on the sand so it didn't take long for us to get settled. We laid out our towels and I stripped off my T-shirt and ran into the water while Nate lathered up with sunscreen.

I have olive skin that rarely burns anyway, and it was already close to four p.m. so I wasn't worried about the sun too much. Nate is pretty fair, so he has to be careful about sunscreen. After a couple of minutes in the water, I went back to our towels and put some sunscreen on my hands. Nate automatically turned his back to me and I rubbed it in.

I'd been putting sunscreen on Nate's back since we were about eight years old. Our moms took us to the Bryerville city pool when it finally got warm enough to swim. We were getting to that age where we didn't want our moms kissing us and fawning over us in front of people. Well, at least I felt that way. I think Nate didn't mind so much.

Anyway, we got to the pool and our moms got out the sunscreen and prepared to slather it all over us. I refused and told them we were old enough to put on our own sunscreen. Nate agreed with me. So we both squeezed the sunscreen onto our hands and started rubbing it in.

I was able to get my whole body, including my back, but Nate wasn't quite as flexible and didn't have as much control over his body, so he couldn't get his back. Not wanting our moms to think we couldn't get the job done, I took some more sunscreen and rubbed it into Nate's back. We did that during the next few trips to the pool and then it just stuck. Nate would put sunscreen everywhere else but he wouldn't even try to reach his back; that was my job. And the truth is, even then, I loved the excuse to touch his skin.

I thought back to that memory and smiled as my fingers moved over Nate and my hands finished rubbing in the sunscreen. Then I remembered his moans from the prior night, when his dick had been buried in my mouth and my hands were caressing his chest, and I immediately got hard.

My God, what is wrong with me? I'm like a teenager with no control over my body. I adjusted myself in my swim trunks, hoping to hide the obvious, and I looked up to see Nate's face turned to me, with a knowing smile and raised eyebrows. I put my chin on his shoulder so my mouth was right by his ear.

"I can't help it. That's what you do to me, buddy."

I looked over his shoulder and down to his lap, extremely pleased with what I saw pointing up at me under his trunks.

"And from the look of things, the feeling is mutual."

I stood up and reached my hand down to him. "Are you getting in the water or just relaxing here for a while?"

"I think I'll just stay here and enjoy the breeze."

Which meant Nate would sit and think. I wasn't sure whether it'd be about the lab, the latest book he was reading, a new scientific theory he was formulating, or something else entirely, but it made me smile to realize that, even on a beach, Nate's mind was always working, turning over new ideas. The man was incredible.

I ran into the waves and spent the next hour swimming laps against the current. It felt good to get exercise, work my muscles. Swimming wasn't usually my sport, but having the ocean push back against me and move my body around wasn't the same as doing laps in the still water of a pool. I really enjoyed it.

Eventually, my stomach reminded me I hadn't eaten much dinner the previous night and I'd skipped breakfast and lunch that day. I wasn't usually a guy to skip a meal, but I'd been pretty distracted with other things...better things. I swam to the shallow part of the water, walked out of the surf to our towels, and dropped to my knees by Nate. He was lying on his back, propped up on his elbows, leering at me.

"I know it's kind of early, but are you hungry?"

He grinned mischievously.

"Depends. What're you offering?"

He raked his eyes over my chest, down to my trunks, and licked his lips.

"I'm offering dinner, at a restaurant, with other people sitting nearby, you little perv."

I reached my hand onto his lap and rubbed his dick through his trunks, surprised to find it hard.

"But if you really can't wait, Nathaniel, I'm sure we can work something out."

"'S okay. Anticipation is half the fun. Well, maybe not half the fun, but I can wait."

He smiled and I felt like I was glowing. He was flirting with me, making thinly veiled sexual references. He was still the same Nate, my Nate, but things were different between us and I was seeing a new side of him. Not surprisingly, I loved that side of Nate, just like I loved everything else about him.

We put on our shirts, scooped up our towels, and wandered around the shops and restaurants along the beach until we found a place with patio seating and a decent menu. The waitress came over to the table and was annoyingly chatty before she finally took our orders.

I asked for a burger and Nate ordered pasta, asking the waitress to make sure they left off the mushrooms. Nate doesn't mind mushrooms, but I hate them. I have a tendency to eat off his plate, so whenever we go out, Nate makes sure he doesn't order something I don't like. He doesn't say anything about it, he just does it, always has. Kind, considerate Nate. My heart felt like it was swelling.

I put my elbows on the table, leaned over, and looked into Nate's eyes.

"You've been really quiet today."

He put his hands on the table and it seemed like he was going to hold my hand, but then he hesitated and stopped.

"I'm just really happy to be here. Really happy to finally be like this with you, Jake."

I picked up both of his hands, kissed his palms, then turned them over and kissed the backs of his hands, leaving them pressed between both of mine.

"I'm happy too, Nate. So unbelievably happy."

CHAPTER SIX

Nate

I **WOKE** up naked and in Jake's arms. I could hardly believe I was awake and not floating through some sort of very vivid dream. I sat up and looked at Jake, wanting to reassure myself that he was still there. His chest heaved up and down while he slept and, for the millionth time, I gasped at just how beautiful he was.

When I'd kissed Jake that morning, I really had no idea how he'd react. Thinking back to what I had done, licking his ass, pushing my tongue into him…I guess I also had no idea how I'd react to that kiss. I'd never rimmed a guy before that morning. Truth be told, I'd always thought it sounded gross and unsanitary.

But I hadn't been thinking that morning. I'd been lost in the feeling of being with Jake, of touching him and tasting him, listening to him whimper and moan. Somehow my mouth and tongue seemed to have their own ideas of what to do, and having Jake's ass in my mouth, tasting him with my tongue, well, it wasn't gross at all. It was sensuous and wonderful and the audible pleasure I'd brought him, the way he had come so quickly and without either of us touching his dick, was the most fulfilling sexual experience I'd ever had.

It really is better when you love the guy, I was thinking to myself, and then Jake opened his eyes.

"Good morning, Casper. Or should I say good afternoon? What time is it?"

His deep voice was still raspy from sleep, sounding so damn sexy; his hand was rubbing my leg, making my dick instantly hard, and his comment took me back to Halloween, all those years ago, reminding me of my childhood, of our shared histories and memories. It was an incredibly powerful combination of feelings.

"It's two thirty. We slept most of the day away. Mmmm, that feels so good, Jake. It feels so good to have you touch me. God, I still can't believe you want to touch me like this."

I wondered how long he'd want to touch me. Just that day? Just that week on vacation? I knew it couldn't last. Eventually he'd come to his senses, remember that he likes to fuck girls, and expect things to go back to the way they were. But could I ever go back? Jake's voice interrupted my impending panic attack.

"I guess I'll just have to keep touching you, to make sure you believe it."

He sat up and wrapped his legs around me, and I started to relax. I let go of the sheet, and Jake's eyes moved lustfully over my body. The combination of that look, his legs wrapped around me, and his hands rubbing me sent my body into overdrive and left no room for my anxiety. We were kissing, touching, coming. And then I just tried to catch my breath.

"I've always liked seeing you when I wake up, Nathaniel, but man, this really adds to the experience."

Jake's comment made me laugh, but it also made me think of our new relationship. I wondered whether that relationship was limited to the hotel room. Whether stepping out into the light, into public, would make things revert back to the way they'd always been. It was the last thing I wanted. And yet, I thought being reminded of what I really was to Jake—a friend—was probably just what I needed. Otherwise, I wasn't sure I'd be able to recover when we returned to New York and he expected things to go back to normal. So I suggested leaving the room.

"Unless you dragged me here just to seduce me and then keep me in bed the whole time, maybe we should try to venture out of this room for a little bit. How do you feel about going to the beach for a couple of hours?"

"You're a real spoilsport, you know? Fine, we can go out, but if you're just wearing your trunks at the beach, I can't promise to keep my hands off you."

God, how I wanted those words to be true.

We took a quick shower together, another first for me. I'd never showered with another guy as an adult. It always seemed so intimate, and I hadn't ever dated anyone all that long. Besides, I hated spending the night away from home—away from Jake—so even with those few boyfriends I'd had, I rarely slept over at their places. And, with a few exceptions, I rarely invited them to spend the night at our place, because I wanted to spend my mornings with Jake.

When we were kids, though, Jake and I took baths and showers together all the time. We sat together in the bubbles, playing with our rubber ducks and other bath toys while our mothers chatted. We always had so much fun splashing and laughing that we refused to get out until the water was cold and our fingers looked like raisins. I think I have a picture somewhere of the two of us sitting in one of those bubble baths with our arms around each other's shoulders. I sighed as I thought back to those days in our past while I felt Jake, in the present, washing my body tenderly.

When we got out of the shower, I noticed there was only one clean towel left in the bathroom. Jake didn't take it for himself, which didn't surprise me, because Jake had always taken care of me. What did surprise me was that he didn't just hand me the towel. Instead, he used it to dry off my body, slowly and gently.

I watched the water dripping off his muscular chest and felt angry at myself for telling him we needed to leave the room. I'd wanted him my entire life, and when I finally had him naked in a hotel room, I had to force us to go out. What was I doing? Why was I testing him? I should've just been grateful for whatever time we had together.

I wanted to thank him, to tell him how much he meant to me, how much I loved him, how desperately I wanted him. But the words didn't come out.

Eventually, we made our way out of the hotel room and onto the beach. Jake ran into the water and I slathered on sunscreen. After a couple of minutes, Jake came back to our towels and squeezed some sunscreen onto his hands. I instinctively turned my back to him and he rubbed it in.

Even though Jake had always put sunscreen on my back, and even though I'd always enjoyed it more than I'd ever admit, it felt different. After he'd touched me the way I'd always wanted him to touch me, feeling his fingers on my skin turned me on more than I'd ever thought possible. I wanted to turn around and kiss him, right there on the beach, in front of everyone.

I'd been openly gay since I'd first realized I was gay; I'd never hidden it. But being with Jake was different. He'd never dated a guy. He was Mister Macho. I knew he'd be uncomfortable with public displays of affection. The realization that having a relationship with Jake might not be the kind of relationship I'd always wanted, in that it'd never be open and public, made me feel a little gloomy.

I turned to look at Jake, to remind myself that I damn well better be thankful for whatever he was willing to give me, even if it'd never be exactly what I wanted, and I noticed he was adjusting a sizable erection in his swim trunks. My dick immediately swelled as I thought to myself that he really did seem to be physically attracted to me. Despite our groping session in the hotel room that morning and the action the previous night, I still found it hard to believe he could actually want me. Jake put his chin on my shoulder, and I could feel his hot breath in my ear.

"I can't help it. That's what you do to me, buddy." He glanced down at my lap. "And from the look of things, the feeling's mutual."

He stood and offered me a hand. I declined and told him I wanted to stay on the sand, enjoy the breeze, which was true, but more than anything, I just needed time to think.

Jake ran into the water and swam in pretty far, so I couldn't see him well. I lay back on the towel and thought about what would happen between us and whether I could deal with having what I knew would be a secret boyfriend. I realized that Jake would never own our relationship. That he'd never introduce me to his friends and coworkers as anything other than a friend. There really weren't gay people in Jake's world. Well, other than me, of course.

I weighed the pros and cons in my mind. Then Jake started walking out of the surf, his muscles looking even more taut than usual, water dripping and glistening off his body, the shape of his big cock outlined by his wet swim trunks, and I knew having any kind of intimacy with Jake, even if only in our private hotel room, was more than I'd ever thought possible. I'd accept whatever relationship he could offer.

I propped myself up on my elbows and watched him walking toward me like a dream. A come-in-my-pants dream. He dropped down on the towel and smiled at me.

"I know it's kind of early, but are you hungry?"

I looked at his incredibly gorgeous body and kicked myself internally once again for insisting we leave the hotel room. He was the only thing I was hungry for. I wanted to taste his skin. I wanted to suck his cock, taste his cum. I wondered if there was any way to just get him back to the room.

"Depends. What're you offering?" I asked as I leered at his perfectly chiseled chest and wondered how he could be so defined and yet not overly bulky.

"I'm offering dinner, at a restaurant, with other people sitting nearby, you little perv."

He reached over and rubbed my dick.

"But if you really can't wait, Nathaniel, I'm sure we can work something out."

I didn't want to wait. I wanted to go back to the room, where I could touch him and he'd touch me back. I wanted to spend the next six days of the trip completely connected with him, not knowing how long the whole thing would last. But I realized he was probably very hungry, and actually, so was I.

"'S okay. Anticipation is half the fun. Well, maybe not half the fun, but I can wait."

We gathered our things and walked along the boardwalk, looking for a place to eat. I wanted to hold his hand as we walked, but Jake never held hands or really displayed affection outside of the bedroom with any of the women he'd been with. He sure as hell wasn't going to start with a guy, so I held back and just enjoyed his company.

Eventually, we found a restaurant and sat down. I looked up and saw our waitress walking over, eyeing Jake. That happened so frequently I was used to it, and it usually didn't bother me. Well, not too much, anyway.

She came to our table, never taking her eyes off Jake, and asked him if he lived nearby, how long he'd be in town, if he knew about the great club down the way (with a not-so-subtle implication that she'd be at that club later that night), and on and on.

I hated it, hated that she felt like she could flirt with him and hated that he didn't stop her, didn't tell her he wasn't interested, that we were together. Not that I expected him to say those things, of course, but I still wanted it. And after what he'd said to me about having a relationship, after what'd happened between us in that hotel room, I guess I'd been hoping for more. The annoying waitress finally took our orders and pulled herself away from Jake.

"You've been really quiet today."

He was leaning on the table with his hands in front of me. I wanted so much to touch him, to hold his hands. But I knew he wouldn't like it, so I resisted the impulse. I told myself it was enough that we were together, eating dinner, enjoying the evening, knowing when we got back to the room I could touch him, feel his skin. That was more than I'd ever had before and it thrilled me. That was what I would focus on.

"I'm just really happy to be here. Really happy to finally be like this with you, Jake."

And then he did something I never expected. He took both of my hands into his and kissed them, front and back, before he held them between his hands and didn't let go. He didn't seem to mind or care if anyone saw him sitting at this restaurant holding hands with another man.

"I'm happy too, Nate. So unbelievably happy."

And the way he said it, the look in his eyes as he held my hands, I couldn't help but push my insecurities aside and believe him.

CHAPTER SEVEN

Jake

AFTER WE finished eating dinner, Nate and I strolled along the beach, taking our time walking back to the hotel. I didn't want to come on too strong, too fast, but being close to him overwhelmed me, and I couldn't stop myself from holding his hand and rubbing his arm as we walked. When we got close to the hotel, we saw a convenience store and I suggested stopping in to buy some snacks and drinks. The truth was, I wanted to get more than just drinks and snacks. Nate leaned into me, talking quietly.

"Are you getting supplies to keep us from having to leave the room for the rest of this trip? Not that I'm complaining."

He had no idea how true that was. Just thinking about being alone with Nate in the hotel room got me incredibly hot. I let go of his hand, cupped his face in my hands, and pulled him into me for a long, deep kiss. He returned my kiss with a passion and desire that matched my own, which surprised and excited me even more.

"Let's get this shopping done. I want to get you alone and undressed. Now."

We decided to divide and conquer when we got into the store, both of us picking things out and meeting at the register. I handed the cashier my credit card and turned to Nate as the cashier was ringing up and bagging our items.

"You make me crazy, you know? I want you so much, Nathaniel. So fucking much."

His blue eyes seemed to sparkle even more than usual, and he kissed me hard, grinding his dick against mine. After a few minutes, the cashier cleared her throat, and I pulled away from Nate long enough to sign the bill, put the card back into my wallet, and take the bags. I managed to do all of that with one hand, keeping my other hand on Nate's arm. I didn't want to break our touch, both for myself and because I sensed a similar need for physical contact coming from Nate.

When we got back to the room, I put the bags down and kissed Nate again, feeling my dick strain against my swim trunks and Nate's respond in kind. He slipped his hands under my shirt and pulled it up over my chest. We broke our kiss as I raised my arms so he could lift my shirt over my head. He untied my swim trunks, pulled them over my hard cock, which was pressing straight up against my stomach, and let them drop to the floor. I undressed him in the same manner, and noticed his breathing was fast and heavy and his dick was weeping. He pressed himself against me, pushed his tongue into my mouth, and sucked almost desperately on mine. Our hands roamed over each other's body and it was all I could do to stop myself from exploding.

Nate led me to the bathroom and suggested a shower to wash off the ocean and the sunscreen before we got into bed. As the warm water ran over us, Nate pressed his mouth against mine again, his tongue seeking entry. He took the soap and lathered up my arms, back, chest, legs, and finally, focused on my cock. He took his soapy hands and rubbed the length of my cock, my balls, and then reached around and massaged my ass. I took the soap from him and returned the favor before we rinsed off, letting our hands continue to wander. I wasn't sure how I managed to keep myself from releasing during that shower, but my erection was getting painful. I was on the edge and wouldn't be able to hold back much longer. We stumbled out of the bathroom, dried each other off while still continuing to mash our mouths together, and tumbled into the bed.

Although I was absolutely crazy and out of control with desire, I was completely in tune with Nate. I needed to come, but even more, I needed to feel Nate climax, to taste him again. I moved my head down to Nate's cock and swung my legs around so my feet were at the head of the bed. Before I could get Nate into my mouth, he grasped my ass and pulled my cock toward his face. Then he took me into his mouth as far as he could. With a deep moan, I swallowed his cock down to the base.

We were both grunting and sucking, moving our heads up and down on each other's dick, when I felt Nate's balls rise and his body tense. My body immediately reacted, and we both came hard in each other's mouth. Nate's cock was deep in my throat as he ejaculated, and I could feel shot after shot hitting the back of my throat. I pulled my head back a bit so I could take some shots on my tongue and really taste him. I think he sensed what I was doing and liked it, because I could hear him moaning even more, with my cock still wedged inside his mouth.

When we both finished, we reluctantly pulled off each other, and I flipped around, putting my head next to his. He was breathing heavily, almost gasping for air, but that didn't stop him from pulling me in for another passionate kiss. Our tongues tangled and I could taste myself in his mouth. I stroked his body gently as I tried to catch my breath.

"Oh my God, Nate. What you do to me. I am so fucking crazy about you. You feel so damn good. You taste so damn good. I can't get enough of you."

I rubbed his arms, his neck, his back, and I could feel him rubbing my chest. We kissed again. I was lost in the moment, deliriously happy.

Nate

JAKE WAS still holding my hand when the waitress walked over to the table, carrying our meals. I could tell she'd combed her hair and applied fresh lipstick after she'd last left our table, no doubt in an attempt to impress Jake. She was wearing a short jean skirt and a tight white tank top stretched over her big breasts. She was pretty, if you liked that sort of thing, and she looked at Jake seductively, ready to make some comment as she put the food down. Then she noticed he was holding my hand.

She seemed confused, and I could tell she was trying to read the situation, to understand what was happening between us. I thanked her for the food with a curt tone to my voice. She hesitated a moment before turning around and walking away. Jake didn't take his eyes off me the whole time.

We let go of each other so we could eat, and Jake asked me about the lab and why I'd been working all those late nights. I told him about our projects and a few problems we were having trying to get funding to finish our work.

I wasn't supposed to talk to people about what we did at the lab; I signed a bunch of confidentiality agreements promising they could take my firstborn or something if I gave away any secrets. But I'd always told Jake everything (well, almost everything), and even as I was signing those documents, I had no intention of keeping anything from him. I just explained that we couldn't tell anyone anything about it, and he agreed, no questions asked.

We finished eating and walked back to the hotel room. Having Jake hold my hand at that restaurant had calmed me down, put my insecurities at bay. But when we were back on the boardwalk, I felt that same anxious "I'm not ever going to be enough for him" feeling return. Then Jake took my hand in his, and those anxious feelings dissipated. His touch was magical; it made me feel secure and wanted.

I was basking in the warm glow of being with Jake, getting excited in anticipation of what I knew we'd be doing when we got into our room. After the way Jake had been looking at me all day, how he'd fondled my dick through my trunks on the beach, kissed my hands and held them at dinner, and was holding my hand as we strolled along that crowded boardwalk, I didn't want to test him any further to see how he'd act in public. I just wanted him alone, preferably naked, for the rest of the trip.

Jake suggested we stop by a store to get food and snacks, and I was thrilled with the prospect that he had the same idea.

"Are you getting supplies to keep us from having to leave the room for the rest of this trip? Not that I'm complaining..."

Jake didn't answer. Instead, he pulled me against him and kissed me passionately. We were standing in front of the store with dozens of people walking by. I couldn't believe this beautiful, perfect man I'd wanted my entire life was mine, and he wasn't trying to hide it.

"Let's get this shopping done. I want to get you alone and undressed. Now." His deep voice was raspy with lust.

I picked out some fruit and crackers and brought

them to the cashier. I could tell she was watching Jake walk through the store, checking him out. I really couldn't blame her. After all, I couldn't take my eyes off him either. Jake tossed his items on the counter and gave the cashier his credit card. Then he turned to me.

"You make me crazy, you know? I want you so much, Nathaniel. So fucking much."

I didn't understand what was bringing that on, and I didn't care. Jake wanted me. A flood of warmth washed over me. I clutched Jake and shoved my tongue into his mouth as I brushed my fingers through his hair and pushed my dick against his. I wasn't sure how long we stood there, making out, before we heard the cashier clear her throat. We pulled apart, but Jake kept his hand on my arm while he finished paying and gathering our things.

When we finally got back to the room, I was dizzy with excitement. Jake and I were kissing and groping each other. We got our clothes off and stumbled into the shower. I took the soap and washed his body.

I loved being able to touch every part of him, to feel all of his muscles under my fingers. After I finished with most of his body, I lathered and caressed his dick and balls. I even let my hands wander over to Jake's ass, and felt surprised when he didn't pull away. I assumed that area was going to be no-man's land—completely off limits. Well, maybe after letting me lick and suck his ass that morning, he wasn't very worried about my hand rubbing him.

I let my fingers and hand caress his ass cheeks,

and then I slid my hand in between them, massaging each side. I wondered what it would feel like to slip my fingers into his hole, followed by my cock, but I didn't want to push my luck. Even if he was willing to have a sexual relationship with a guy, there was no way Jake would let me fuck him. If there was such a thing as a total top, that would be Jake. He was always in control of every situation, incredibly aggressive, a complete alpha male.

I'd always been versatile sexually. I loved feeling my dick push into a nice, tight ass, but I also loved getting my ass fucked. Well, lots of people get into certain roles when they were in a relationship; at least that was what I assumed. And I knew lots of guys who were total bottoms and had great sex lives. I told myself I could live with being a bottom for the rest of my life if it meant being with Jake.

I was so lost in my passion for Jake, in the feeling of his skin and the taste of his tongue during that shower, that I don't remember getting out of the water and into the bed. I snapped out of my fog when Jake pulled his mouth away from mine, and I noticed his rigid cock right in front of my face. I had licked it that morning and tasted his cum when I licked it off his body, but I hadn't sucked him off.

I needed to taste Jake, needed to feel his cock in my mouth. I hadn't ever sucked someone as thick and long as Jake, so I probably should have taken it slow, but I was too far gone. I pulled him into me and heard him moan. Then he pushed his mouth over my dick and all my senses vibrated. I tried to hold off the inevitable, to let the feelings I was having continue, but I couldn't, and I released in Jake's mouth. I was thrusting my dick into his throat when I felt him pull his mouth back. I thought he was trying to get my dick out, that he didn't want my cum in his mouth, but then he stopped when the head of my dick was pointing at his tongue. Oh my God, he wanted to taste my seed. That realization, combined with Jake shooting in my mouth, took my breath away.

After we'd both finished and pulled off each other, I was lying on my back, trying to process what had just happened. I'd always been reserved in bed, like I was in life. When I was having sex with a guy, I'd often catch myself thinking about something else—whether the relationship would go anywhere (and always knowing that it wouldn't), whether he was clean (even though I always used a condom); hell, sometimes I'd even find myself thinking about work, politics, or a book I'd been reading. That, combined with the fact that I couldn't climax unless I was thinking of Jake, meant I'd never had any problem lasting a long time, certainly longer than the guys I'd been with. One of those guys once told me my stamina almost made up for my lack of passion in bed. Almost.

But making love with Jake was totally different. I was focused completely on Jake, on his body, on our bodies together. I could smell him, taste him, hear him. That made me lose all control over my mind and body, and I felt nothing but passion. I didn't recognize myself. And I mean that in the best possible way.

Like he had with so many things in my life, Jake

made me a better lover. The irony of that statement—my straight friend was making me a better lover—wasn't lost on me, but more than anything, I felt so grateful in that moment. Grateful for how he had always taken care of me, and was finding a way to take care of me on a whole other level.

Jake flipped around so his head was by mine. He looked into my eyes and I wanted to tell him how I felt. I wanted to tell him how much I loved him. But the words wouldn't come out, so instead, I pulled him over and kissed him deeply.

"Oh my God, Nate. What you do to me. I am so fucking crazy about you. You feel so damn good. You taste so damn good. I can't get enough of you."

My thoughts exactly.

CHAPTER EIGHT

Jake

AS WE boarded the plane back to New York, I felt sad to leave our beach vacation, where so much had happened between us, where our friendship had grown into something even deeper, but I was happy we were going back home to finally live our lives together. I mean, we'd been living our lives together since birth, but not completely, not the way I'd always hoped. Knowing we were truly together in every way thrilled me. Nate and I got into our seats and I looked into his eyes, held his hand, and kissed him.

"You're everything to me," I whispered into his ear. Then I put my head on his shoulder and closed my eyes.

I wasn't sure how many times I'd come during that week, but I knew it was, hands-down, a lifetime record for me. I didn't even realize my body could have sex that frequently. Nate would just touch my cock and I would get hard, regardless of how soon after our last lovemaking session it was. All those nights and days of kissing, licking, and touching were running through my mind. I settled on one memory as I drifted off to sleep.

We'd gone out to dinner just to get some air and, frankly, let housekeeping change the sheets on the beds. When we got back, we took a shower together and then got into bed and right back to it. We were kissing and groping when Nate pulled away, breathing heavily.

"I want you to make love to me, Jake."

I smiled at him.

"I thought that's what we've been doing the last few days."

"No, I mean, yes, we have been making love, but I want you to…I want you to…"

He sounded a little nervous. I rubbed my thumb over his mouth and then kissed him deeply.

"I know what you mean, Nate. I was just teasing. I want to make love to you too."

I got up and walked over to the bag of snacks and drinks we'd bought at the convenience store and pulled out a box of condoms and a bottle of lube I'd purchased in anticipation of that moment. I brought them back to the bed and handed them to Nate.

"I've never done this, so will you please show me what to do?"

He looked surprised.

"I didn't realize you'd bought these. And I didn't know there was anything you hadn't done in bed. I guess maybe it's different with women."

He lay down on his back and took the bottle of lube into his hand.

"I can get myself ready, and then it shouldn't be that different from what you're used to. Not that I know what you're used to, because I've never been with a woman, but I assume it won't be that different."

He still sounded nervous and also confused and a little anxious. I crawled on top of him and put my hands on each side of his face as I kissed his forehead, his nose, each of his cheeks, and then his lips.

"Being with you is *nothing* like what I'm used to. Not in any way. Being with you is special and wonderful and it makes my whole body soar. Besides, what I want is for you to *show* me what to do."

He had a puzzled expression on his face, and I knew he still didn't understand what I meant, so I ripped open a condom package with my teeth, took out the condom, and rolled it onto Nate's hard cock. He looked completely shocked.

"What are you doing? Wait, you want me to...to... really? Are you sure, Jake?"

"Yes, I'm sure." I smiled at his surprise. "I want to do everything with you, Nate. I've fantasized about having you inside me since we were in middle school."

IT WAS the beginning of our seventh-grade school year, and school was closed for Labor Day. Our parents still had to work, so Nate and I stayed home together. We were playing video games, and Nate kept bumping his shoulder into me.

He had finally started growing over that year, so even though he was still a fairly small guy, he was catching up, which made him feel more comfortable throwing his body around. Anyway, after a few more shoulder bumps, we started wrestling on the floor. I held back because I realized I was still much, much bigger and stronger than Nate, but it was fun and we were laughing and climbing all over each other. At some point, Nate had me pressed on my stomach on the floor, and he was lying on top of me, holding my wrists down with his hands.

"Say uncle and I'll let you go, Jake. Say uncle."

He was out of breath and his voice was a little raspy.

I could get up any time. Nate's body weight wasn't actually keeping me there. But I wanted him to feel like he was finally strong enough to take me down; I knew how much it meant to him. Besides, even then I loved feeling Nate's body against mine. So I pretended that I was struggling and wiggled my back and my ass around.

Nate had to push down with his entire body to keep me on the ground, and I loved feeling him move on top of me, hearing him breathe heavily as he struggled to keep me pinned to the ground. I was focused on Nate's body, enjoying it, when I suddenly realized the pressure on my ass was changing. It felt like there was a hard pipe or something pressing on me. I was about to ask Nate what it was, and tell him that using weapons was cheating, when I realized his hands were occupied holding mine down, so there was no way he could've reached for anything. And that was when I knew what was pressing down on my ass.

I think I spent the rest of the afternoon with a partial erection, just thinking back to the feeling of Nate's hard dick pressed against my ass. I whacked off that evening in the shower thinking about it, and then whacked off again thinking about it when I went to bed. I fell asleep thinking about it, and once I was asleep, I dreamt about it. In my dream, we were still in the family room, wrestling, but we were naked, and when I felt Nate's erection on top of me, he wasn't just pressing down on top of my ass, he was entering me. When I woke up that morning, my pajamas and sheets were wet and sticky. For months, I thought of that dream whenever I masturbated.

ONCE NATE'S obvious shock at what I was asking him to do wore off, he looked incredibly aroused. He rolled me onto my back and straddled me. He combed his fingers through my hair, rubbed my face, leaned in, and kissed me very gently at first, and then softly covered my lips with small, fast licks. I felt like I was melting.

Eventually he pushed his tongue into my mouth. I sucked on his tongue and rubbed his back. We lay in bed together, kissing, for a long time, and then Nate licked my neck. My cock was hard as steel and leaking. He sucked on my neck in the spot where it meets my shoulder and I lost all control. I started whimpering and thrusting up at him. He made his way down my stomach and started to lick the wetness off my cock, but I stopped him.

"I'm so close, Nate. If you touch my cock, I'll shoot."

Nate moaned in response. He moved back up the bed with his body in between my legs, put a pillow under my ass, and kissed me deeply as he rubbed his fingers firmly into my thighs, moved his hands underneath them, and pushed my legs up. He rubbed lube at my opening and slowly pushed his finger in.

I gasped. "Oh God, Nate. Please."

I could hear him breathing heavily as he gave me time to adjust; then he added another finger and pressed deeper into me. I thrashed my head from side to side as he moved his fingers in and out and twisted them. The whole time, his face was close to mine, he was kissing me softly and looking into my eyes, making sure I was enjoying the experience. And I was enjoying it. Really fucking enjoying it.

"Oh, Nate...I...I need something...need you...oh, please, Nate...please."

I felt the head of his cock press gently against my opening, and he removed his fingers, slowly replacing them with his condom-covered cock, which he had coated with lube. My body stretched impossibly thin to accommodate him, and it hurt, but it also felt good, so fucking good. He pushed into me until just the head of his cock was inside, and then he stopped, giving me time to accommodate him and kissing me again. After a few minutes, he looked into my eyes.

"Is this okay? Are you okay, Jake?"

"It feels wonderful. Oh, Nate, you feel wonderful. I've wanted this for so long, wanted you for so long. Don't stop. Please don't ever stop."

He smiled at me with tears in his eyes. He held my head between his hands as he stroked the sides of my face with his thumbs and kept pushing into me slowly, not letting his eyes stray from mine. My body felt a little sore and very, very full, but more than anything, I felt incredible. I realized I'd been whimpering and moaning, and then Nate kissed me again.

"I'm all the way inside you now. You're so tight. Oh, Jake, you feel so good."

I could tell he was waiting for me to adjust to the feeling of him being completely inside me. After a few moments, I thrust myself up to let him know I was okay and he could move. He understood my cue and slowly pulled his cock out a couple of inches, then pushed it back in. I groaned and dug my fingers into his back. He increased the speed and length of his strokes; then he pulled out almost completely and pushed himself back in at a different angle.

"Oh my God! Oh, Nate. Nate. Ohhh! What are you doing? Oh!"

"I'm pushing my dick against your prostate."

He was breathing heavily but his voice was soft. He was still holding my head between his hands and rubbing the sides of my face with his thumbs. He hadn't moved his eyes away from mine.

"Being inside of you is making me crazy, Jake. I

don't know how much longer I can do this. I need you to come for me. Can you do that? Can you come for me?"

He kept making short thrusts against my prostate as he talked. I could smell his skin and his breath against my face. He smelled like safety, like childhood. He smelled like home.

I could do anything for him, would do anything for him. Besides, he wasn't giving me a choice in the matter—my body couldn't hold out any longer either. I moaned loudly, thrust my hips up against him as I dug my fingers even deeper into his back, and I came. Nate was moaning right along with me, pushing into me hard as he released. We stayed tangled together for a long time, looking into each other's eyes, stroking each other's face, both of us crying a little. Then I whispered to him.

"I am completely in love with you, Nate. Madly, deeply in love with you."

CHAPTER NINE

Jake

I CARRIED our bags up to our place while Nate followed and held all of our mail. Man, I'd never noticed how much mail we got. We'd only been gone a week.

"I'll get the door. You sure you're okay with those bags, Jake?"

I smiled—there were only two bags.

"Thanks, Nate. I'm good."

Once inside our apartment, I took both of the bags into our small laundry room and made piles of colors and whites. Well, maybe a laundry "closet" was more accurate, but for a New York apartment, it was still pretty fucking awesome.

Our place wasn't in the best neighborhood, but it wasn't a scary neighborhood where you had to worry about being mugged when you were coming home—I'd never let Nate live in a place like that. And our building was decent too. Not a fancy place with a doorman or anything. Shit, we didn't even have an elevator, but I actually preferred living in a walk-up. What was wrong with walking, right?

As far as the apartment itself, it was great. Small kitchen that opened to a really decent-sized living space, two smallish but functional bedrooms, each with an attached bathroom, and then this laundry setup in a room that was probably the size of a small walk-in closet. The place wasn't big, but actually, I liked that about it too, because it meant I could always hear Nate, even if he was in another room. That was only a problem during the few times Nate had a guy sleeping over. I wanted to fucking rupture my eardrums on those nights, but I settled for headphones and old-school punk playing at maximum volume.

As I put in the first load of laundry, I smiled at the thought that those days were over. I'd be the only guy sleeping in Nate's bed. Or would he sleep in mine? We didn't need both beds, so maybe we could turn one of the rooms into an office or something. Hmm, neither of us really had jobs where we worked from home...

"Thanks for getting the laundry going. You hungry?"

Nate was leaning against the doorframe so his shirt rode up, and his pants were a little loose, just hanging on his hips. Part of his smooth, flat, firm stomach was showing. I immediately got hard.

"That depends. What're you offering?" I stole Nate's line from that day on the beach.

"I'm offering my dick, in the shower. You interested?"

That was such a better fucking offer than the one I'd made on the beach. I followed Nate to the shower, stripping off my clothes along the way, once again amazed at how uncontrollably attracted I was to him, and how lucky I was to be able to touch him, taste him, and do all sorts of other great stuff with him too.

After the shower, we threw on some sweats and headed into the living room to watch a movie. Movie nights were always nice because we sat together on the couch and shared a blanket. I'd used that closeness to "accidentally" rub my leg or my arm against Nate for years. But I no longer needed to make excuses to touch him, and I didn't have to make do with an arm or a leg. I relaxed on the couch with my head up on one arm and my legs stretched along the entire length of it and pulled the blanket over me as Nate put in the movie. When he came back to the couch, I lifted the blanket and leered at him.

"C'mere."

He smiled a smile that made my heart skip and got under the blanket, cuddling up against me, pressing his whole body against mine. He rested his head on my chest and settled in to watch the movie. But I couldn't focus on the television, not with Nate on top of me. I could only think about him, the warmth radiating from his body, the fresh smell of his hair.

I'm not the smartest guy around, I've always known that—I mean, how could I not know that with a genius for a best friend? Still, I have a good sense about people. I can read people easily and, I always thought, accurately. I had misread Nate's feelings though. That much was clear to me. I'd spent my life thinking that he wasn't attracted to me, that he didn't want a romantic relationship with me. But I'd been wrong.

Insecurity is not one of my personality traits. If anything, I'm an arrogant fucker. Most, if not all, of that is because I don't give a shit about what other people think about me, or for that matter, about other people, period. It's easy to be arrogant when you have nothing to lose.

Of course, none of that is true with Nate. Not that I'd ever thought I'd lose him. We'd always been in it for life—till death do us part, only without the marriage. I'd always known that. But I *did* care what he thought about me.

When I saw Nate being kind, selfless—just being himself, really—I sometimes wondered what gene I was missing that kept me from giving a shit about people. I could try to blame it on my parents' death, and the reality is that I became angrier and colder after that, but I was a fucking prick before they died. Nate, on the other hand, just wanted his friends to be happy and the world to be a better place. I'm not making that shit up or being sarcastic. Seriously, that's why he spent all that time in the lab, working on a cure for this disease, or a solution to that problem. He didn't make nearly as much money in that job as he could have if he'd worked for some big corporation, and I knew he'd received offers. But it wasn't about money for him; it was about helping people.

I know the only reason—and I mean the *only* reason—I hadn't ended up dead or in jail for killing someone was because even in my darkest, angriest moments, I had Nate in my heart and in my mind, and I tried, I desperately tried, to do what he'd want me to do. I tried to be the man he'd want me to be. I built my entire life around that, around him. So maybe, somehow, I had a blind spot in my people-reading skills when it came to Nate.

But not anymore. Even though Nate hadn't verbally reciprocated the feelings I told him I had for him, I believed he loved me. Maybe not as much as I loved him, but then again, that was impossible. I loved him more than anything, I'd die for him, and that was no exaggeration.

Still, I knew him, and I knew he couldn't engage in the physical relationship we'd shared over that past week if he didn't love me. I didn't know about every sexual partner Nate'd had over the years, and I didn't know the details of his alone time with those partners, but I had a pretty good idea. If I had to guess, I'd say he'd been with between five and ten guys over the years, and I knew he wasn't fucking all of them.

And then there was the look in his eyes. I'd never seen Nate look at anyone else the way I suddenly noticed him looking at me. I wasn't sure whether it was a new look or whether I'd been uncharacteristically oblivious over the years. Whatever the case, he loved me, but he was too scared to say it. I thought that maybe my past was getting in the way. It was funny, I'd decided to fuck women because I'd thought it didn't mean anything, but to Nate, it somehow seemed to mean everything.

I stroked Nate's hair and squeezed him into me as a nonverbal apology for my mistakes, for making him doubt my feelings for him. He responded by moving his hand down my stomach in a circling pattern and then cupping my balls. He continued watching the movie while holding my balls in his hand, sometimes rubbing his fingers over them and sometimes just holding them.

"You have no idea how appropriate this is, Nate."

He looked up from the movie.

"What?"

"You've always had me by the balls. It's nice to see you're finally willing to embrace it."

He stopped watching the movie and scooted his body so he was lying flat on top of me, nibbling on my neck and still rubbing my balls. I put one hand on the back of his neck and caressed him softly. My other hand was under his shirt, rubbing his back. I moved it down and slipped it into the back of his sweats and massaged his ass.

As I was rubbing his ass with that hand, I moved my other hand up from his neck and onto the back of his head. I pushed my fingers through his hair and gently pulled so he had to lift his face from my neck. I gazed into his eyes and drew him down to my lips, kissing him hard. My tongue invaded his mouth as I pressed the back of his head, rubbing his hair with one hand, and moving my other hand into his ass crack and softly brushing my fingers over his opening. I felt him shudder and moan as he pushed his ass up to my finger. Man, that got out of hand fast.

"Your place or mine, Nate?" My voice sounded raspy and, well, horny.

"Mmmm. Wha...what?"

I realized he was too far gone to answer, so I replaced my tongue in his mouth, put both of my hands on his ass, and picked him up as I raised the top half of my body off the couch and swung my legs onto the floor. We were still kissing, and he was sitting in my lap, straddling me.

"Hold on, baby."

He wrapped his arms around the back of my neck and locked his ankles behind my back. I stood, keeping my hands cupped under his ass, and walked into his bedroom, then kneeled on the bed so I could gently lower Nate. He was kissing me and moaning while he ground his dick into me. I rubbed his cheek with my hand and kissed him again, then sat up a little, pulled off his shirt and removed his sweats so he was lying on the bed completely naked, completely hard, looking up at me. I gasped at how beautiful he was. He had the best skin I'd ever seen, smooth and firm.

"I fucking love your body, Nate."

I stripped off my shirt, and he put his hands on the sides of my sweats and shoved them down to my knees. Then he reached his hand around my cock and slowly stroked me while he used his foot to push my sweats all the way down to my ankles and completely off. I groaned and kissed him again, returning my fingers to his ass and rubbing softly over his hole for a minute. I reached over to the nightstand and got the lube, coated my finger, and pushed it into Nate.

"Ohhhh, Jake. Ohhhh, yeah."

He was thrusting his hips up and pushing himself onto my hand so that my entire finger was in his ass. I added a second finger, even though he didn't seem to need it; he was more than ready.

"Oh, Jake. Jake. Unghhh. I need you, Jake."

Even though I had been inside him at least a dozen times during our trip, and even though I was crazy-horny and wanted nothing more than to be in there again, I was worried about hurting him, so I didn't want to go too fast. I kept moving my fingers inside Nate's ass while he writhed around on the bed and I used my other hand to get a condom.

All of his moaning got to me eventually, and I couldn't wait any longer. Besides, Nate was literally begging me to put my cock inside him, so I lay down on top of him, holding most of my weight up on my forearms, and pressed my cock against his hole. I wanted to push in slowly, give him time to adjust, but Nate had other ideas. As soon as the head of my cock pressed against him, he wrapped his legs around my back, locked his ankles, and used his leg muscles to pull himself up and impale himself on my cock.

"Oh fuck, Nate. Oh fuck."

I was all the way inside him, and he was moaning and pushing himself up; there was just no way for me to maintain a slow pace. Instead, I started meeting his thrusts with hard, fast pushes until I was slamming him down onto the mattress with every stroke. I didn't know how much longer I'd be able to keep that up, and I needed him to come, so I reached my hand between us and grabbed Nate's cock. It only took two strokes and he was going off between us and clenching his ass around my cock. That set me off too, and I groaned as I filled the condom.

After I caught my breath, I kissed Nate and then walked into the bathroom to throw out the condom and get a wet washcloth to clean him up. I walked back to the bed, kneeled over him, and gently wiped his neck, chest, stomach, and cock.

"You have the most beautiful cock in the world, Nate."

It was true. His cock was so smooth and thick and long. I think my words about his cock, combined with the attention I was paying to it with the washcloth, were getting to Nate, because I could feel him hardening again.

"Fuck, I want you."

I moved the washcloth and took Nate's cock into my mouth. He wasn't fully erect yet; he was still recovering from his last orgasm. But my powerful sucks alternated with soft licks got the job done, and a few minutes later, he was almost screaming and shooting off in my mouth.

Nate was gasping for air. I snuggled into the crook of his arm and licked and kissed his neck. I was fading fast and I knew Nate was in the same boat.

"I love you, Nate."

I promised myself those would be the last words he'd hear every night before he fell asleep from then on, and I wondered how long it'd take for him to believe them, to believe me, and maybe, just maybe, to say them back.

CHAPTER TEN

Nate

AFTER BEING away for a week, Jake and I both had to play a lot of catch-up at work. I was immediately back to early mornings and late nights. On the plus side, I got to come home to Jake every night. I loved those nights. Even though we couldn't have sex as frequently as we'd had on vacation (which was all day, every day), we were able to get in a couple of orgasms each every night, sleep in each other's arms, and then make love again in the morning.

None of the hundreds or thousands of sexual dreams I'd had about Jake over the years came anywhere close to matching the reality of making love with him. I'd always imagined Jake in bed to be the same Jake I saw with the women he fucked. Meaning, I imagined Jake being in complete control, aggressive, and unemotional.

Jake was actually nothing like that. Well, I guess he was aggressive, but he was so concerned about what I was feeling, so diligent about making sure I felt good, that his aggression came across like desire more than anything else. It seemed like he wanted me, really wanted me. And I had never seen Jake as emotional as he was when we made love. He moaned, gasped, whimpered, and sometimes cried. He held me tightly, caressed me, and kissed me so deeply that he made my toes curl. And even though I could tell he wanted to stay in control, of his own body if nothing else, he couldn't. Or rather, I wouldn't let him. It seemed like our bodies were programmed to know how to touch each other, where to touch each other, and once we started, the rest of the world disappeared and neither one of us was in control. We were floating through some euphoric state, clinging to each other, and hoping to never come back down.

I tried to focus on that feeling, to remind myself that he loved me (he'd told me so himself, during our trip and every day since we'd been back) but I was certain he'd get over it. How could he not? What was he going to do? Stop seeing other people? Stop having sex with women for the rest of his life? I mean, really. If anyone knew Jake, it was me. He didn't do relationships or commitment. And he avoided anyone who'd ever wanted a committed relationship with him.

The first girl who'd given that a shot was Sylvia Caster, during our senior year. It seemed Sylvia hadn't gotten the metaphorical memo that every other girl in school had read and abided by—the one that told them Jake would fuck them, but he played the field and he wasn't going to be anyone's boyfriend. So Sylvia had been after him all year, and he'd even agreed to take her to the prom. She was bringing her best friend, Julie, and the four of us were going to double.

We were at the dance, and Sylvia and Jake were

crowned prom king and queen. No surprise there—the captain of the football team and the head cheerleader were kind of a given for those titles. Julie snapped pictures of Jake and Sylvia dancing the honorary dance, or whatever it was called. When they came back and sat down, Sylvia grilled Julie about the pictures—were they close enough, could you see both of their faces, could you see her dress, and on and on.

Jake was talking to me about our plans for after the dance. He'd gotten a hotel room and was about to tell me about it when he was distracted by Sylvia telling Julie she'd better have nice pictures of her with her boyfriend. Jake froze, and a dark storm of anger took over his face. I would've worried that he was going to get blood all over his rented tuxedo, but I knew Jake didn't hit girls.

I was sitting on one side of Jake and Sylvia was on the other. Because he was facing me when she made her comment, she didn't see the look on his face, so she was taken completely off guard when he turned to her and muttered something under his breath in what sounded like the human equivalent of a growl. I didn't catch all of it, but I'm pretty sure he told her he wasn't her fucking boyfriend or even her fucking date. Then he put some money down on the table and told Sylvia and Julie we were taking off and they could take a cab home if they couldn't find a ride. That's the lesson here, folks—try to push Jake into a relationship and you'll be abandoned on what you thought was the best night of your life, wearing pink, fluffy taffeta and a cheap crown, no less.

So I knew my new relationship with Jake couldn't

last, but I figured I'd give my best shot to make it last as long as possible. The way I saw it, it was like what I did at work all day. I was great at analyzing problems and coming up with solutions. It was how I created new medications and everything else we did at the lab.

The first thing I needed to do was consider the data I already had. Once I thought about everything I knew about the illness I was trying to address (i.e., the problem), I could best determine how to find a cure (i.e., a solution). I spent the rest of the night thinking about Jake, what I knew he liked, what I knew he didn't like, what made him comfortable, what made him uncomfortable... you get the picture. Anyway, by morning I had a plan to make our relationship as easy and pain-free as possible for Jake. Maybe, that way, he'd be willing to stay with it, to stay with me...at least for a little while.

I was finally caught up enough at the lab so I could spend an entire weekend at home. Jake didn't have to go into the station that weekend, so when he woke up the next morning, we went grocery shopping. Well, to be more accurate, first we sucked each other off and then we went to the market. We had no food in the apartment and had been living off of takeout, protein bars, and cum. As we walked through the store, filling our baskets with food, I felt really warm inside to be sharing that coupley, domestic moment with Jake—grocery shopping on a Saturday morning. It wasn't like we hadn't ever shopped for groceries together before, but everything had taken on heightened meaning.

Just as I reached over to hold Jake's hand, I caught

the eye of the owner, who was organizing some cans next to the register. We'd shopped in that market for as long as we'd lived in our apartment and that man was always there. It was like he never took a single day or even a single hour off. He nodded at me and smiled, and I nodded back as I thought about my strategy for getting Jake to stay in our relationship—keep things comfortable for him. Well, in all the years we'd shopped in that market we hadn't held hands, obviously. So I stopped and dropped my hand. I heard Jake sigh and looked over at him, but he was already a few steps ahead of me, going into the next aisle.

I wondered whether he'd known what I was about to do and if it'd caused him to speed up so I wouldn't embarrass him in front of the shop owner by holding his hand. I mentally kicked myself for not being more careful. I wouldn't make that mistake again; I would stick to my "do not make Jake uncomfortable" plan.

I'd left my cell phone at our place while we shopped, and when we got back, I saw I had four missed calls and a voicemail. All four calls were from my friend Patrick. He'd also called several times over the past couple of weeks and left messages, but I hadn't had time to call him back. I listened to his latest message and laughed.

"Nate, it's Patrick again. Why haven't you returned any of my calls? You've been home for three weeks and we haven't seen you out once. You better be going out tonight. Ken, Scott, and I are meeting at Club 57 at eight. I expect you to be there so we can reintroduce you to the gay world. I'm concerned a week alone with Officer

Football might have turned you straight. Do you even remember how to suck cock? Club 57 at eight, Nate."

If only he knew…

"Funny message?"

Jake had finished putting away the groceries. He came up behind me, wrapped his arms around my chest, and rested his chin on my shoulder.

"What? What makes you say that?"

"You were laughing. Why are you getting all fidgety, Nate? Who was that?"

He swiped his tongue up the side of my neck, from the base all the way up to my ear, and licked and nibbled my earlobe.

"Mmmmm. It was just Patrick. Mmmm. Feels good, Jake."

"Yeah, what does Patrick want?"

His voice sounded throaty. He continued licking my neck and my ear as he dropped one of his hands down the front of my jeans and started rubbing my dick.

"Ungghh. He's going to Club 57 tonight with Scott and Ken. Mmmmmm. He wants to reintroduce me to the gay world. Uhhhh. He's worried I forgot how to suck cock."

Jake's body stilled.

"Well, you haven't forgotten anything. No need for Patrick to make introductions. What time are we meeting him?"

He had stopped kissing and licking me, and his voice sounded tense. Oh, no. Had I made it seem like I expected him to go out to a gay bar with my gay friends? That was definitely not "make Jake comfortable" territory. Jake didn't go to gay bars and he'd never been comfortable around my gay friends. I had to get out of this. I didn't want him to think I expected him to drop his old life and enter my world, like some sort of Mister Gay Pride.

"We don't need to go out with them, Jake. Really. It's not a big deal."

He pulled his hand out of my pants. Oh, no. Why hadn't I stuck to my plan? Why did I have to ruin this?

"I want to go. What time?"

I swear, he was gritting his teeth.

"Eight. They're meeting at eight. What should we do until then?"

His face relaxed and he put his hand back down the front of my pants.

"Oh, I have some ideas."

Then he leaned in and kissed me in a way that was somehow simultaneously tender and desperate, and I forgot all about my friends, my plan, and everything else but the two of us, and how good and right we were together.

CHAPTER ELEVEN

Jake

NATE AND I were naked, sitting on the bed cross-legged, playing poker. We'd played poker together for years, though until very recently, we'd never played naked. That certainly added a level of distraction to the game, but we'd spent the past few hours all over each other, putting every body part possible into every other body part possible. So we were both very sexually satisfied and mostly able to concentrate on the game.

Playing poker with Nate was great because we each had different strengths, which made us fairly evenly matched competitors. I was great at reading people, so I focused on Nate's expressions and mannerisms to help me decide my next move. Nate, on the other hand, counted the cards. He remembered every single card that'd been played and he knew what was left in the deck. If we could combine into one person, we'd make a killing in Vegas.

I was down one game when I looked at the clock and realized we had to get dressed if we were going to get cleaned up in time to meet Nate's friends by eight p.m. I was looking forward to hanging out with those guys. I'd always thought Nate's friends seemed nice, but I couldn't stand being around them because the conversation always turned to a guy Nate had been with, or a guy they thought he should be with. All that talk about Nate and other guys made my stomach hurt, so I steered clear of the whole situation. Now that Nate had a boyfriend, though, I knew they'd stop talking about him with other guys, so I could just have fun and get to know them.

"Okay, Nate, I admit defeat for this round. We should get in the shower and get going."

I started stacking up the cards and putting them back in the box. I was happy he'd won that round of poker. I think I'd beaten him the last couple of times and he was due. It was funny, there was something about Nate that entirely eliminated my normally over-the-top competitiveness. I didn't generally admit or even accept defeat. But it was different with Nate. I was uncharacteristically happy when he beat me at something because it meant he won, which was even better than me winning.

"Umm. Yeah, I guess. Listen, Jake..."

I had a feeling he was going to say we shouldn't go out with his friends. I could tell he wasn't thrilled with the idea, but I knew I could be different around them now. I'd be friendly. After all, Nate was friends with those guys, so they must be important to him, and anything that was important to Nate was important to me.

"I'm really looking forward to tonight, Nate. What were you going to say?"

Preemptive strike. Always a good strategy.

"Oh, umm. Nothing. Let's go."

We got into the shower and Nate was very quiet. He seemed anxious. I picked up the soap and cleaned his arms, chest, stomach, cock, balls, and legs. He started unwinding a little.

"Turn around, baby. I want to wash your back."

He turned and faced the showerhead as I gave the same careful attention to the back of his body. I poured some shampoo into my hands and massaged Nate's hair with it. He sighed heavily, and I could feel his whole body relaxing. I rinsed his hair and body, put my chin on his shoulder, and whispered in his ear, "I love you so much, Nathaniel."

Then I licked a path from his neck down to his shoulder. I kissed and sucked on the top of his shoulder and caressed his arms. He sighed softly as I kept licking and kissing down his body until I was on my knees behind him. He pressed his arms against the shower wall and rested his head on them.

The angle of his slightly leaning body made his ass stick out, which gave me great access. I put my hands on his cheeks, spread them apart, and ran my tongue down his cleft. Nate moaned and pushed his ass back into my face.

I kept licking him for a couple of minutes, focusing more and more on his puckered entrance. When his moans became loud and almost constant, I penetrated him with my tongue, while I reached my hand around and stroked his cock.

"Oh, Jake. Jake. Unghh. Unghhh."

He was thrusting his hips so that he was alternating between pushing his ass back against my face and pushing his dick harder through my fist. When he came, his entire body shuddered and he was gasping for air. Most of his seed was dripping down the shower wall, but some of it was on my hand.

Nate turned to look down at me just as I let go of his cock, pulled my tongue out of his ass, and licked his offering off my fingers. My God, he tasted so good. All of him, his skin, his ass, his cum, it all tasted so good to me.

Making love with Nate had seriously changed my entire perspective of how it felt to touch and taste another human being. Before him, I had fucked women. That was the extent of it. I guess I kissed them, but only as much as I absolutely had to. And I never licked them, not anywhere. I know, I know, I was selfish. But it wasn't like I gave a shit about them, or cared whether or not they'd want a repeat performance. In fact, I'd sometimes wondered why I'd even bothered fucking them—like, maybe my hand would've been better. I didn't know how I'd changed so quickly and completely to the point where I got hard just *thinking* about tasting Nate, other than the obvious fact that I was deeply in love with him.

Nate finally caught his breath and joined me on the shower floor. We sat silently, our foreheads touching, our hands stroking the backs of each other's head as the water ran over us. I could feel our love for each other radiating between us. At that moment, I realized I'd been a complete chickenshit during all of those years I'd been yearning for him but fucking countless, nameless women.

Those were mistakes, huge mistakes. I should've been fighting for him. I should've made sure he understood what I felt for him. But I didn't know how to change the past, how to undo that damage.

My clothes were still in my old room, so after we got out of the shower and dried off, I went in there to get dressed. I thought about my schedule for the coming week and whether I could come home at a decent hour to go through my stuff so I could sort it out and move it over to Nate's room, which we'd been sharing since we'd returned from our trip.

I put on a pair of Levi's, my black boots, and a gray, short-sleeved T-shirt I'd picked up at a diner we'd once stopped at during a car trip home from school. Then I combed my fingers through my hair and headed into Nate's room.

He was wearing dark, low-rise jeans that hugged his ass in the best possible way and buttoning a slim-fitting blue shirt, which highlighted his incredible chest and stomach and picked up the blue sparkles in his eyes. He had combed his hair and spiked it in the front.

"You look great. Here, let me help you get that shirt buttoned. It might be a welcome change from my usual goal of getting you *out* of your clothes. Of course, I'll be going right back to my wicked ways as soon as we get home."

I waggled my eyebrows and gave him my best leer. Nate grinned. Then he noticed my T-shirt and ran his hand over it.

"I remember this place. They had those great chili

cheese fries, which I managed to spill on you. I think the waitresses stopped breathing when you stripped your shirt off and bought this. We're just lucky we got out of there before they started fighting with each other about which one of them would get to go home with you."

I kissed him softly and stroked his cheek, hoping he could feel my love for him. I wished he could let go of my past mistakes and understand how deeply I loved him, and that I wouldn't stop, not for anyone, not ever. I knew we needed to talk, I needed to find a way to make him understand what I felt, and I really needed to understand what he felt, but there wasn't time right then. Our talk would have to wait.

"It would have been a fruitless fight, Nate. I was already going home with *you*, remember? Are you ready to go?"

WE GOT to the club and found Nate's friends sitting at a table overlooking the dance floor. They smiled when they saw Nate walking up. Then they noticed me behind him and looked surprised. I wondered why. Did they expect Nate to go out without his boyfriend? I know straight guys often want a night out away from their women—a guy's night out. But I guess I thought, since we were all guys, we could all hang out together.

Nate gave each of his friends a hug and sat down. Patrick looked uncomfortable as he reached his hand out to me. I shook it.

"How're you doing, Patrick?"

I waved to Ken and Scott. They looked tense. Man, this was going to be harder than I thought. Had I really been that much of a dick to them over the years?

"I'm going to head over to the bar. Vodka and cranberry, Nate?"

He nodded.

"Does anyone else want a drink?"

The other guys shook their heads no and smiled weakly at me. I walked over to the bar and felt relieved to be away from all the tension. I thought back to my past interactions with Nate's crew and recognized that I hadn't been particularly friendly, but it wasn't like I'd hit any of them. If anything, I'd just stayed out of their way. The bar was crowded, but the bartender came right over to me.

"Hey there. I haven't seen you in here before. You, umm, don't really look like our normal clientele."

I wondered what the hell he meant by that, and my face must have shown my anger at his comment because he raised his hands up and stepped back.

"I didn't mean anything by it, man. It's just we don't normally get guys dressed like you in this place. What can I get you to drink?"

I ordered Nate's drink and a beer for myself and wondered whether my clothes were an issue. I could honestly say it was the first time in my life I'd given any thought to what the fuck I was wearing.

As I approached the table with our drinks in my

hands, I noticed Nate and Patrick sitting next to each other, with Ken and Scott sitting across from them. All four guys were hunched over the table with their faces close together and it seemed like they were having an animated conversation. When I got closer, I heard Patrick almost yelling.

"So what does that mean, Nate? You're bringing this guy here because he, what? Let you suck him off or something, after you told him you were done drooling after him like a pathetic puppy? That doesn't make him gay, Nate. It just proves he's a self-absorbed asshole who doesn't want to lose his number-one fan."

Ken had noticed me coming up and he grasped Patrick's arm. All four guys turned in my direction, and the color drained from Patrick's face. They looked terrified. Okay, let's face it, I *was* a self-absorbed asshole. But not when it came to Nate. Never when it came to Nate. Did he actually believe that?

My chest felt like I'd been stabbed, and I was having trouble breathing. I set the drinks down on the table and squatted down so I wasn't towering over them. The last thing I needed was to scare Nate's friends.

"Is that what you told them, Nate? That I *let* you suck me off one time on vacation?"

Nate was frozen. He looked panicked and didn't respond. I rubbed the base of my hands over my eyes and held back tears that were working their way down. Then I turned to Nate, held his hands, and spoke softly.

"I shouldn't have come here. I get that now. I don't know what you told them, Nate, or why, but they're

your friends and it's your call. I guess I just expected...
something else."

I wanted to tell him I expected to be included in
that part of his life, in every part of his life. I expected
him to hold my hand at the market that morning rather
than pulling away when the shop owner looked at us. I
expected him to tell his friends I was his boyfriend, lover,
partner, whatever word people use to mean "everything,"
and that I wasn't some sort of one-night stand. But I knew
a bar wasn't the place for a heart-to-heart, so I stood up
and looked at Nate's friends.

"It was nice seeing you guys. Have fun tonight."

I was walking away when I heard Nate calling my
name. But I couldn't turn around. If I looked at him, I'd
break down right there and embarrass him in front of his
friends.

"I'll see you later at home. I'm sorry, Nate."

CHAPTER TWELVE

Nate

I **WAS** sitting on the shower floor with my forehead leaning on Jake's forehead, stroking his hair. I felt like my heart was going to beat itself right out of my chest because I was so full of love and emotion. I had been in love with this guy forever. *Forever!* How was it possible that I loved him even more?

I didn't even realize more was possible. I thought I was at the infinite end of how much one human being could feel for another, and then it was like the entire scale was reformulated and the way I'd previously felt seemed like nothing. I thought getting to touch him, to physically express my feelings for him, would satisfy those feelings, but instead it just added to them, made them stronger, more layered and complex.

It was all too much for me to process on my own. I'd tried to treat our relationship like a scientific challenge, but that wasn't going to work. It wasn't about numbers or formulas. It was about my feelings. There was so much running through my mind and my heart, and I wasn't capable of processing that kind of stuff without Jake. When it came to feelings and emotions, I needed to talk to him. But how could I talk to Jake about the fact that I was terrified of losing him, that I couldn't go back to the way things were, but I couldn't seem to control myself and I was bound to scare him away?

Well, we didn't have time to talk anyway. We were going out with my friends and we had to get ready. I got dressed and wondered how Jake would react to the club and what I was supposed to say to my friends about him being there. I couldn't very well tell them we were... Hell, I didn't even know what we were.

I was buttoning my shirt when Jake came into the room. He was wearing these old Levi's he had that were soft and faded in the crotch from all the years of his big cock and balls pressing against the fabric. He was facing me, but I knew exactly what his ass looked like in those jeans. It was an image I'd memorized. The jeans weren't tight at all, but the way they draped over his ass, they came in a little at the bottom of his crack so you could really make out the shape of his perfect, muscular globes.

He was helping me button my shirt when I noticed he was wearing a T-shirt we'd bought during a road trip we once took. It was soft from the years of wear and clung to his body in a remarkably sexy way. I smiled, thinking these were the clothes Jake chose to put on to go to a gay club. I knew he didn't give one thought to what he was putting on his body. Somehow, that made him look even more hot and masculine. I rubbed my hand over Jake's chest and felt his hard muscles through the soft fabric of his T-shirt.

"I remember this place. They had those great chili cheese fries, which I managed to spill on you. I think the waitresses stopped breathing when you stripped your shirt off and bought this. We're just lucky we got out of there before they started fighting with each other about which one of them would get to go home with you."

Jake kissed me and whimpered in my mouth as he ran his hand over my cheek. I loved him so much.

"It would have been a fruitless fight, Nate. I was already going home with *you*, remember?"

I did remember. We'd had a great time on that trip, playing the radio loud and singing along to the songs, sometimes making up our own words. We'd talked about school, our dreams for the future. I'd graduated from college early and started medical school by then. Jake loved calling me Dr. Richardson, and when we checked into motels along the way to get some sleep, he always put the room under my name, focusing on the doctor title. I told him to stop, but I actually loved it. He was so proud of me and that made me feel proud of myself.

"Are you ready to go?"

We went to the club and quickly spotted my friends. I sat down, and Jake went to get our drinks. As soon as he stepped away from the table, Patrick turned to me.

"So, umm, why is Jake here?"

I didn't know how to answer. I knew he wouldn't want people to know what'd been going on between us, but I couldn't find a way to explain why, after all of these years, he was coming with me to hang out with those guys. Truth be told, I wasn't sure myself. Scott spoke up to fill the silence.

"Look, Nate, it's not like we have a problem with him or anything, you know that. It's just..."

He paused and seemed nervous. Then Ken jumped in.

"It's just that we worry about you. You're a great guy, Nate, but no one is going to see that if you keep holing up in your apartment with Jake. We all know how you feel about him, but it isn't going to happen and you need to get that and move on. We asked you here to get you out, help you meet someone. That isn't going to happen with him here, and you know it. You won't even notice anyone else in the room. Nate, you really need distance from Jake. I know you don't want to hear that, but it's true."

My mind was still swimming in confusion about what was happening with Jake and how I could make sure it kept happening. I thought maybe I could try to explain it to my friends.

"No. You guys don't understand. It isn't like that. Well, I mean, not anymore. I get what you're saying, and actually, I said the same thing to Jake during our trip— about needing distance or whatever—but then things changed. We, umm, I mean, we did stuff, and I'm not so sure he's really completely straight, you know? I think I have a chance at...something."

Ken and Scott leaned into the table and looked at Patrick.

"What are you saying, Nate? He's your boyfriend

now?"

Oh, no. If Jake heard that he'd run for the door.

"No, no. I'm not saying that. I'm just saying things... changed. Things got...physical."

I couldn't figure out what to say so they would understand and lay off while I still refrained from telling them things I knew Jake wouldn't want them to know. All of a sudden, Patrick was raising his voice.

"So what does that mean, Nate? You're bringing this guy here because he, what? Let you suck him off or something, after you told him you were done drooling after him like a pathetic puppy? That doesn't make him gay, Nate. It just proves he's a self-absorbed asshole who doesn't want to lose his number-one fan."

I felt heat running through my body, with an anger that was unmatched. How the hell could Patrick say those things? Jake was the most giving, caring person I knew. I opened my mouth to tell Patrick to fuck off, when I noticed Ken's face go pale as he grabbed Patrick's arm. I turned in the direction of Ken's stare and saw Jake standing there. Oh my God. Did he hear that? Did he think I was telling them he was having sex with a guy? I didn't know what to say, how to react, how to fix that disaster.

Jake hunched down so he was looking into my eyes. He set the drinks down.

"Is that what you told them, Nate? That I *let* you suck me off one time on vacation?" He reached out and held my hand in between both of his. "I shouldn't have come here. I get that now. I don't know what you told them, Nate, or why, but they're your friends and it's your call. I guess I just expected...something else. It was nice seeing you guys. Have fun tonight."

I thought he'd be mad, livid, but he didn't seem mad at all. If anything, he looked and sounded sad, really sad. I even thought I saw tears in his eyes. We had hurt him. I could feel it. I didn't understand why exactly, but I could clearly feel it. I finally found my voice as he was walking away.

"Jake. Jake, wait."

He stopped, but didn't turn around.

"I'll see you later at home. I'm sorry, Nate."

And then he walked out of the bar. The four of us sat there in a stunned silence until Scott spoke up.

"What the fuck was that? I swear, Patrick, I almost pissed in my pants when I realized he heard you. I thought he was going to kill you for talking that way about him and that the rest of us would be collateral damage. I sure as hell didn't expect that reaction. Nate, what is going on? Seriously, spill."

Well, I guessed the damage was already done.

"He said he loves me. That he has always loved me. Of course, that was before this...fucking disaster of a night. I need to go home. I need to salvage whatever I can. I can't lose him. Not after what we've shared. I just can't lose him."

I was shaking and crying as I got up.

"Oh shit. I didn't understand what you were saying and I just never thought he... We'll take you home. You can't go alone."

We walked out of the bar and everything was wet.

It must have rained while we were in there and it was still drizzling every now and then. I didn't say anything as we headed back to my apartment. I was fixated on the hurt look on Jake's face and the way he'd held my hand while he spoke so softly. My friends walked me to my door and stood there, looking uncomfortable, while I unlocked it. As soon as I opened the door, I knew he wasn't home. The place felt empty.

"He isn't here. I don't know what to do."

I dragged my fingers through my damp hair and stepped inside. Patrick, Scott, and Ken followed. We sat on the couch for a while without talking until Ken finally cleared his throat and spoke up.

"I, umm, I've never seen Jake like that. I mean, I don't really know the guy, but I've been around him now and then since you and I met, and that's got to be at least five years. I've always thought he was gorgeous but mean and, honestly, kind of a jerk. He seemed different tonight. He, umm, he was holding your hand, Nate, and the way he looked at you. He was sad, but there was more to it. I, uh, I don't know what I'm saying."

Patrick nodded and Scott joined in.

"I know what you're saying, Ken. I've never had anyone look at me that way. I've never seen someone look at anyone that way. He looked at you like you were a treasure, like you were the only thing he could see, like the rest of us weren't even there. Why didn't you tell us, Nate?"

"I...I guess I thought he wouldn't want me to say anything. I'm confused. I have all of these thoughts clogging up my mind. I'm terrified of losing him." I groaned and rubbed my hands over my eyes. "I don't know what the hell I'm doing."

I got up and walked to the bathroom to splash some cold water on my face. I was clutching the counter and looking down at the running water, trying to get a hold of myself, when all three of them walked over.

"We're going to take off, Nate. We shouldn't be here when he gets home. I'm sure he doesn't want to see us. Or at least me."

"It's not your fault, Patrick. It's mine. I made this mess and I need to fix it. I need to talk to him and tell him how I feel."

And then, I suddenly realized Jake was home.

"He's here."

"What? How do you know? I didn't hear anything."

I hadn't heard anything either, but I knew he was home. I could feel it. I turned off the faucet, pushed my way past my friends, and walked toward the front door. Jake was standing with his sneakers and T-shirt in a pile by his feet. He was dripping wet and stripping off his running pants, leaving him wearing only his jock. He must have gone running. When he needed to clear his head, Jake exercised. He added the pants to the wet pile and looked at me. Our eyes connected and I could feel his love for me. We were standing there, gazing at each other from across the room, when my friends came around the corner and gasped.

"Holy shit."

All three of them had their mouths open as they

took in the sight of Jake, dripping wet, wearing only a jock. His muscles seemed even more firm and defined than usual, maybe because he'd been exercising, and his wet hair was a deep black, making his green eyes shine. Clothed Jake was the hottest thing any of them had probably ever seen anyway, but almost-naked Jake? Well, that was enough to make a guy swallow his own tongue.

"Will you guys please stop perving on my boyfriend and get out of here?"

I wasn't mad but I really wanted them to leave.

A wave of happiness tore over Jake's face. He walked across the room, dropped to his knees before me, and buried his face against my stomach. I stroked his cheek and combed my fingers through his hair. My friends finally managed to put one foot in front of the other and walked toward the door. Jake looked up at me and smiled.

"Boyfriend?"

Shit, had I called him my boyfriend? Well, I was too tired to pretend anymore. I had to put it all out there. To tell him what I felt. I took a breath and responded.

"Yes, boyfriend."

He wasn't running for the door or telling me off. In fact, he seemed happy. That helped me gather my courage. I got down on the ground so we were eye to eye and I kissed him—softly at first, and then passionately, pressing my tongue into his mouth, letting him suck on it.

"I love you more than I can say, more than I ever thought possible, Jake. I have always loved you. I will always love you. I love you. I love you. I love you."

He didn't pull away. He didn't laugh at me. He just smiled and rubbed his big hand against my cheek.

"It's about damn time, Nate."

CHAPTER THIRTEEN

Jake

AFTER I left Nate and his friends at the bar, I went home, changed my clothes, and went jogging. I had to clear my head and get out some energy and frustration. I knew he loved me. I knew it in my core and I wasn't going to let any silly insecurities grow and convince me otherwise. No, he loved me; I could tell. He was just too fucking scared to say it.

I think that was what hurt the most. The thought he was scared to say something to me. We'd always been able to tell each other everything. Well, I guess that wasn't true, was it? But still, how could he be scared of me? Didn't he know I would never, *could* never, hurt him? Not for anything.

I wanted to sit him down and shout it at him. "You love me, Nate. That's what you're feeling. You love me!"

It seemed like that might be the only way to get it through his thick skull. But I knew I wouldn't. That was one feeling I couldn't explain to him. He'd have to figure it out on his own. He'd have to find the words and I'd just have to wait until he got there. Well, I'd been waiting for most of my life to have Nate reciprocate my feelings; I could wait a little longer. Hell, I could wait a lot longer. I could wait forever. After all, what the fuck else was I going to do?

It was raining outside and the cars were splashing through the puddles. By the time I got home, I was soaked. I walked in and peeled off my clothes so I wouldn't drip all through the apartment. I was taking off my pants when Nate came into the room. I looked up and saw the love in his eyes and it warmed me. I wasn't sure how long we were standing there, just looking into each other's eyes.

"Holy shit."

His friends had come around the corner and they were staring at me with their mouths open. Not particularly charming, but at least they weren't calling me a self-absorbed asshole, so I guess that was an improvement.

"Will you guys please stop perving on my boyfriend and get out of here?"

He told his friends that I was his boyfriend! Not some guy he sucked off in a hotel room. I was so fucking happy that I walked over to him and collapsed, with my head leaning on his stomach. I looked up.

"Boyfriend?"

I saw a hint of anxiety cross his face, and then resignation.

"Yes, boyfriend."

Nate sat down and kissed me. Man, do I love kissing him. My entire body tingles, my chest almost hurts, and my cock hardens to full mast immediately.

"I love you more than I can say, more than I ever thought possible, Jake. I have always loved you. I will always love you. I love you. I love you. I love you."

Well, I guess I didn't have to wait forever after all. I'm sure I was grinning from ear to ear.

"It's about damn time, Nate."

"You aren't mad?"

"Mad? Why on earth would I be mad to hear that you love me? Nate, do you have any idea how long I've wanted to hear you say those words to me?"

He was looking down at the ground and his eyes were misty.

"Nate, you can talk to me. About anything. Please talk to me."

He scooted over to the couch and sat with his back against it. His eyes raked over my body with such power and such lust behind them that I swear his look alone almost drove me to orgasm. Then he looked back down. I sat next to him and stroked his arm as I waited for him to find his courage. His voice was choked with emotion when he finally spoke, still looking down.

"I'm terrified that you'll leave me. That I'll scare you away. That you'll change your mind."

I mentally cursed myself for probably the hundredth time in the past six weeks for the damage I'd clearly done to Nate with my stupid, thoughtless actions over the years. Why hadn't I seen that I was hurting him when I was fucking those women? I lifted his chin so his eyes met mine.

"Nathaniel, if there is one thing you can be sure of

in this life, one fucking constant that will *never* change, it's that I will always be here, loving you with everything I have and everything I am. That's not going to change. You can't scare me away, you can't push me away. I won't let you. Do you hear me, Nate? I won't let you. I'm the dumb jock you got saddled with in that hospital bassinet and I'll be drooling after you to the grave. Cradle to the grave, Nate. That's the way it's going to be. No matter what."

"You're not dumb," he mumbled it into my shoulder, followed by a kiss, and I smiled.

He should have a bumper sticker made, considering the number of times he'd said those same words to me over the years. We both sat on the floor, leaning on the couch, with our shoulders touching and our fingers twined together. I could tell that Nate was thinking, processing what I had said.

"Do you remember senior prom, Jake?"

I turned to him.

"Yeah."

"You let your date have it because she called you her boyfriend, and then you left her there."

So that was what this was about. That was why he'd relegated me to some fucking one-off with his buddies instead of owning our relationship. I sighed.

"Is that what you remember?"

He looked at me, confused.

"That's what happened."

"Come here, Nate."

I stood and reached my hand down to help him

stand. Then I gently pulled him to my room and sat him on my bed. I walked over to my dresser and picked up a framed picture.

"This is a picture of me with my prom date, Nate."

It was a picture of the two of us, wearing our tuxedos and smiling, with our arms draped across each other's shoulders. Nate looked at the picture and smiled, rubbing his thumb over it. Then he seemed confused again as he looked up at me.

"Your prom date? What do you mean?"

"Nate, I asked you to go to prom with me. Tell me you remember."

No response. Just that same confused look in his eyes. Fuck. I knelt at his feet.

"Okay, I'll remind you. Prom was coming up and everyone was talking about it. I asked you if you were going to go and you laughed, said you didn't have a date. I thought, well, you don't have to be attracted to me to go to prom with me. I mean, it's just dancing, right? So, I asked you to be my prom date. Do you remember what you said?"

I knew he was remembering, but he was still sitting there, just looking at me. No words were coming out of his mouth. So I kept talking.

"You said you didn't want to be some sort of gay poster child, going to prom with another guy. I didn't understand that. But I knew you were uncomfortable, so I told you we'd get a couple of girls to go with us and then we wouldn't be making a statement. We'd just have fun. Sylvia and Julie didn't have dates, so I told them they could come with us. I didn't ask Sylvia to be my date, Nate. And I sure as fuck wasn't her boyfriend."

Nate looked down at the picture for a couple of minutes before he finally spoke.

"You were serious? When you asked me to the prom, I mean. You were actually serious?"

I knew he was sensitive and I knew those years growing up in Bryerville were hard on him, that he felt inadequate. But I guess I never fully grasped the depth of the damage, of his insecurity.

"Of course I was serious. You know what, Nate? You never danced with me. I asked you that night but you laughed. I think you still owe me a dance."

His eyes were misty.

"Yeah. I guess I do."

So we got up, turned on the radio, and danced slowly in my room. Nate was still wearing his nice jeans and button-down shirt. I was coated with dried muck from the puddles and the rain, wearing nothing but a jock. It didn't matter. Everything except Nate faded away, just like it always did when we were in each other's arms. And we danced.

I fell asleep that night dreaming about the prom. In one particularly vivid dream, Nate was in his tuxedo, looking incredibly handsome, and we were dancing together, gliding across the room. All of a sudden, Nate dropped to his knees, unzipped my pants, and started licking up and down the length of my cock, swirling his tongue around the crown, licking the pearly drops that were being steadily released. He took my cock down his throat, and I moaned deeply, thrusting toward him.

My body trembled with the feel of Nate sucking me hard as he bobbed his head up and down. I could feel myself climbing toward the edge of an orgasm, and just as I started falling, shouting Nate's name, I heard his muffled moans and I realized—this wasn't a dream. It was a wake-up call. I caught my breath, opened my eyes, and looked down to see Nate cleaning my spent cock with his tongue. I groaned deeply when he pressed his tongue into the slit, tasting the last drops of my seed.

"It's still dark out. What time is it?"

Nate crawled up my body, covering me with his. He licked my neck and sucked on my earlobes as he answered.

"It's only five. You don't have to work any cases today, though, so you can sleep in as late as you want. Right now, I need you."

He kissed me softly, covered my lips with fast licks, and then sucked on my tongue. I trembled, feeling his passion, his desperation for me. Our cocks were pressed together, and as we were kissing, Nate was rubbing against me, letting our cocks caress each other.

"You feel so good, Nate."

"Mmm. So do you. I bet I can make you feel even better."

He licked his way down my body, avoiding my quickly recovering cock and taking one testicle at a time into his hot, wet mouth. I moaned and whimpered at the attention. After spending time on my balls, he pushed my knees toward my chest and swiped his tongue down the length of my ass. He worked my ass with his tongue. Kissing, sucking, penetrating. By the time he pressed a lubed finger inside me, my cock was already hard as steel and aching for another release.

I reached my hand over to stroke my cock and Nate pushed it away. I groaned, but kept my hands away from my dick. He added another finger, and I was writhing on the bed, asking him to help me find relief. He moaned loudly in response, got on his knees in front of me and raised my legs against his chest, resting them on his shoulders. His lubricated, condom-covered cock grazed my opening, and I tried to push back onto it but he was pressing on my thighs, not letting me move, making it clear he was controlling the experience.

He entered slowly, stopping every couple of inches to make slow thrusts. It felt like torture. Marvelous, delicious torture. I tried to wait but I couldn't. I needed to come right then, so I moved my hand back to my aching cock. Nate was watching me and growled.

"Don't touch yourself. I'll let you come, Jake, but not yet. Don't worry. I'll know when you're ready."

Oh, dear God. I didn't know how much longer I could take this. He was pressing his thick, long cock inside me, brushing against my prostate, but he refused to pound himself against it and his slow pace was just enough to keep me hard and wanting, but not enough to let me find my release. I needed to get off. But he just kept up the maddeningly slow pace, holding my hips down so I couldn't thrust against him, not letting me stroke my cock. My body shook and my moans got louder and louder, until I couldn't take it anymore. All coherent thought left my body and I started to beg.

"Please, Nate. Please. I need to come. Let me come. Nate…oh please…please."

Just as I thought I would pass out from the pleasure and frustration, he pulled almost all the way out and started pounding into me, hard and fast. It only took a few strokes and I was shooting against my stomach, chest, and chin while I screamed his name. I clenched and that was it for him too. He moaned as he released while he was in my ass.

Nate licked my seed off my body until I was completely clean. He stroked my hair, kissed my cheek, and settled his head in the crook of my neck.

It took all the energy I had left to whisper in his ear.

"You own me, Nate. You fucking own me."

CHAPTER FOURTEEN

Nate

HIS BREATH was warm on my neck, his arm was draped over my chest, clutching me tightly, and I could smell his hair, his skin, all of him, as he slept beside me. I don't sleep much. My mind is always going over things and it won't let my body rest. But I'm used to it, and I usually like it because it means I can get more done. When I was a kid, it was more studying, more reading. In college, it was a double course load that allowed me to graduate early. In medical school, there wasn't all that much time anyway, but I was still able to do some work at the lab on the side because I was studying when everyone else was sleeping. And since I'd started working at the lab full-time, I'd spent those sleepless hours going over whatever project we had on hand.

Lately, though, it seemed like I'd been spending my restless nights thinking about Jake. Or, more accurately, about my relationship with Jake. A few weeks earlier, I'd finally gathered the courage to tell him how I felt, that I loved him, that I wanted us to be a couple. I'd expected him to be angry, to push back, to run away. But he didn't do any of those things. Instead, he danced with me. He held me in our little apartment and danced with me to whatever song was playing on the radio.

I wrapped my arms around Jake and thought about how good he tasted, how much I loved going to sleep feeling just a little sore after he'd been inside me. Jake was sleeping with his head resting on my shoulder, holding my hand. I put my face down on his head and smelled his hair. He smelled so good, so masculine. Jake has this incredibly strong presence that he exudes in every way. When I hear his deep voice or smell his skin, I immediately feel safe, like nothing bad can happen to me.

I thought about the reactions most people had to Jake, and decided they fell into one of two categories. Either, one, they were scared shitless of him, or two, they were very attracted to him (and still a bit scared). Almost every woman on the planet seemed to fall into category number two, and if they were good-looking, then Jake had probably fucked them. As for category number one, well, I think every guy who met Jake but didn't know him really, really well fell into that category. Even the guys Jake had known for years from work, and his buddies, were somewhat scared of Jake. But despite being scared of Jake, guys still admired him. It was like they wanted to be him and they tried to hang around him, hoping something would rub off.

As I looked down at the sleeping figure cuddled up on me, and thought about how he whimpered when we were in bed together, I chuckled at the idea of him being scary. The truth was, though, that he was rough. I knew that; I had seen it since we were kids. Well, actually since we were in middle school.

I'd tried to pinpoint it once and decided middle school was when it had really started, the darkness that seeped out of him and scared the daylights out of people. Something changed in Jake at around that time. He'd always been a strong guy, inside and out. But he'd pretty much kept to himself, and he hadn't gotten physical with anyone. That changed in middle school.

He was quarterback of our varsity football team, even though we were only in sixth grade, so he was younger than all of the other guys on the team. I assumed that was what altered him—that he needed to show those older guys he could be just as tough as anyone else on the field, and the aggression just started following him in his daily life.

He always seemed on guard, like he was waiting for someone to do something or say something he didn't like. He even got into a couple of physical scuffles with other guys. That didn't end in middle school, and I knew he was still just as rough, if not rougher, because I'd seen him come home on several occasions looking like he'd been in a fight.

So yes, I knew all about Jake's violent side. It was just that he'd never—and I mean never—been rough with me. With me, he'd always been incredibly caring and sweet, and that had certainly carried over into our new physical relationship.

My God, our physical relationship. I wanted him

all the time. I spent my days half-hard, thinking about his body, about how he'd touched me the night before, about how I'd touch him that night.

The night after the incident with my friends at the bar, I woke him with a blow job and then made love to him slowly. Very slowly. By the end, he was begging me to let him come, and then he shouted my name and told me that I owned him.

That was what I'd wanted to hear. I'd wanted to know that he needed me, that he belonged to me. The way that I belonged to him. There was something unbelievably arousing to me about the fact that this strong, rough, Rambo of a guy turned into a gentle, compassionate puppy when he was with me. It made me feel special, because it meant he thought I was special.

After that night, he moved his things into my room. Not that he had many things. The guy had the most minimalistic wardrobe of anyone I knew. And he didn't really have much else either. A box of papers, his gun locker, and a few pictures—that was it.

I looked over at the pictures—one of the two of us at prom, one of his parents on their wedding day, and one of our whole family during our high school graduation. In that picture, Jake and I wore our robes and held our diplomas, with both sets of parents crowded next to us, smiling proudly. That was a great day, and I'm still grateful I got to share it with Jake.

My parents and I had always gotten along. I was an easy kid. I didn't rebel, didn't mouth off. In fact, I did pretty much everything they said, until they wanted me to leave Jake. That I wouldn't do, couldn't do.

I **TOOK** the SAT during our sophomore year in high school, just for fun. I hadn't given the test any thought and I hadn't prepared. Yet I somehow managed to do well. Very well. I got a perfect score, which resulted in letters and phone calls from a bunch of colleges and programs. Some of the colleges were tops in the country, and they offered me a free education.

Our school principal was a combination of excited and relieved. She was thrilled one of her students would have an opportunity to study with the best young minds in the country, and she was grateful that she could stop trying to find someone to teach me something I hadn't already managed to learn on my own. She said I could graduate early, even without taking the remaining couple years of high school.

My parents had never had an opportunity to leave our town, let alone our state. They'd gone to Bryerville Community College and they were happy with their lives, but I knew they wanted more for me. And those special programs offered more, much more. As exciting as it seemed to grow my mind, to study with our nation's top academics, the idea of going anywhere without Jake was numbing. I couldn't even breathe without him, let alone think without him.

And he needed me. I'd helped him with his

homework since elementary school. I'd studied with him for every test. Jake was a smart guy. Really smart. But for some reason, he'd always struggled with schoolwork. The way the books were written didn't make sense to him. But when I explained things, he always understood. We had our own special language, our own way of communicating.

If I left, Jake would struggle to finish school. He wouldn't have time to focus on football, which he loved, if he had to spend all his time trying to understand his schoolwork. I wasn't willing to do that to him, and I wasn't willing to live without him.

I told the principal I wanted to finish high school. And I told my parents I wouldn't go. We fought, we yelled, they cried. But ultimately, my mom relented and my dad followed. I made them all promise not to tell Jake about the offers. I didn't want him to feel like he was keeping me from something. The truth was that he wasn't. There was no program, no college, nothing that could ever matter to me as much as him. He was my priority.

So I stayed in Bryerville, helped Jake finish high school with good grades so he could get into a good college, and then we went together. It wasn't Ivy League, it wasn't a special program with other gifted kids, but it was the two of us together, and that was all that mattered to me. It was all that had ever mattered to me.

As I lay in bed next to Jake, all those years later, I felt incredibly grateful that I'd been able to share my life with him. My entire life. Jake knew me. I mean, he really knew me. He knew my flaws, my fears, my shortcomings.

I could name all the good parts of me that he knew too, but that wasn't the point. It was easy to love the good parts, to want the good parts. But he didn't just love the me I tried to project. No, he loved me completely, warts and all.

I finally realized that when I shared my insecurities and fears with him and the love in his eyes didn't falter. It was the same love and acceptance he'd always shown me, even on my worst days. The love that made him the best friend I'd ever had. The best friend anyone could ever hope to have.

He'd said he was in love with me and promised he wouldn't stop loving me. I hadn't always believed in myself, but I had always trusted Jake with everything. He was the strongest, most reliable person I'd ever known. He had always been there for me. He'd never let me down. Even if I didn't understand how someone as wonderful as Jake could want me, I knew he wouldn't lie to me, hurt me, or betray me.

So there I lay, next to the man I'd always wanted, my doubts fading into oblivion as tears of joy streamed down my face with the knowledge of the happiness that lay ahead, of the life we'd continue to share together. Then I closed my eyes, and finally fell asleep with a deep sense of comfort and security for what the next day, and all the days ahead, would bring.

CHAPTER FIFTEEN

Jake

AS THE weeks and months went by, Nate seemed happier and more at peace with our relationship. He held my hand when we went out, rested his head on my shoulder when we saw movies, and he even kissed me on the street and in restaurants. I think he finally believed my feelings were sincere. As for me, well, I'd never been happier. I knew it was obvious because when I was playing pool with my buddies one night, they actually commented on it.

"Who is she, Jake? Who is the piece of ass that gave you that dumb fucking grin on your face? And, um, can I share her or at least have her when you're done with her?"

I leaned down and lined the pool cue up with the ball.

"Fuck off, Jason. I'm not sharing. And I'm never going to be done with *him*. Nine ball, corner pocket."

I sunk the ball and looked up to see two of my buddies with shocked expressions on their faces, and the third with a smile.

"So, you and Nate finally got to it, huh? I wondered

what the fuck was stopping you. Congratulations, man."

Anton was smiling, but Jason and Todd were still standing there, dumbstruck. Eventually, Todd spoke up.

"Wait. Seriously? What the fuck are you saying, Jake? And how the fuck did you know, Anton?"

Anton took his turn at the table and then drank a swig of his beer.

"How the fuck did you *not* know, Todd? Haven't you ever noticed the way Jake looks at Nate? It's like Nate hung the fucking moon," he picked up his beer again and slurred, "with his dick."

Todd shifted from foot to foot, processing the information. Jason snickered as he picked up the cue and hit the ball. Then he scratched his balls and laughed.

"Well, I sure as shit don't want any of *that* action, then. Todd, when you're done imagining our friend with a dick up his ass, do you think you can manage to pick up the pool cue? It's your turn, asshole."

Todd turned a couple of shades of red and growled at Jason.

"I'm not imagining...oh fuck off, Jason!"

He took a long drink from his beer and then he turned to me with his eyes lowered.

"He, umm, he seems like a good guy, Jake. I'm glad you found someone. It means Abby can stop hounding me about finding you a nice girl."

We got back to the game. And even though Todd seemed a bit distracted, he was over it by the time we finished, giving all three of us shoulder bumps as he took off to get home to his wife and kids. They were good guys, deep down. I'd always known that, otherwise I wouldn't have spent any time with them. Still, it felt nice that they were happy for me. And that I didn't have to beat the shit out of any of them.

The three of us decided to play one more game, and Anton went up to the bar to get our beers. Just then, two guys who'd had too much to drink and were horsing around got a little carried away, and one of them fell back on Anton, knocking him to the ground. I knew that was bad news. Anton never met a fight he could avoid, and he was already pretty drunk. I started to walk over when Anton got up and punched the guy hard in the stomach, knocking him against the bar.

"What's your fucking problem, man? You want to start something?"

I stepped in between them and showed the two guys my badge.

"All right, guys. This is over. Everyone needs to get out of here and sober up."

The two guys we didn't know were about to say something, but then they looked at my badge and decided defending their pride wasn't worth getting into it with the police, so they turned around and walked out of the bar.

"What's your fucking problem, Jake? You don't think I could handle those guys? They're two pussies. And don't pull that cop bullshit with me. Get the fuck out of my way."

He pushed past me, but I grabbed his shoulder.

"You really want to get into a fight now, Anton?

I don't give a shit, but you're on probation, asshole. You want to go back in for two more years? I can't stop them from arresting your ass if someone calls the cops. Go home and sleep it off, man."

He knew I was right.

"Fine. I'm getting out of here. I need to get laid. Fucking assholes."

He kept grumbling as he walked out. I thought about the irony that I spent my days working cases and arresting criminals while most of my friends had arrest records. Truth was, I understood those guys. I wasn't actually any different. I just managed to keep it in check most of the time, for Nate.

"You have time for one more beer, Jake? It's on me."

"Sure thing, Jason."

I sat down at the bar, knowing what he wanted to discuss and thinking about how to stop him. He ordered two beers and turned to me, looking nervous.

"I...umm. I just wanted to thank you for..."

I put my hand on his shoulder to stop him from talking. He was a nice guy, but dumb as fuck, and he didn't know when to keep his mouth shut.

"No need to thank me, Jason. I didn't do anything. And even if I had done something, it wouldn't have been for you."

He nodded and we drank our beers quietly. I hoped he wouldn't bring it up again, and that he had enough sense not to talk about it with anyone else.

Jason's sister had caught her twelve-year-old

daughter's basketball coach with his hands all over the girl and his pants around his knees. So she'd shot him. Turns out the piece of shit had been diddling girls on the team for years, but she still got arrested. Apparently vigilantism wasn't acceptable. There weren't any witnesses other than the girl, who wasn't talking, so the only real evidence against Jason's sister was the gun they found in her house. I lifted the key to the evidence room, went in one night when no one was around, and got rid of the gun. Truth was, no one actually wanted to go after the girl's mother, they just didn't feel like they had a choice. But without the only real, tangible evidence, they had an excuse to let it go.

But Jason didn't need to thank me, because I didn't do it for him. I didn't even do it for his sister, not that I didn't admire what she'd done to that asshole. Like everything else in my life, I did it because of Nate. My stomach hurt with the memory as I finished my beer and left the bar.

IT WAS the first day of sixth grade, and I had to stay at school for football practice after classes ended.

Football was a big deal in our town, so lots of guys wanted to play. That meant our school was able to field two teams. The varsity team was mostly made up of ninth-graders, with a couple of eighth-graders. The sixth- and seventh-graders the coach thought would be good enough for varsity, eventually, got to play on JV. Everyone else was shit out of luck.

We had tryouts for the teams at the end of the summer, and the coach pulled me aside after the first day and told me if I continued to play like I had that day, I'd be the youngest guy ever to play varsity. True to his word, the coach put me on the varsity team and made me the starting quarterback. That meant practice after school every day.

Nate and I had always walked home from school together. So, he said he'd stay late too, and study. After classes ended for the day, I found Nate and asked him where he'd be studying so I could come get him after practice. He was very excited and told me the science teacher had offered to stay late with him and show him a cool experiment. I chuckled at how happy he got from the prospect of, basically, doing extra schoolwork.

After practice, I walked over to Mr. Smith's room and noticed that all of the blinds were down. That was odd, because the blinds were up during class, and none of the other rooms had their blinds pulled down. I walked into the classroom, and Nate turned to me and smiled. He was standing in his underwear, looking into a microscope.

The hairs on the back of my neck stood up and I got a really bad feeling in my stomach. I hurried over to Nate and wrapped him in my jacket. Nate hadn't gone through a single growth spurt at that point, so he was very, very small for his age. I was bigger than most of the ninth-graders and even some of the teachers by then, so my jacket was huge on him and it covered him to his knees.

"What is going on? Why are you standing here in your underwear? Where are your clothes, Nate?"

Nate looked confused, like he'd honestly forgotten that he was standing in a classroom practically naked.

"Oh, Mr. Smith opened a soda and it sprayed all over my clothes, so he told me to take them off and he'd dry them for me in his office." He gestured distractedly toward a door at the end of the room. "Since the school is closed and no one else is here, he said I could use this microscope to look at these slides while he does that. Look at this, Jake, it's really great…"

Nate was explaining the slides and what he was seeing under that microscope, but all I could focus on was what I was seeing in front of me. How does someone "accidentally" open a soda so that it sprays completely over another person to the point where their clothes are too wet to wear? Since when do teachers tell their students to take off their clothes in a classroom? When did Mr. Smith close the blinds? And how exactly was he going to dry off Nate's clothes in his office?

I interrupted him.

"He told you to use this particular microscope?"

"What? Oh, yeah this one. He even put the first slide in and put the others right next to it. These are amazing."

Nate kept talking about the slides as I scanned the room. There were several microscopes out on the tables. Why this particular microscope? I looked around more slowly and noticed that, to use the microscope Mr. Smith had selected, Nate had to stand exactly parallel to the door leading to the teacher's office.

I walked over to that door and saw a vent right above it, with a strange shadow inside. I put my fingers into the vent and pulled myself up. There was a small black piece of metal propped right inside. I pulled on it with my finger and slid it down, noticing that it was connected to a wire. I quickly turned around and was relieved to see Nate still looking into that microscope, completely fascinated. I yanked the wire and stuffed it, along with what I figured was a very small camera, into my jeans pocket.

"Hey, bud, I'm going to go see if your clothes are dry and I'll be right back, okay?"

I walked into Mr. Smith's office without knocking and closed the door behind me. His desk was pushed up against the same wall as the door, though it would have fit much better in almost any other part of the room.

He tried to act normal, but he stuttered a bit as he asked me what I was doing there. I didn't give him a chance to finish his question before I grabbed him around the throat and squeezed tight. Mr. Smith was a short, pudgy guy, and even at the age of twelve, I was stronger than him.

"Where is the tape?"

It took every bit of willpower I had not to raise my voice. The last thing I wanted was for Nate to hear me yell and somehow figure out what'd happened.

I realized that my grip on Mr. Smith's throat was

so tight he couldn't speak.

"I'll loosen my grip, but you better not yell. In fact, you better fucking whisper."

I relaxed my hand, but only enough to let him get his words out.

"What tape? I don't know what you're—"

He was still stuttering, clearly terrified. I tightened my grip on his throat.

"Do you actually think I don't know what a camera looks like? I know that was a camera in the vent. I know the wire runs through the vent and down this wall."

I used my empty hand to lightly touch the wall, next to the door.

"I know there's probably a hole in the back of one of your desk drawers, where you feed in the wire and connect it to a VCR. And I know you pulled the tape out when you heard me come into the classroom. Now, I'm going to ask you again, and you better think about what your science training taught you about how long a man can stay conscious with restricted oxygen flow to his brain. Where is the tape?"

He instinctively looked down at his briefcase, which was sitting on the floor. I pushed the case over to him with my foot and kept my grip on his throat.

"Get it out of the case."

He was shaking as he pulled the case onto his lap, reached around inside, and pulled out a VCR tape.

"Put the tape on the desk."

He put the tape down and tried to say something, but I didn't give him a chance. I had never hit anyone before that moment, but thinking of what he had done to Nate, what I knew he could've done, lit a fire deep within me. I held his throat so he couldn't make any noise. Then I gathered all the strength I had, all that anger, focused it on my arm, and punched his face. My first shot hit his eye, the next hit his nose, and the third his jaw. I wanted to keep going, but I was worried that I was taking too long and Nate would realize that something was going on. Besides, the fucking pervert was already unconscious from either the oxygen deprivation, the blows to the face, or both.

I let go of his throat and his head dropped down on the desk. I tucked the tape against my lower back, into the top of my jeans, and covered it with my shirt. Then I picked up Nate's damp clothes off the desk and headed back into the room. Nate was still looking into the microscope, mesmerized.

"Here you go, Nate. They're not too wet to wear home. Besides, you can keep my jacket on to stay warm. Mr. Smith said we should get going."

The next morning, we had a substitute teacher in science class, and eventually they hired a replacement. That piece of shit didn't come back to school, but the angry fire in my gut still burned. We were just kids, and Nate was so sweet and naive. He loved school, loved learning. The thought that a teacher, someone in authority whom he trusted, could take advantage of Nate that way changed my entire perception of the world around me.

I was angry to my core and I could never really trust anyone after that. Well, anyone except for Nate, of course. I'd trust him with everything. After all, he was my Nate.

I HATED thinking about that day. It still terrified me. And I wasn't a guy who scared easily. Actually, I wasn't a guy who got scared at all. It was why I was good at my job, and why I got assigned to undercover details with the scum of the earth—I had the ability to stay cool in a crisis. Other guys got nervous, or anxious, or scared, and it gave them away. That didn't happen to me, because there'd never been anything anyone could do to me that would've mattered. Not as long as Nate was safe and happy.

That day in middle school, he came so close to losing his happiness, his sweetness, his peacefulness. I wanted him to carry those feelings and that safety for his entire life. Tears burned my eyes as I walked into our building and up the stairs. I brushed them away, reminding myself he was safe, that nothing had happened to him. I'd gotten rid of the video, no one saw it, and he never knew how close he'd come to... I wouldn't even let myself think of what he'd come close to.

The apartment was dark and quiet when I got in, so I knew Nate was already asleep. He'd been working so hard, trying to develop a new vaccine. His brilliance never ceased to amaze me.

I took a quick shower, dried off, and quietly walked over to the bed. Nate was lying on his side, his blond hair mussed and tousled over his face and the pillow. He was so damn beautiful. And he was mine.

I lifted the blanket, slid in behind him, and felt his body immediately react. He mumbled as he turned toward me, eyes still closed, and snuggled into my chest. I kissed the top of his head and rubbed his back while he slept peacefully. I pushed the bad memories away, that day in school with Mr. Smith, the night of the accident, the bashers outside of the bar, all of them.

He was safe. He'd always been safe. And he'd always be safe. I'd keep making sure of it. I whispered to him before I closed my eyes.

"I love you, Nate."

CHAPTER SIXTEEN

Nate

"I SWEAR, Jake, if I didn't know better, I'd accuse you of weighting these dice or something. How is it possible that you've landed on every railroad?"

It was Sunday morning, and we were sitting around the coffee table in our living room, eating toast with jam, and playing Monopoly. Jake was on fire with his rolls and I was pretty sure I didn't have enough money left to pay the rent for another loop around the board.

"What can I say? I'm just exceptionally talented with my hand and wrist, Nate. I can maneuver them in a way that makes things come out just the way I want."

He gave me a predatory smile as he spoke and looked down at my dick, which immediately responded by tenting my sweat pants.

"Are we still talking about the dice, or are you referring to other skills?"

He shrugged and smiled.

"If you don't know after the last six months, Nate, then I guess I'm just talking about the dice. Your roll."

He moved a bit as he spoke and raised his knee,

leaving a great view through the leg of his exercise shorts. He wasn't wearing any briefs, so I could see his thick, long, slightly plump cock resting against his leg. I wanted to move my tongue over the vein running down its length. I guess I must've rolled the dice, though I had no recollection of anything other than Jake's dick.

"Oh, looks like you landed on one of my railroads again, buddy. Do you have enough cash on hand to pay for a ride, or will you need to take it out in trade? I might be willing to let you ride my railroad for free, if you're willing to give me a ride on your, ehm, train." He waggled his eyebrows at me. "What do you say?"

How was it that he could make playing board games hot? I crawled over to his side of the coffee table on my hands and knees, lifted his shirt, and nibbled my way up his stomach and chest. When I reached his neck, he raised his arms and I lifted his shirt off. I continued the nibbles and kisses up his neck and around to his ear.

"I say yes," I murmured into his ear as I licked and sucked on his earlobe.

Jake was leaning against the couch, his eyes closed. He moved his hands to the back of my head, curled his fingers into my hair, and pulled me to his mouth. As our tongues danced, I reached down to his shorts and he raised his ass so I could push them down. Once I got the shorts down to his knees, I broke the kiss to get them the rest of the way off.

No matter how many times I saw Jake's body, he still took my breath away. The man was truly a work of art. Every muscle was perfectly defined. His skin had a beautiful, dark tone even though he didn't spend any time in the sun. He was breathing heavily, his eyes darkened with lust, and he was gazing at me with deep intensity.

I traced each of his nipples with my tongue and gently brushed my fingers over his cock. He was trembling and whimpering. I could tell he was full of need and desire. He was ready.

"I want you on your hands and knees."

My voice was low and husky in his ear.

He groaned and kissed me desperately, pushing his pelvis up so his naked cock rubbed against mine through my pants. Then he pulled back and assumed the position. I was still fully clothed, kneeling behind him. I ran my hands through his hair, down his neck and back, leaving a trail of goose bumps in their wake. His cock was dripping, so I reached my hand around, collected his seed, and rubbed it into his ass. Then I pulled my sweats down so they were right below my ass, and I lined up my glistening cock with his opening.

We had gone through the whole panoply of STD testing a few months prior. Making love without any barriers was a first for both of us, and one of the advantages to monogamy—in addition to truly getting to know your mate's body and how to make him feel good, feeling safe and comfortable enough to let go completely and not hold anything back.

I let the pearly drops collect on the crown of my cock and then I pushed my way into Jake. He gasped a bit from the sensation—we usually used more lubrication. I pulled back, trying to decide if I should just keep going, use spit, or go into the bedroom for the lube. Then I noticed the jar of jam. I took a big spoonful of jam out of the jar and rubbed it onto my dick and into Jake's hole.

Jake gasped. "Aren't you creative?" His voice was very low.

I pressed my fingers into his mouth and he sucked off the jam as I pushed the head of my cock past his ring. He moaned and relaxed his body, letting me push in the rest of the way. I could feel his pubic hair against me and my balls were pressed against him. I was home.

I found his spot and made short, rabbit thrusts against it as I gnawed on the back of his neck and shoulders. I wanted to tease him, make it last, but my need was too great. I couldn't hold off for long. After several minutes of pumping into him, I felt my balls pull up, and I made one last push as I called out his name and filled him with my seed.

I caught my breath, and flipped him over so he was lying with his back on the floor. Then I plunged my mouth down on his cock, taking it into the back of my throat. Jake was moaning and grasping my hair with his fingers as he pushed himself up to meet my mouth. I sucked hard, twirled my tongue around his cock on the upstrokes, and bobbed my head up and down. After a few seconds, my mouth filled with his release as he shouted out.

"Oh God, Nate. You're so fucking good at that. Ughh...ughh...oh, yeah."

I finished swallowing and sucked a bit more, getting the last of his cum out. Then I dragged my tongue up his body and ended at his mouth, kissing him as our bodies pressed together, rubbing jam over both of us.

"So does that ride qualify me for a free trip on your railroad?" I mumbled.

He laughed and opened his mouth to answer me, when his phone beeped.

"Damn it."

He sat up, taking me with him, and reached for the phone. His face grew dark as he read the message.

"I'm so sorry, babe, but I have to go in to work. Something's going on."

I scooted off him, lifted my pants back up, and shifted uncomfortably because of the sticky jam. I needed to clean up. Jake kissed me on the head, got up, and walked into our bedroom. I heard the shower start.

I'd expected to spend the whole day with Jake, just the two of us, doing nothing...and everything, together. I was disappointed, but I tried not to show it as Jake finished what had to be the fastest shower of all time and walked out of the bedroom wearing faded jeans, a black sweater, and his old black boots. He was putting on a worn, lined, canvas jacket, and I noticed that he wasn't wearing his shoulder harness. He walked over to me and stroked my cheek.

"I promise I'll make this up to you, okay? I shouldn't be gone too long. I love you, baby."

"Love you too."

He walked out and I sighed deeply. I'd barely seen him over the last week. He'd been leaving early, coming home late, and even when he was home, we were constantly getting interrupted by texts or phone calls and he'd suddenly leave. He never told me who was calling, but I could hear a woman's voice coming through the phone.

Some nights I stayed up, waiting for him to return. He always went straight to the bathroom and took a long shower. I loved the smell of Jake's body, even when he was sweaty, so on one of those nights I asked him to come to bed and skip the shower, but he refused. By the time he crawled into bed, his skin was red and almost raw from the scrubbing.

I started packing up the game and smiled as I put it into the box. It was the same Monopoly game we'd had as kids. It had doodles on the back from a day when we were about three or four years old and decided the game needed to be more colorful. We'd lost most of the playing pieces over time and replaced them with coins, so instead of the metal thimble, iron, shoe, dog, top hat, and wheelbarrow making their way around the board, it was a penny, nickel, dime, quarter, and silver dollar. When we still lived at home and all six of us played together, we added other random items to the mix so we'd each have a playing piece.

Those family game nights were fun. We all sat around the dining room table at Jake's house, his mom baked snickerdoodle cookies, and his dad made us all milkshakes. We spent hours laughing together, playing games, and talking. We hadn't had a night like that since his parents had died. I missed them, and I knew Jake did too.

That gave me an idea. I called my mom and got the recipe for the cookies. I knew she'd gotten Mama Bev's (that was what I always called Jake's mom) recipes after she died. When Jake got back, we would eat cookies, drink milkshakes, and play board games.

I cleaned up around the apartment, got some laundry going, and headed out to the store. Man, am I domestic or what? I laughed a bit to myself, but the truth was that I loved doing those household things, just like I loved sitting around the house playing board games with Jake. Those were the things of daily living, the things families did, and that was what we were—a family.

We'd grown up that way, we'd lived that way our entire lives, and I knew we'd always be that way. The two of us, together. Completely together.

After I got everything I needed at the store, I went home and mixed the ingredients. Once I had the first batch of cookies in the oven, I took a quick shower to finally get that crusted jam off of me and got dressed. When I walked into the kitchen, I could see the message light blinking on my phone.

"Hi, Nate. I'm sorry but, um, something came up and I won't be home for a while."

What did that mean? I called him back, but his phone went straight to voicemail. I sighed, took the first batch of cookies out of the oven, slid another batch in, and called Patrick. I needed to go out and do something to occupy my mind. I had a really bad feeling about the whole situation with Jake.

"Hey, Pat. What're you up to today?"

"Hi there, stranger. Not much. I just need to pick up some movies to send to my mom at home."

"Sounds scintillating. Do you want some company?"

He laughed.

"Sure thing, Nate. I'll come by your place in a little while and we'll head out."

I was just putting the last few cookies on a plate when I heard a knock on the door. I picked up my jacket and headed out with Patrick. We decided to stop for lunch, and ended up sitting and chatting in a cafe. I figured Jake would call me when he was done, but my phone hadn't rung. I checked it just in case I hadn't heard it ring, and noticed it was off.

"Damn. Looks like the battery died on my phone again. I need to get this thing replaced. I swear the battery can't hold a charge for more than a couple of hours. It's ridiculous."

I slammed the phone down on our table. Patrick laughed and handed me his phone.

"Don't take it out on the poor phone, Nate. It's not the phone's fault that you miss your boyfriend. Here, you can use mine to check your voicemail and see whether he's called."

"Sorry. He's just been working a lot."

I smiled sheepishly at him as I took his phone and checked my voicemail. No messages. I gave him back the phone and tried to get the frown off my face.

"Okay, so are you ready to go pick up those movies for your mom?"

We chatted as we made our way to a sketchy neighborhood where Patrick bought movies from a guy who either pirated them somehow, stole them, or both. I was already in a bad mood, so I started nagging.

"Seriously, Pat. You know this isn't legal, don't you? I think you can afford to buy movies from a retail store like the rest of us."

Patrick was looking away and he didn't answer.

"Hey, Nate, isn't that Jake? Let's go catch him so you can tell him your phone isn't working." He continued, almost under his breath. "Then maybe you'll stop being so grouchy and obsessed with the possibility of missing his call."

He was pointing across the street, and I thought he was just trying to distract me so I'd stop giving him a hard time, but when I looked over, I saw Jake walking into a bar with several other guys and a woman. We waited for the light to change and then walked across the street and into the bar.

It was dark inside so it took my eyes several seconds to adjust, but when they finally did, I couldn't believe what I was seeing. Jake was with those guys in the back of the bar. His back was to me and he was pulling the woman over to him. He kissed her and she squeezed his ass.

I suddenly felt sick to my stomach, and my chest was so tight I could barely breathe. We had to get out of there. I yanked Patrick's arm just as he was about to say something and I pulled him out of the bar.

CHAPTER SEVENTEEN

Jake

I WAS sitting at my desk, finishing up some paperwork and thinking about what Nate and I should have for dinner, when a pair of long legs covered in ripped pantyhose and a very short skirt slid in front of me.

"Hey there, Detective Owens."

I looked up to see a tight shirt, exposed flat belly, big breasts, and a face that looked very pretty unless you noticed the eyes. The dull, tired eyes.

"Hey, Suzie Q! Long time no see."

I gave her a warm hug. With the amount of clothing she was wearing (or, more accurately, not wearing), she could use all the warmth she could get.

"I thought we talked about getting you off the street, honey. Maybe going back to school? Come on, let's get you some coffee and a donut, and we can catch up."

I'd met Suzie about a year earlier, when she was a pregnant, seventeen-year-old runaway working the streets. I'd tried to get her into a group home for teen moms and had hoped it would help her and the baby lead a different life. It seemed as if things hadn't worked out. I took her into the backroom, poured a cup of coffee, and gave her the box of donuts. She looked hungry and anxious.

"What can I do for you, sweetheart?"

She fidgeted in her seat a bit, and then started to cry. That surprised me. Suzie was a tough girl. She'd been on her own since she was fourteen, and had lived through any number of nightmares before then, but I'd never seen her cry or express any kind of emotion. I sat quietly and waited for her to calm down and tell me what she needed. Finally, she started talking between her sobs.

"I really fucked up, Detective Owens. Big time. They've got Alexis and they won't give her back to me unless I help them. I don't know what to do."

"Okay, honey. It's going to be okay. Let's start at the beginning. Who is Alexis, who are they, and what kind of help do they want?"

Turned out that Alexis was Suzie's two-month-old daughter. She'd managed to stay in the group home long enough to have the baby, but when Suzie turned eighteen, mom and baby were back on the streets. She'd gotten a job at a coffee shop when she lived in the home, but it didn't pay nearly as well as her old "career," and once she was responsible for her own rent and her own childcare expenses, it was easier to go back to her old way of life. Things fell apart not long after that.

"I thought it'd be different this time. I wasn't answering to anybody. I worked for myself, got to keep all the money coming in. No one could tell me what to do. It was great. Then I met this guy. He seemed nice enough.

Clean. Always paid without causing problems. Anyway, after about a week, he told me he knew a way for me to make good money. All I had to do was introduce him to new girls. Young girls. Like me, when I was starting out.

"At first, I thought he just liked 'em young, you know? And I know some girls who could use the money. I thought they'd be grateful.

"But then, I noticed after I'd introduce him to a girl, she'd disappear. It happened to a few girls and we checked their places. Their stuff was still there, but no one had heard from them. I got a really bad feeling and stopped returning his calls.

"That's when it all changed. He caught up to me outside my place one night. I'd been dumb enough to take him there a few times. At first, he just asked why I wasn't taking his calls, why I wasn't introducing him to new girls.

"When I told him why, he hit me, said it wasn't my business, and that I just needed to take care of myself and my kid, which meant giving him more girls. Well, no one tells me what to do. I told him to fuck off, and when he left, I made it into my apartment. I couldn't work for three days after that because of the bruising, but I still didn't answer when he called. I didn't need that shit. The guy was bad news.

"Then, when the bruises faded, I went out again. But when I came home, Alexis was gone. She's a great sleeper and I only ever go out for a few hours at a time. So I leave her in the apartment when I go out at night. I was freaking out and I almost called the cops, but then my phone rang, and it was that guy. He said he had Alexis, and if I didn't get him more girls, he'd just keep mine. He also said if I called the cops, they'd take her away because I left her alone and because of, umm, my job.

"I tried to get him more girls, but everyone is sort of scared off now. So I haven't found anyone and it's been two days. He isn't giving Alexis back. I don't know where to find him. I don't know what to do. Will you please help me, Detective Owens?"

She gave me her most seductive smile and stroked my arm.

"I'm not a kid anymore, Detective. I turned eighteen a few months ago. That means we can have some fun."

That broke my heart. I gently removed her hand from my arm.

"I'm flattered, really. But you're still way too young for me, Suzie. And, more importantly, I'm taken. Very taken. But I'll help you. That's my job, remember? We're going to figure this out and see what we can do. Okay? Give me a minute to call home and then we'll start at the beginning again, so I can get all the details and we'll take it from there."

I called Nate and let him know I wouldn't make it home for dinner, and then spent the next several hours talking with Suzie, running down the number in her phone, and talking to some of the women in vice. By midnight, I had a pretty good idea of what was happening.

Gary Higgins, the guy Suzie had met, was working with some sort of human trafficking operation. They'd floated through a couple of different states, picking up girls along the way, always disappearing before anyone could catch up with them. They focused on runaways and prostitutes, people no one would miss.

They'd never taken a baby, until now, as far as I could find. So this was a change. I wasn't sure whether Gary was getting sloppy, desperate, or whether they'd found a market for someone who wanted to buy a baby. None of those options were good news for Alexis. We needed to find her, and fast. And if we were lucky, we might be able to find the girls, and lock up at least some of the people involved in the ring.

The only way for us to get to the girls and the baby would be to get into the ring from the inside. Just catching Gary or one of the other guys wouldn't get us anywhere. By the time we'd get him to talk, the whole operation would've picked up and moved away, taking their captives with them. Our best shot was for Suzie to make the introduction and then for me to try to get into the ring. I'd never had a problem breaking a few rules, and it looked like that was what it would take. My captain agreed.

The next morning, Suzie called Gary Higgins and begged him to come over. When Gary arrived, I was waiting for him in Suzie's apartment (and I use the term "apartment" very loosely; hovel would be more accurate). I made sure I smelled of beer and I gave him my angriest look so he'd believe I was truly raging. The guy was pretty strong, but I was stronger. I hit him as I yelled.

"So you're the motherfucker who thinks he can just come in and mess with my merchandise? Suzie's my girl, you understand? Where the fuck do you get off hitting her? Do you know I lost three days of business because of you? No one wants to fuck a girl whose face is all banged up! And where are my other girls? What are you offering them, more money? You think I'm just going to let that go? This is my neighborhood and those are my girls."

I had him bleeding and lying on the floor, and took his gun from him. He broke when I got my pocketknife out.

"Hey, man, I didn't know. I thought she worked alone. I didn't know about you or your interest in the girls, but I think I can make this worth your while, especially if you can get us more girls."

I knew we were in. I let Gary call a couple of guys and we set up a meeting for the next day. I brought another detective with me—Kathy Devito, a woman who'd been working undercover in vice and could handle this crowd. I introduced her as my girlfriend, said she was great at bringing in young girls because they trusted her.

Over the next couple of days, we had a few meetings with Gary and some of the guys in his operation. We had teams set up, tailing every guy who left our meetings, hoping they'd make their way back to the girls. They told me how much they'd pay and showed me pictures of some of their girls to give me an idea of what they wanted. Every girl looked so young, and in the pictures, they were bruised, dirty, and terrified. It made my skin crawl.

I told them we could get some girls and I listened carefully to their side conversations. That was how I realized they were holding the girls nearby. The good news was that they hadn't sold them yet. The bad news was that I wasn't sure about the baby.

When I came home at night after those meetings, after seeing those pictures, after hearing about the girls, I got into the shower and scrubbed myself raw to get the scent of my day and every part of them off me. The last thing I wanted was to bring any part of it into our home, into our bed. I couldn't expose Nate to that kind of sick, depraved life.

We'd reached a point where we were just waiting for Gary and his friends to come up with the money. Then, on Sunday morning, I got a text from Kathy saying we were on. I hated leaving Nate. I could tell he was disappointed. He'd actually managed to get a whole day off work and we'd planned on us spending it together. We'd hardly seen each other over the past week. I kissed him and apologized. I thought we'd get through things quickly. It didn't work out that way.

It turned out there was an issue with the place they were holding the girls, so Gary and his crew were late meeting us. On the plus side, when they arrived, they were still pissed about whatever had happened, so they were talking to each other pretty freely about the new location. As we walked together to the bar where they liked to meet, I started getting a very good idea of where they were holding the girls.

When we got to the bar, Gary knocked and one of his guys unlocked the door. As we were walking in, the phone rang in the bar's office and Gary's guy ran to answer it, while the rest of us walked into the back of the bar. Kathy and I were standing with the crew, talking about the drop spot where we'd bring them the new girls.

My back was to the door when I *felt* Nate walk in. I was reeling and trying to figure out what Nate was doing there. Gary's guy was still on the phone, so he hadn't locked the fucking door, which was how he'd gotten in. But why was he there?

I panicked. For the first time in my life, I really fucking panicked. I had a gun tucked into my boot, but there were five guys around me and every one of them was armed. If Nate said my name or walked over, he'd blow my cover, and with it, his safety. They'd take us all out. There was no way I could get to all of them before they shot Nate. There were too many of them. His only hope was stepping back out the door before anyone noticed him. And there was only one way I could think of to make that happen fast.

I grabbed Kathy's hand and yanked her to me. She looked confused, but she went with it. I kissed her, she squeezed my ass, and I felt the air leave the room. Nate was gone. I'd probably broken his heart, but at least he was safe. I felt like I was going to cry. I wanted to run after him. But I couldn't.

It took another fifteen minutes before Kathy and I left, promising to bring the girls to the designated location within an hour. Instead, we called our team, told them what we'd heard about the new location, and helped with the search.

I tried to call Nate, but his phone went straight to voicemail. He didn't want to talk to me. For the first time in our lives, he was shutting me out. I honestly felt like I couldn't breathe. I'm not sure how I managed to keep going, but I had no other choice—I had to find the baby and the girls.

It took forty minutes for us to find them. They were tired, sick, and scared, but they were alive. We had people watching the bar and everyone who walked out. As soon as we had the girls, we radioed the team and they picked up Gary and his crew. One officer was injured and one of the scumbags was killed, but considering the situation, that was a great result.

I should've been happy—we'd saved all those people and it was probably the most important bust of my career. But all I could think about was Nate. His biggest fear was that I'd betray him, that I'd go back to women, and he'd caught me doing just that.

I knew I could explain it to him and he'd understand intellectually and forgive me. But I also knew that I'd hurt him, deeply hurt him. We had come so far in our relationship, so fucking far. But that hurt wasn't going to go away. And I wondered whether it would ever be possible for him to truly trust me again on an emotional level. My heart ached as I finally made it home and walked into our apartment.

Nate must've heard the door open, because he ran in from the bedroom. I was almost surprised he was home, that he hadn't packed up and left me. But what was even more surprising was the look in his eyes. He didn't look hurt or even mad. He looked relieved.

"Oh, thank God! I'm so glad you're okay."

He threw his arms around me and started sobbing into my neck.

"I'm so sorry, Jake. I knew you were working. I wasn't thinking when I walked in there. I just wanted to see you." He was squeezing me tight and mumbling into my neck. "I was so worried I'd blown your cover. I was so scared. Thank God you're okay."

I hadn't hurt him. He knew why I'd kissed Kathy. He'd understood the whole time. I pried his head off my neck so I could look into his eyes.

"You knew. How did you know?"

That got a smile out of him. He sniffled.

"I know you, Jake, and I trust you. Besides, why else would you be kissing a woman?"

He was smiling and his eyes were twinkling.

"We both know you like cock way too much to be straight."

I guess we'd come further than I'd realized. I wiped away the tears from his face and whispered to him.

"Thank you for trusting me." I kissed him softly, then took his hand and led him to the bathroom. "I need to take a shower. Join me, and I'll show you just how much I like cock."

We walked into the bathroom and I stripped off Nate's clothes and mine. He was trembling. I could tell he'd been really scared that afternoon. I stroked the back of his neck and looked into his eyes.

"It's okay, baby. Nothing happened. You don't need to be scared."

He didn't seem convinced, but he nodded. We got under the hot water and I scrubbed my body. I usually wash Nate first when we shower together, but I really needed to get the remains of the day off me before I touched Nate. I felt dirty all the way underneath my skin. Nate put his hand on mine.

"Let me wash you, Jake. I promise to get you clean...without rubbing off any more layers of skin."

There's so much love in Nate's eyes when he talks to me. It's impossible for me to say no to him. When I look at him, I'm filled with an overwhelming desire to please him, to do anything and everything for him.

"Thank you, Nate."

He washed my body softly and slowly. Then he rinsed me off and did it again. I would've thought the things I'd seen that day would have extinguished even my over-the-top sex drive. I'd felt physically ill most of the day because of what Gary and his crew had done to those girls, the way they'd treated them, their battered physical and emotional conditions.

But as Nate washed me, my mind focused on him. On his glowing, smooth skin. On his blond hair, dampened by the water. On the way my skin tingled from his touch. I loved him so much, and by the time Nate was done rinsing me, I was so hard that I wasn't sure there was blood left in any part of my body other than my dick. I looked down at Nate's cock and saw that he was in the same condition.

I put my hands on the sides and back of Nate's neck and stroked his cheeks with my thumbs. We leaned into each other at the same time and shared a long, deep kiss. I took the soap and lathered my hands, then rubbed them all over Nate's body as we continued to kiss. Soft pecks intermingled with long, deep kisses where our tongues danced.

After I was done washing every other part of him, I reached around to his ass and ran my soapy hands down his crack. He shuddered and moaned. That was all the encouragement I needed.

I took my soapy finger and penetrated Nate's ass. I got past the first knuckle quickly and moved my finger around. Nate moaned and pushed back against my finger. I added another finger and found his sweet spot. His eyes were closed and he was moaning quietly. I dropped to my knees and sucked on the head of his cock as I continued to work his ass.

Nate bent down and held onto my shoulders for support. He slowly thrust his hips forward and back so he was softly pumping in and out of my mouth. I sucked him hard and moved my head back and forth to meet him. His fingers dug into my shoulders as his quiet moans turned into loud gasps. It only took a few minutes for my mouth to be filled with his seed.

I looked up at Nate as his dick softened in my mouth. His eyes were closed and there was a look of exquisite pleasure on his face. It still thrilled me that I could do that to him. That I could evoke those types of feelings in him.

A couple of strokes and I was going off, kneeling in front of him, looking at his face, and holding his dick in my mouth. Then I stood up. Nate wrapped his arms around my waist and buried his face in my neck. We held each other like that until the water got cold.

Nate was quiet as we dried off. I knew that he was thinking about that afternoon at the bar. Not about the kiss, though. That hadn't fazed him. He was still scared about what could've happened. He was worried about my safety.

I wasn't sure what to say to make him feel better. The first thing that came to mind was to tell him it really wasn't the most dangerous thing that'd ever happened to me on the job. I'd been in much tighter squeezes. Often. Of course, hearing that would make him feel worse, not better.

I'd never really cared all that much if I got hurt while I was working. Oh, I was always careful, but I did what needed to be done to finish the job. And that meant taking chances. Not with other people's lives, of course, but with my own. That fearlessness was a big reason I was so good at my job.

I looked at Nate's worried face, and it dawned on me that my life was no longer just my own. He'd be hurt if something happened to me. I'd never considered the possibility that I was risking Nate's happiness when I risked my life. The question was...what could I do about it?

CHAPTER EIGHTEEN

Nate

I WOKE up and moved my hand around the cold sheets. No Jake. I could see bits of sunlight coming in from behind the dark curtains.

"What time is it?" I wondered to myself, realizing I'd just woken from a very deep sleep.

I'd been doing that more and more lately—sleeping soundly through the entire night. I thought it might have something to do with the fact that Jake was there with me during the night. I could feel him and smell him next to me, and I knew he was safe. It was the only time I could truly relax. And then there was the fact that I was exerting tremendous amounts of energy with Jake every night in bed...or in the shower...and sometimes in the living room or kitchen. Well, you get the picture.

I grumbled incoherently as I made my way to the bathroom, emptied my bladder, and brushed my teeth. I stumbled into the living room naked and saw Jake in the kitchen, talking quietly on the phone. He smiled when he saw me, raked his gaze down my body, paused at my crotch, and licked his lips. I met his gaze and raised my eyebrows as other parts of me also rose in response to his stare.

I wondered if the time would eventually come when my body would stop reacting so strongly to him. Over six months into our relationship, things seemed to be intensifying between us rather than cooling off. In addition to my incredible attraction to him, I no longer wondered what it would be like to touch, taste, and smell every part of him. I knew those answers. And the reality was much more intense and erotic than my imagination had ever been.

I was also learning things about my own sexuality through my relationship with Jake. I'd always been a bit shy, and I hadn't ever dated anyone long enough to truly trust that person and let go of all my inhibitions. I wasn't sure whether that would've been possible with anyone other than Jake anyway. But with Jake, safety and trust were a given.

He'd always known everything about me. All of my faults and mistakes over my entire life were an open book to him. And he'd always accepted and liked me in spite of them. So letting go physically with him came very naturally to me. And that meant I was finally learning what I enjoyed sexually—not what I was supposed to enjoy, not what was normal or safe, but what actually felt good to me. And what I was discovering surprised me. I knew at some point I'd need to find time to sit and think about those feelings and desires.

"Looks like Sleeping Beauty finally woke up, Mama C."

He held the phone out toward me.

"Nate, your mom is on the phone."

I walked into the kitchen and his fingers lingered on mine as he handed me the phone. I put it to my ear.

"Hi, Mom."

I tried to walk away, but Jake put his hands on my waist, holding me in place as he sucked on my neck. I put my hand on his chest, pushed him back gently, and shook my head.

"You're going to leave a mark."

I was covering the phone with my hand and speaking to him in a barely audible voice. He rolled his eyes and lowered his mouth to my nipples.

"What? Oh, yeah, I was listening. Aunt Polly and Uncle Mark's anniversary...that sounds fun."

My mom was telling me about an anniversary party, or a family reunion, or maybe about an impending war. I couldn't concentrate because Jake had me pressed against the sink. He was sucking on my nipple and rubbing his cock against mine, his hand loosely holding our dicks together.

"It hasn't been that long, has it? Nine months? I didn't realize that... Yes, you're right, Mom... We will... I'll talk to Jake about it... This morning. Right now, in fact... We'll call you later tonight. Tell Dad I love him... Bye, Mom."

I closed the phone, hoping that she couldn't tell I was losing my breath.

"Unggghhh. Jake. I was talking to Mom on the phone. That's just not right."

Not that I was pulling away. If anything, I was encouraging him. Rubbing my cock against his, meeting him thrust for thrust. He was holding my hip with one hand and keeping our dicks together with the other, while he pushed against me. I put my hands on the back of his head, pushed my fingers into his thick, black hair, and pulled his mouth against mine. We exchanged hard, penetrating kisses as we thrust against each other, moaning into each other's mouth and panting.

I tripped first, coating our stomachs, chests, and Jake's hand with my cum. He scooped it up and rubbed it up and down his cock, using it as lube to get himself off in another few strokes. Our bodies were covered in our joined juices.

"Did I say good morning already, Nathaniel?"

I laughed and kissed him.

"No, as a matter of fact you didn't. Come on, horndog, let's get in the shower and you can tell me about your talk with Mom. If it was anything like mine, then you already know she wants us to come home for a visit."

I dropped my hand to his and he immediately wrapped his fingers around mine. I walked to the bathroom with him behind me. I let go of his hand to turn on the water and he wrapped his arms around me, stroked my nipples, and nibbled on my neck.

"I've always wanted to do you in your old room. It'd fulfill all of my childhood fantasies. A trip home sounds perfect."

I stepped into the shower and started to rinse off. Jake followed me.

"We haven't been home in almost a year. We're going to see family, friends, all that stuff. And all you can think about is having sex in my childhood bedroom?"

I wasn't actually complaining, and he knew it.

"What can I say? I'm oversexed when it comes to you, buddy. Can't get enough." He was soaping up my body. "Is that a problem, Nate?"

His voice was husky and low. It warmed my heart and sent shivers up my spine. He was looking into my eyes, smiling.

"Not a problem. It's actually one of your best qualities."

Jake laughed. A deep, body-shaking laugh.

"Great. I hang around my whole life, waiting for you to notice me, and at the end of the day, you just want me for my dick."

"No, not just your dick, Jake. Don't forget your ass. You have a great ass."

I slipped a soapy finger into his ass just to make my point. He groaned.

"Are you working late today?"

I nodded. I'd worked really hard to get to where I was in my career. I was on the cutting edge of medical research. Every day was a major intellectual challenge, and I was by far the youngest person in my field. In other words, I was on top of the game, career-wise. More and more lately, though, the long hours bothered me. I wanted to spend more time at home with Jake.

We were done with the shower, so I turned off the water as Jake reached over and pulled our towels off the rack, handing me mine before he used his. He'd always been like that—incredibly considerate, putting my needs first. I realized I sometimes took it for granted.

"Thanks for the towel." I dried off my chest and smiled at him. "What do you have going on today, Jake?"

"Other than work, the only thing I'm planning today is another visit to check in on Suzie and her baby. She doesn't seem to be doing too well. I can tell she's on something. I've been trying to get her to go into a program, but she refuses. And I know she's still working the streets. I just hope the baby is okay. Suzie's a good girl, deep down, but she's so young and so...I don't know, damaged."

I'd never seen Jake take a case home the way he had with Suzie and her baby. He'd checked on her almost every day since he'd helped find Alexis, after she'd been kidnapped. He never told me the details of what had happened. Jake rarely told me about his work. At least not in detail. I understood that he didn't want me to know about the things he saw. Truth be told, I was grateful. I would've been happy to listen if Jake needed to unload, but I couldn't imagine doing what he did, seeing the worst of humanity firsthand.

And I was still recovering from that day I'd almost blown his cover at the bar. I think it was the first time I had truly realized how much danger he put himself in every day to protect other people. It amazed me how he was able to do that and still come home with a smile on his face. It was yet another demonstration of his incredible strength. It was inspiring. So I held myself back from complaining about his work and sharing my almost-paralyzing fear about his safety. Instead, I caressed Jake's cheek and tenderly kissed his neck.

"You're amazing. The way you're helping that girl and her baby. Everything you do. You're amazing, Jake."

He gave me a funny look.

"I'm just a dumb brute, Nate. You're the amazing one. The things you come up with. You're really helping people, making a difference." He had a soft look on his face as he stroked my arm. "I'm so damn proud of you."

"You're not dumb," I responded instinctively. The incredible thing was, he really meant what he said about me. Most people thought I had the most boring job on earth. I spent my days in a small, windowless room, mixing chemicals and looking in microscopes. Whole weeks went by where nothing really happened; I'd just watch things grow, or not grow, as the case may be.

The guys I'd dated never asked me about work. Jake had always been interested, though. And not just when I started working at the lab. Even when we were kids, Jake had loved hearing about my theories and ideas.

During our freshman year in high school, I spent hours reading about alternative fuels. I wanted to try to generate methane gas from the manure at a local dairy farm. My hope was that I'd be able to generate enough gas to warm a pot of water. Coming up with the theory and design was interesting, and for me, very enjoyable. But actually building the collection equipment and handling manure, well let's just say it wasn't my thing.

Jake had been listening to me talk about my design

and theory for months. Then one Saturday morning, he woke me up early and told me we were going to get started turning the theory into reality. He'd taken my design and gathered the materials we needed to build the collection equipment. He spent every weekend for two months doing the majority of the physical work to build it, while I explained where things should go and tested our progress. And when we finally had it put together, he dealt with the manure, while I measured the gas we were generating.

By the end of the semester, we'd succeeded. It was the first really substantial project I'd developed and implemented. In fact, I think the reason I ended up going into research was because of how much I'd enjoyed that project and the others I'd worked on during high school and college. But the truth was; I didn't enjoy my work at the lab nearly as much as I'd enjoyed those earlier experiments.

Looking back, I think it wasn't only the intellectual challenge I'd enjoyed so much back then. It was also the fact that Jake had helped me with every one of those experiments. He not only did the majority of the construction, when that was necessary, he was also my sounding board. And even when I knew he didn't understand exactly what I was saying, talking through my thoughts with him always helped crystallize those thoughts in my own mind.

Working at the lab was different. We developed things as a team and we talked through our theories with each other. Everything we did had to stay at the lab. So while I still had that intellectual challenge I'd always enjoyed and I was doing work that had widespread impact, I no longer had the ability to share my ideas with Jake in the same way. That made the job less enjoyable than I'd expected. I sometimes wondered whether I should go in another direction and practice traditional medicine, where I could work with people, take care of them individually.

My thoughts were interrupted by Jake's deep voice.

"If you want to take a trip home, maybe we should go next month. I got an e-mail from Dwayne that a bunch of folks from our class are planning a get-together. Kind of like a reunion. We haven't seen some of them in ten years, might be nice."

That did sound nice. When we'd moved to New York, I was itching to get away from our town. I wanted adventure, new experiences, life in the big city. I wanted to meet new people instead of being where everyone knew me and I knew everyone. I wanted to get laid. But now the thought of being back with family, under an open sky where I could see the clouds or stars for miles around, without the interruption of tall buildings and smog, sounded absolutely magical. And as far as getting laid was concerned, I liked Jake's idea of fulfilling our childhood fantasies.

"I'd like that, Jake. It really has been too long. Let me know the date of the get-together and I'll let the guys at the lab know when I'll need the time off."

We finished getting dressed and walked out of

our apartment together. I straightened his collar. It was actually fine, I just liked touching him. He took my hand and kissed it, his eyes gazing into mine.

"You have the most beautiful eyes, Nathaniel."

The sound of his voice washed over me and made me feel loved. He combed his fingers through my hair. Then he took me in his arms, kissed me deeply, and licked my ear, darting his tongue inside. My dick was bulging in my pants, pressing against him.

"Oh my gosh, Jake. You have me in a constant state of arousal. I can barely concentrate at work all day. Do you have any idea what you do to me?"

He nibbled on my ear and pushed his dick against mine. It took every ounce of control I had not to drop to my knees and take him in my mouth right there in the hallway. I was actually salivating at the thought of his taste.

"Mmm-hmm. I know. It's my job to keep you horny. Glad to know I'm succeeding."

He reached down and gently fondled my hard cock through my pants.

"Don't worry. I'll take care of this tonight when you get home. You can rely on me, baby."

I loved hearing him call me "baby." It made me feel protected and safe. And I knew I could rely on him. For that, and everything else.

CHAPTER NINETEEN

Jake

I GOT to the squad room the morning we'd decided to take a trip home and e-mailed a few of our cousins and friends to let them know. Then I spent some time catching up on paperwork, attending a briefing for a new case, and meeting with my captain. He told me the higher-ups were very impressed with my work on the human trafficking ring, along with several other cases, and that I was getting a promotion. Detective Second-Grade.

I hadn't been expecting a promotion because guys usually had more years on the force under their belts before reaching that rank. I was happy, but not as much as I knew I should've been. I was worried about my job, about the fact that my risks could hurt Nate. I'd been trying to figure out what to do about it for days, but still had no answers.

Nate was working late again, and by the time he got home that night, he looked absolutely exhausted. I met him at the door and he fell into my arms.

"I'm so tired. It's like there's never enough time to get everything done. We need three more guys just to keep up with our current projects, but it's just not in the budget."

He always worked so hard. I wished there was some way for me to help carry his load. Well, there was no way for me to help him at work, but I could make his home life as easy and relaxing as possible. I stroked his hair, moving his blond locks off his forehead.

"Did you eat dinner? Are you hungry, baby?"

He gazed at me and then buried his face in my neck. I loved it when he did that. I put my face down on his head and inhaled deeply, enjoying the scent of his hair.

"Yeah. I ate some stuff from the vending machine."

I made a mental note to start packing him food to take into work. He couldn't live off candy bars and potato chips.

"Okay. Then let's get you washed and put to bed."

I led Nate to the bathroom, removed his clothes, and then dropped my own briefs to the ground. I'd already showered earlier, but I wanted to get in again so I could wash Nate.

He stood in the shower with his eyes glazed and his lids drooping. I lathered his body, enjoying the feeling of his smooth, warm skin, his long, lean limbs, and his soft cock and balls. Then I rinsed him and worked on his hair, massaging his scalp until he sighed and relaxed his body. Once that was done, I turned off the water and dried us off. We brushed our teeth, pissed, and then I led Nate to bed.

His eyes were closed as soon as his head hit the

pillow. I spooned behind him, wrapped my arm around his chest, and held him tightly to me. My face was touching the back of his head and my cock was nestled against his ass.

"I love you, baby."

I spoke softly to him, thinking he was already asleep. Then I felt Nate's ass pressing back against me. My dick immediately responded by poking him.

"Mmm. I love your dick, Jake. I've been thinking about it all day."

His voice sounded almost dreamy, and he wiggled his ass, making contact with my cock. I was so fucking horny, I couldn't stand it, but Nate was really tired. So I forced myself to hold back.

"Yeah? What were you thinking?"

His breathing had slowed down. I wasn't even sure whether he was still aware of what he was saying. It was almost like he was talking in his sleep.

"I was thinking about how good it feels when you're inside me, stretching me, filling me, completing me."

As he spoke, Nate continued to wiggle back against my ever-hardening dick. When he felt my crown against his pucker, he pushed back. It was like his body was acting on its own, sucking my cock inside. He was making me so hot with his words and movements that I wanted nothing more than to push inside him, and to keep pushing until he exploded all over us and I filled him with my seed. But he had stopped talking and his breathing was slow, so I knew he was almost completely asleep. I kept still.

Nate continued wiggling and pushing back, and after a few more minutes, my balls and pubes were pressed against his ass. Just as I realized he'd managed to bury my cock completely inside him, I felt Nate's body tense and I looked over his shoulder and saw his cock pulsing and releasing.

His eyes were still closed, his breathing slow. Neither of us had touched his dick. I wasn't sure what was happening, but I was so fucking hard. The feeling of his ass spasming around my cock while the smell of his cum filled the air was too much. I ached with the need for release, but I swear, he was asleep.

"I'll go get something to clean you up," I whispered into his sleeping ear, my head swimming in confusion over the coupling we'd just shared. He reached his hand backward so it held my hip.

"No. Stay inside me. I need to feel you inside me while I sleep."

I tightened my grip on his chest and made sure my cock was buried as deeply as possible in Nate. In that position, even if I softened, I'd stay inside him. Not that softening seemed possible given how fucking hard I was at that moment. Somehow I managed to fall asleep despite my extreme arousal.

The sound of Nate's moans woke me. I opened my eyes and saw the clock—two a.m. We'd only been asleep for a couple of hours. Nate was pushing back and forth against me, forcing my still-hard cock to pump in and out of his ass. Yet it seemed like he was asleep.

"Are you awake, Nate? What's going on?"

"I need you. I need you, Jake."

His voice was thick with sleep or lust or both. He was thrusting back and forth against me, moaning, and the whole idea of him wanting me so much that he was impaling himself on my cock in his sleep was fucking hot. I was incredibly turned on, but also confused. I didn't want to hurt him, so I held back and let him set the pace. It took every ounce of restraint I had not to slam into him.

After a few more minutes of his slow, sleepy thrusting, Nate started to beg.

"Please, Jake, please. I *need* you."

"I'm here, baby."

I squeezed his chest with my arm that was still wrapped around him and kissed his neck.

"More. I need more, Jake. I need you to move!"

I needed to move too. But I didn't want to hurt him.

"Nate, I don't know what's going on. I don't know whether you're awake or asleep. If I start moving, I'm not sure I can hold back and I don't want to hurt you."

He groaned in frustration and shoved himself back against me.

"Oh God, please. I need you now! Give it to me, Jake. Hard and fast. Push inside me. Deep inside me. Please, please, oh please."

I hadn't ever heard him talk like that. It wasn't just dirty, it was desperate. My heart was racing. I moved my hand from his chest to his hip and held him still as I slowly pulled my cock out of him. When I popped out, he actually cried out from the loss.

"No, no."

He was pushing back against me, trying to find my cock with his ass again but I had a firm hold on his hip.

"Don't worry. I'll give it back to you."

He sighed in relief, but his body was still tense with need and anticipation. His cock was pressed all the way up against his stomach, dripping.

I turned Nate over so he was lying on his stomach, his head resting on the pillow. Then I settled behind him, kneeling over him. He raised his beautiful ass in anticipation, but kept his chest and face pressed down on the bed. I put my hand on his head and softly ran it down his neck and back and all the way down his firm ass. Then I lined up my cock, grasped his hips, and pushed my way in with one hard, deep, fast stroke.

"Ahhhhhh."

Nate was almost screaming as his cock erupted. Holy fuck! I'd made him come with just one stroke and without touching his cock. And it was the second time that night. He wasn't done though. His ass was still in the air with my cock buried in it. That was when he started yelling.

"More, Jake! Give me more! I need more!"

At that point, I could hold back no longer. All logic was gone and I fell into some sort of primal stupor. I put my left hand on his shoulder and my right hand on his hip, gripping him firmly as I pulled my cock out and thrust it back into him. I moved in and out at a feverish pace. My grunts and growls were mixing with Nate's shouts.

"Yes, yes, yes! Oh God, yes. Like that, Jake. Give it to me like that!"

I was pistoning in and out of him using all the force I could muster. I could feel sweat dripping down my face. I wasn't sure whether it was from the exertion or from the pain it was causing me to keep my orgasm at bay. I wanted to come, needed to come. But I could tell Nate wasn't done yet, so I held back.

Nate's forehead was pressed down on the pillow, and he was gripping the sheets with his hands as I pounded him into the mattress. I moved my hand from his shoulder around to the front of his body and down to his cock. I wanted to stroke him, to get him off so I could climax.

"No, Jake. No. Don't touch my dick. Make me come again, but don't touch my dick."

I almost lost it just from his words. I was so fucking turned on that my balls actually ached. I grasped both of his hips and pulled him backward toward the end of the bed. Then I stood next to the bed, lined my cock up to his raised ass, and penetrated him. Standing on the ground, I had all the leverage. I held him still so that I could pummel him completely. I made sure to angle my cock so that I was hitting his prostate every time.

By that point, we were both moaning so loud I was sure the neighbors could hear us. I didn't care. The only thing that mattered to me at that moment was getting Nate off.

He'd been grasping and pulling on the sheets so wildly that the pillows had fallen from the bed. Most of his moans and shouts were indecipherable. They were guttural noises. But occasionally, he added words— "harder, deeper, faster, more."

Tears ran down my face from the agony of not allowing myself to release, but I didn't let go. I just held onto Nate and gave him what he wanted. I pummeled into him as hard as I could, as fast as I could, as deep as I could. Over and over and over again. Finally, he raised his head from the bed and screamed.

"I'm coming! Ahhhhh. Oh, Jake, yes, yes, yes. I'm coming!"

"Oh, Nate, Nate. Oh fucking, yes! Unggghhh!"

I joined him in his ecstasy. Pure pleasure replaced the pain of restraint as I drained my balls into him.

I stood still, my cock buried inside him, sweat running down my face as I tried to catch my breath. The bed was a mess, tangled sheets, cum everywhere. I knew we'd need fresh sheets and I wanted to get a warm washcloth to clean Nate and soothe his ass, which had to be sore. He must have sensed my impending movement.

"No. Don't go anywhere. Stay with me, in me."

"Are you sure, baby? I don't want you to be hurt. I want to clean you up, let you rest."

I gently caressed his ass so he'd understand.

"I'm not hurt, Jake. You have no idea how much I needed that, how good I feel right now. Please, just stay in me."

So I sort of crab-walked on the bed, my pelvis pressed against his ass tightly so my softening cock could remain buried. Then he collapsed on his stomach and I lay down on top of him, moving us both slightly to the side so he wasn't supporting my full weight.

He fell right back asleep. But I was awake for a while, gripping him to me and processing what'd just happened. I'd come to realize that while Nate enjoyed our tender moments, he also craved an aspect to our physical relationship that was not soft and gentle. I hoped I was able to give him both of those things so he'd have everything that he wanted, needed. I thought about his words and cues, about what made him harden the fastest, moan the loudest, climax the hardest. And about how I could do all of those things while still making sure he felt respected, loved, treasured, and cared for.

Eventually, I fell asleep.

The next time I woke up, the clock read six a.m. and Nate was once again pushing back against me and wiggling his ass, with my cock still wedged inside him. He'd already ejaculated three times in the past six hours. I kissed his neck and softly stroked his chest.

"Nate, what's going on?"

He put his arm on mine and rubbed it before he took my hand up to his mouth and kissed it.

"Am I wearing you out?"

I moved my hard dick a couple of inches in and out of his ass.

"Does it feel like I'm worn out? I've just never seen you like this. I want to make sure you're okay."

He sighed contentedly and pushed back and forth to meet my gentle thrusts.

"I feel so safe with you, Jake. So protected. I feel

like I can do anything, say anything. Like I can let go completely."

I squeezed him tightly and felt my eyes moisten.

"Of course you can, baby."

He sighed again and relaxed in my arms.

"I've been working too much. I hate being away from you." He hesitated, and then continued in a soft voice. "And I'm scared when you're at work, Jake. I'm not a whole person without you. I know it sounds trite, but you honestly complete me. There is no me without you. I can't exist without you."

Tears were now filling my eyes. I hated how scared he was by my job. I knew I had to make a change. I couldn't let Nate spend his days feeling anxious and scared. And I couldn't take the chance that something would happen to me. I couldn't leave him.

"I know what you mean, baby. All these years of being two halves of a whole. It's nice to finally be able to put the two pieces together."

I pulled him back tightly so he was pressed against me and my dick moved inside him. I understood he wanted, needed to feel that physical connection. That connection that had finally put an end to whatever space we had between us, so there was truly no way of knowing where he ended and I began.

"Exactly. That's exactly how I feel."

CHAPTER TWENTY

Jake

I **WOKE** up Saturday morning and looked at the warm, sleeping body next to me. His eyes were closed, his hair was tousled, and he had a crease from the pillow across his fair cheek. I gently brushed his soft hair off his forehead and sighed as the memory of Nate's angelic face over the years flashed through my mind like a slide show.

My first real, distinct memory, one that I knew was mine and not just an image based on a story told by my parents, was of Nate's face. It was our third birthday party, and we were standing on either side of our shared cake, ready to blow out the candles. Nate's cheeks were pink because we'd been running around with our cousins all afternoon, his hair was even lighter then and it was a bit matted down on his head, his eyes were closed, and his lips were sort of puckered, ready to blow out the candles. I looked at him and felt warm inside, then I held my breath when it was time to blow so he could get all the candles out and have his wish come true. After he was done with the candles, he opened his eyes and smiled at me.

Just as that memory of then-three-year-old Nate's eyes pulled at my heart, present-day Nate opened those crystal-blue eyes. I stroked his cheek.

"Good morning, beautiful."

His voice was raspy with sleep as he answered me.

"Good morning."

He scooted toward me, bridging the few inches that separated us, and nuzzled into my neck.

"Whatcha thinking about, Jake? You have a faraway look in your eyes."

I stroked his hair.

"I'm just remembering. What's the first thing you remember, Nate? Your earliest memory?"

He was quiet for a minute, thinking. Then he pulled back a little and gazed at me.

"You. My first memory is you."

He kissed me softly.

"Remember when we turned three and our folks had the whole family over? All the uncles and their wives and kids? We'd just blown out the candles on our Bert and Ernie cake and I'd made my wish—that we'd be friends forever. Then I opened my eyes and saw you across from me. I remember looking into your eyes and deciding that green was my favorite color. So that's my first memory— your green eyes, your face, smiling at me over that cake."

He leaned down to kiss my chest as he mumbled, "What's your first memory, Jake?"

His lips touched my chest just as he finished his question. My heart was racing. Nate must've noticed because his head jolted up and he looked at me with concern.

"What's wrong? Your heart, it's...."

I couldn't speak. Our first memories were identical: three years after the day we were born together, Nate and I, standing over our birthday cake and looking into each other's eyes. All I could do was stare at him. Our eyes locked and he froze. Then he leaned his forehead against mine. We both reached over to each other's head and stroked each other's hair. Nate's eyes were misty as he whispered to me, "Yours too?"

It was moments like that when I was most grateful about the progression of our relationship. Moments when there was nothing either of us could say, when there was no way to articulate the depth and strength of our connection. But I could try to show him.

I rolled us over so Nate was lying on his back and I was on top of him. I stroked his cheeks and looked into his eyes for a couple of minutes. Then I leaned down to his neck and began licking and kissing. All the way down the front, then to the side of his neck and up to his ear. I licked, nibbled, and even bit him lightly. When I got to his earlobe, I sucked on it and he moaned in approval.

While my mouth focused on his neck and ear, my hands roamed down his chest. I slid my fingers over his nipples, tweaking them gently. He groaned and bucked up against me. I bit his neck softly in response and ran my hand down his chest to his stomach, with my mouth following. As my lips made their way down to Nate's nipple, my hands firmly rubbed the sides of his body, all the way down to his ass.

I could hear Nate's breathing getting heavier; he put his hand on my head, brushing his fingers through my hair, and it made my cock harden and pulse. My kisses and licks kept going lower, but I passed by his dick and balls, instead licking down his inner thigh, nibbling on the side and back of his knees, and sucking on his calves.

I had scooted so far down the edge of the bed that my legs were on the floor. I kneeled down and picked up Nate's foot. Then I licked the arch of his right foot, causing him to shudder. I moved to the left foot and took each of his toes into my mouth, one at a time. Sucking and licking them as I massaged the arch and ball of his foot.

I could hear his moans getting louder and more constant as I grasped his calves firmly and slid my hands up his leg, rubbing his muscles. When I got to his thighs, I moved my hands so the pressure focused on his inner thighs. By the time my hands reached his groin, I'd moved my body back up the bed so I was on my knees, crouched over his cock.

I bent my head down and laved his balls. I sucked one and then the other into my mouth. Just as I pulled off his balls and darted my tongue out, tasting the tip of his cock, he spoke to me through his pants and gasps.

"Turn...around... I want to...ungh...taste you."

I flipped my body around and then dove down on his cock. He almost shouted, but the sound was muffled as he pulled my dick into his mouth and down his throat. And then slurping sounds filled the room as each of us licked and sucked on the other. Our bodies were perfectly in tune, and when one of us felt the other reaching his climax, we slowed down, replacing the hard sucks with gentle licks, until the moment passed and we could resume the passion.

I could've stayed like that forever, with Nate's cock in my mouth and his balls in my hand. But eventually our need for release was too great. I felt Nate's balls draw up and, instead of stopping, I increased the suction and moved my head up and down on his cock. Realizing what I was doing, and that his climax was finally approaching, Nate hummed and moaned, causing vibrations on my dick. We each came, seconds apart.

I pulled my head back after the first couple of volleys, so I could taste Nate's seed on my tongue. When he finished, I removed my mouth and nuzzled my face into the underside of his balls. He smelled so fucking good.

"Mmm. Come up here, Jake."

I moved up the bed, and Nate pressed himself against me, burying his face back into my neck. I stroked his back in a circling pattern and whispered to him, "I love you so much, Nate. So fucking much."

NATE HAD to go into work that Saturday. He was trying to get ahead because we were going to take Friday off, so we could spend a long weekend at home. I went over to Suzie's place to check in on her and Alexis and bring them some food. I knocked on the door and heard noises inside. After a couple of minutes, the locks turned and Suzie stood in front of me, completely naked.

"Good morning, Detective. It's nice to see you again. Come on in."

She was smiling seductively and she stroked my arm as she asked me to come in. She leaned in to hug me and my body had absolutely no reaction. I wondered how I'd ever found this attractive enough to get it up. I patted her back, pulled away, and looked around the filthy apartment. Alexis was sleeping on a blanket in the corner.

"Hi, Suzie. Go put some clothes on, sweetheart, and then we can talk."

I had absolutely no interest in fucking Suzie, none. I guess when you know what it's actually supposed to feel like, it's not as easy to accept anything less. But she wasn't giving up that easily.

"We can talk, Detective. I don't mind having you see me like this. And you shouldn't mind, either. Guys pay good money to see me with my clothes off, and I'm giving you a freebie." She got very close to me. "And, umm, we can also *not* talk, if you prefer. No charge, Detective."

I turned and walked into the corner of her apartment that served as a kitchenette. There were dirty dishes piled on the counter, along with empty containers. I unloaded the groceries I'd brought her, putting the milk, yogurt, cheese, and fruit in the fridge and the bread, formula, baby food jars, and rice cereal in the cabinet. Then I started filling a trash bag.

"So how are you doing, sweetheart? From what you just said, I gather you haven't made a career change. Please tell that you've at least found someone to watch Alexis while you're...working."

She didn't answer. She was still standing just inside the door, looking at me strangely. I could tell that she was trying to figure me out.

"I know you like me, Detective. Why else would you keep coming over here? And you don't strike me as the shy type. So why don't you let me show you that I like you too?"

I sighed, turned around, and looked her in the eyes.

"I do like you, Suzie Q. You're a great girl. But I'm *not* interested in having sex with you. As I've already told you, I'm taken."

I finished cleaning the trash off the counters and started on the dishes.

"You know, Suzie, maybe it would help you to get a roommate. Have you thought about sharing a place with another girl? You could save some money on rent and maybe even get help with Alexis."

She grumbled and sat down on the edge of the bed. There wasn't any other furniture in the place. And she still hadn't bothered getting dressed.

"Yeah, I know a lot of girls do that. But I just can't. It wouldn't be good for Alexis."

As happy as I was to know Suzie was thinking about her daughter, I couldn't imagine how having someone else help take care of her was worse than leaving her alone at night. And I was pretty sure Suzie was still doing that, based on her response—or rather, lack of response—to my question. I finished washing the dishes, walked over to Suzie, and sat down next to her.

"Why wouldn't it be good for Alexis? Maybe you could even find another girl with a kid. It might be nice for both of you."

She sort of snorted under her breath and looked at me with those eyes that showed a pain way too deep for a girl that young.

"Yeah, nice for us and whatever asshole the girl brings home." She crossed her arms. "All the girls I know are going to bring guys home, Detective. They want to find a boyfriend, someone to take care of them. The girls with kids are the worst. They're desperate for a sugar daddy to come in and save them. I can't expose Alexis to that. You know how guys can be."

I knew she wasn't talking about exposing her daughter to seeing a prospective roommate having sex. Based on some of the things Suzie had told me, I was pretty sure she'd brought tricks to the apartment when Alexis was home. So that meant she was worried about these men hurting Alexis when she was out.

I felt so sorry for Suzie. For the miserable life she'd lived, and continued to live. I wondered whether Alexis had a chance of a better future, and how on earth Suzie would provide it for her.

"Not all men would go after Alexis. There are plenty of decent guys out there."

She scoffed at me. "Is that right? Well, you let me

know how to find them. I can pass on the information to my mother. She's gone through dozens of guys since I was a kid, and every single one of them was a fucking prick. Believe me, I know all about them...and their pricks. I had firsthand views. I finally left when I was fourteen because I figured if I was going to get fucked by ancient, overweight assholes, I might as well get paid for it. Don't get me wrong, I didn't mind so much and it helped my mom get rent money, but I don't want that for Alexis. You're the only guy I've ever met who hasn't tried to fuck me five minutes after walking in the door...or ever."

This was all beyond me. How could I tell her the world wasn't a terrible place when hers had been nothing but terrible? My phone buzzed in my pocket. I picked it up and saw Nate's number.

"I'm sorry, Suzie, I have to get this."

I stood, and then realized there was nowhere else to go in that place, so I sat back down and answered the phone. Suzie scooted over next to me and pressed her naked body against my side.

"Hi, baby... Yes, I can meet for lunch... No problem, I can be there in fifteen minutes... I love you too, Nate. See you soon."

I put the phone back in my pocket and turned back to Suzie. She was staring at me with wide eyes, her mouth gaping open.

"You're gay." She wasn't asking a question. It was more of a statement. Or a realization. "That's why you're not interested in me. You're gay."

I figured there was no point in mentioning all the

other reasons why I would never have touched Suzie, even when I was fucking women. I knew she didn't want pity from anyone.

"Yes, I'm gay. And, as I told you before, I'm taken. I'm not interested in anyone other than him." I got up. "I have to go, Suzie. I'm meeting Nate for lunch and I don't want to be late. I'll come by again in couple of days, okay?"

She didn't respond.

"And your, umm, boyfriend or whatever, he's gay too?"

I raised my eyebrows at her and chuckled. "It doesn't really work if just one of the guys is gay, Suzie. Kind of gets in the way of the, ehm, relationship."

She didn't seem to see the humor in my comment. "Save it, Detective. That's not what I meant. I mean, your boyfriend, has he always been gay or is he into girls too?"

For a girl with more experience than most people gain in a lifetime, she was asking odd questions. But I figured it wouldn't hurt anything to answer her.

"Nate has always been gay, Suzie. Since we were kids. He's never been into women."

I walked to the door and opened it just a bit so I could slide through. I didn't want Suzie, who was still naked, to be exposed to anyone who might be walking by in the hallway. She didn't seem to mind, because she walked right up to me and grabbed my arm.

"So he has *never* fucked a girl?"

She didn't give up. I actually admired her tenacity and thought about how sad it was that she was using it to get guys into bed instead of to make a better life for herself and her daughter.

"No, he has never fucked a woman. He hasn't ever even kissed a woman. And he's not interested, Suzie, trust me. Nate isn't going to be a future customer." I patted her cheek.

"No, that's not what I...never mind. I'll see you later, Detective. Thanks for coming by."

I walked out of Suzie's building, stepping over the trash that littered the hallways. I was happy to get outside and away from the stench of the place. I tried to think of who I could call to get information on programs that might be available for Suzie and Alexis. I had to be careful, because if Children's Services got involved, there was a really good chance they'd take Alexis. Frankly, I wasn't sure that was a bad idea. I knew Suzie loved Alexis, but I was worried about the baby's safety.

I made it to the restaurant, still thinking about Suzie's situation and what I could do to help. I hung my coat on the rack by the door and looked around for Nate. He was sitting in a booth, pressed against the wall, with a man sitting next to him. Right next to him. Too fucking close to him. I didn't like it but I tried to keep calm as I walked up to the table. Then I saw the guy's face, and my jaw clenched.

It was Bill.

CHAPTER TWENTY-ONE

Jake

THE LAST time I'd seen Bill was ten years earlier. It had been our freshman year of college, and Bill was in graduate school getting a doctorate in philosophy. He was teaching one of Nate's classes and they started going out right after the semester ended. Bill was probably eight years older than us and he was definitely more experienced than Nate. I'd always assumed he was the first guy Nate had had sex with, but honestly, that wasn't the reason I hated the fucker. Well, it wasn't the only reason.

I could tell that Nate was interested in Bill most of the semester, so it didn't surprise me when they started dating. What did surprise me was finding Nate crying on his bed two weeks later. I'd come home from a night out with some girl, and Nate was sitting there with bloodshot eyes and tear-tracks down his face.

I closed the door and rushed over to the bed, wrapping my arms around Nate.

"Nate, what's wrong? Did he...did he hurt you,

Nate? Did he make you do something you didn't want to do?"

I remember thinking I was going to kill that asshole—slowly—if he had done something to Nate.

"No, no. Nothing like that."

His voice broke, like it did when a person had been crying really hard for a long time. I hadn't heard Nate's voice sound like that since we were kids and he'd sprained his ankle trying to climb a tree. It had broken my heart back then to see Nate in pain, and that hadn't changed.

"What happened, Nate? Let me help you. Tell me what happened and I'll take care of it."

I had no idea what Bill had done, but I was pretty sure he was the cause of the tears. I knew Nate had had a date with him that night. I also wasn't sure what I was going to do to take care of it, but at that moment I thought it would involve a lot of blood. Bill's blood. Nate knew what I was thinking—no surprise there. He shook his head.

"Seriously, Jake. He didn't do anything to me that I didn't want. And there's nothing to take care of. He just isn't interested in me anymore. That's all."

Nate stood up and wiped his cheeks with the bottom of his T-shirt. I got a glimpse of his stomach and felt my dick stir. Damn it. Even when he was crying, I couldn't keep my dick under control around the guy.

"He's not interested *anymore*?"

Nate nodded as he walked into the bathroom. "I'm just going to take a shower and go to bed, Jake. I'll be okay tomorrow." He turned to me. "Thank you."

Not interested *anymore*. I repeated Nate's words in my head. Motherfucker. So that was the guy's game? String a student along all semester, ask him out when class is over, and then dump him after he'd had sex with him. I fumed all night. The next day, I found out where Bill lived and stormed over to his place. I pounded on the door and pushed my way in as soon as he opened it.

"Where do you get off using Nate like that? You're a world-class asshole, Bill. How do you think your department chair would feel about his graduate student sleeping with a freshman?"

Bill looked a little confused and more than a little scared, but he held his ground.

"So you must be the famous straight-boy roommate. Well, I can see why…" He was looking me up and down, and his voice trailed off. Then he continued in an angry tone. "I don't know what you're doing here. You're obviously not interested in Nate, so his relationships are none of your business. And I'm not going to stand here and explain myself to a dumb-jock-freshman-breeder. Now get out of my apartment!"

The dumb-jock-freshman-breeder comment didn't bother me. It was mostly true. But my blood boiled when he said I wasn't interested in Nate.

"I'll leave, Bill, but let's get one thing *straight*, no pun intended. I've been interested in Nate since the day he was born, and if you ever come near him again…" I grabbed his cock and balls hard and squeezed them. "Who you like to fuck won't make a difference, because

I'll slice off your dick and shove it up your sissy ass."

He gasped and his face turned purple. I let go of his junk and stormed out the door. I told myself that I'd have to keep a closer eye on the guys Nate was interested in. I hadn't done that with Bill because I was jealous. If I hadn't been so selfish and weak, though, I would've asked Nate to introduce him to me, and I might've realized that he was just using Nate. Then I could have warned Nate or stopped it.

After that incident with Bill, I made sure to know every guy Nate dated. Sometimes Nate would bring them around and sometimes I'd just follow them discreetly. I never saw Nate heartbroken over another guy after Bill, though. Sometimes he was upset after breakups, but there weren't any tears. That was how I knew Nate had been really into Bill.

So when I saw Bill pressed up against my Nate in that booth all the jealousy I'd had ten years earlier came back with a vengeance. For a brief moment, I had a fear that Bill would try to get Nate back, and that Nate would give him another chance. I shook it off. This guy was ten years in the past. And I wasn't going to let go of Nate that easily. I wasn't going to let go of Nate at all.

I marched up to the booth but didn't sit down. Nate looked up at me and smiled. His blond hair was tousled and I wanted to brush my fingers through it, feel its softness. That same loving look I'd gotten used to over the previous seven months spread across his beautiful face. My body warmed from head to toe and my heart felt full. He loved me. I was so relieved that I let out a breath I hadn't realized I'd been holding.

"Hi. I got here a little early and ran into, ehm, an old friend. I don't think you two have ever met...."

Bill turned his head toward me and looked up. He scowled and interrupted Nate.

"Oh, we've met. This is your old roommate. Jake, right? I'm Dr. William Hanson."

Nate looked confused and a little concerned. Bill was making no move to get up.

"I'm surprised you know my name, *Bill*. Last time I saw you, I'm pretty sure you were just going with 'dumb-jock-freshman-breeder.' Now, you're in my spot, and I'd like to sit down, so get up."

I knew I was glaring at him and speaking through bared teeth, but I figured I was being gracious because I hadn't hit the guy...yet.

"You called him dumb!" Nate shouted angrily, his neck turning red. He'd always been incredibly defensive when people said I was stupid. Those dumb jock comments never bothered me. I'd heard them many times in my life, and I didn't think they were far off from the truth. I'm not a brainy guy. Besides, I didn't care what anyone other than Nate thought of me. Dumb, smart, whatever—who the fuck cares?

Bill turned back to look at Nate.

"Oh come on, Nate. I know you were lusting after this guy when you were eighteen, and he is *very* good-looking, obviously, but we both know he only got into school because he could throw a ball. How far does that get you in life? I'm sure that boyfriend you mentioned doesn't appreciate this..." He turned to me and moved his hand up and down. "Appendage. You already sacrificed going out with me when you refused to sever ties with him. I honestly thought you'd have moved past this by now."

So that was why Bill stopped being interested in Nate. He'd made Nate choose between him and me and then broke up with him when he didn't like Nate's choice. Is it wrong that I felt relieved to hear that?

Nate had been trying to stand up, but he was pretty well wedged in between the wall, the table, and Bill. He was visibly shaking.

Now the thing about Nate is, he's a really quiet, reserved guy, but he has an inner strength that most people aren't aware of. I'm not even sure Nate knows it's there. I know, though, because that strength has helped me throughout my life.

Nate used that strength to force me to study all through school, no matter how much I complained.

He used that strength to talk our college admissions office into letting me into the school despite my bad test scores. The football coach, who wanted me on the team, had been doing his best, but he told me that Nate was the one who got the job done.

Nate used his strength to keep me going after my folks died. There was no way I could have made it without him. He made sure that I got some sleep at night and that I made it out of bed in the morning.

And how many guys do you know who came out in the eighth grade? Not just to a couple of close friends or family members, either, but to everyone they knew. I don't know a single guy who did that other than Nate. And he held his head up high for those five years when he was the only gay guy—or, more accurately, the only openly gay guy—in our town.

In his core, Nate was a rock. And the thing that made that rock come out more than anything else was when people said I was stupid. Bill was about to see that firsthand. The redness that had started in Nate's neck had now made it all the way up his face. He was seething. I decided to sit down in the booth across the table from Nate and Bill after all. I had a front-row seat for the show.

"Where do you get off talking about my boyfriend that way? You don't know him. Intelligence shows itself in many different ways, Bill, and if you realized that, you'd know Jake is smarter than both of us combined. And a much better person. But you are right about one thing. I've moved past some things over the last ten years. I'm no longer interested in pseudo-intellectual blowhards with small dicks. Not that I considered breaking up with you a sacrifice, even then."

Bill was shocked. He started stammering.

"Your boyfriend? He's the boyfriend you're meeting for lunch? I, uh, didn't realize he was gay." It seemed like Nate's words were sinking in one part at a time, because Bill paused and then seemed angry. He looked around and then hunched down and spoke in a loud whisper. "And my dick isn't small. Besides, it's not the size that matters, it's how you use it."

Nate rolled his eyes and snickered.

"I wouldn't know about how you use your dick, Bill. But if it's anything like how you use your mouth, then your technique isn't anything to write home about either. Seriously, man, cover your teeth with your lips. No one enjoys getting scraped." Nate paused to let his words sink in. Then he continued. "I'd like to have lunch with my boyfriend now, so please leave."

Bill's face was flushed and his mouth was open but no sound was coming out. After a few seconds he slid out of the booth and walked out of the restaurant without saying another word.

Nate's face was still red. He looked over to me and apologized with his eyes. I pushed a glass of water over to him and smiled.

"Other than that, Mrs. Lincoln, how was the play?"

Nate laughed. "I'm sorry, Jake. That guy's a real jerk, and he's always been jealous of you."

I put my hands on the table, palms up. Nate put his hands on top of mine and I wrapped my fingers around them.

"No apology necessary. I don't give a shit about what that guy thinks of me." I hesitated, and then asked the question that'd been on my mind since Bill had implied that he'd ended things with Nate because Nate wouldn't walk away from me. "Do you remember the night you and Bill broke up? I came home and you were in bed, you'd been crying really hard."

Nate nodded.

"I thought he'd broken your heart. That you were in love with the guy and he'd left you. But just now, he made it sound like he would have stayed if..."

"I wasn't in love with him, Jake." He looked into my eyes and squeezed my hands. "I was crying that night because I was terrified you'd leave me. Bill did give me an ultimatum—him or you. That wasn't a difficult choice, believe me. And when I told him I wasn't going to give you up, that I couldn't live without you, he told me I'd better learn because you'd leave me. He said you'd meet a girl, get married, and move on with your life. I knew he was just trying to hurt me because I didn't choose him, or maybe he was trying to change my mind. But it made so much sense. That's what all straight guys do, right? Get married, have a family. You'd move on, and I wouldn't have you anymore. That's why I was crying, Jake. You're the only person I've ever loved, the only person I've ever wanted to love, and I didn't want to lose you."

I let go of his hand so I could take a drink of water and wash down the lump in my throat. Then, I started talking, my voice choked with emotion.

"You'll never lose me, Nate. You're my family. Always have been, always will be. Nothing could ever change that."

"I know that now, Jake. I didn't then, but I know that now. I can *feel* it." He dipped his head and then raised his sparkling blue eyes to meet mine, a devilish grin spreading across his angelic face just as I took another drink. "And I don't just mean in my ass."

I almost choked on my water. Nate was still laughing when I finally stopped coughing.

"You're really asking for it now, Nate. Wait until

we get home tonight. Your ass will be feeling me for days when we're through. It'll be a miracle if you can walk."

He reached his hand under the table and squeezed my knee.

"That works for me. Walking is overrated."

CHAPTER TWENTY-TWO

Nate

I **WALKED** back to the lab after eating lunch with Jake and thought about how lucky the two of us were to have each other. And not just in that moment. I thought about how lucky we'd been to have each other since the day we were born.

People talk about nature versus nurture. As a man of science, I certainly have my views on that. I do believe that we're born with many of our traits. But I also believe that our environment, our families, our friends help develop and shape the people we become. That's what Jake and I were to each other, what we'd always been— the environment, the family, the friends that developed two baby boys into adult men. In many ways, we'd helped create each other.

That sounds strange, I know, and codependent. But the reality is that I am who I am because of Jake. And I am dependent on him. I always have been. He is as important as air to me. And I know he feels the same way. It's why we've never been able to leave each other; why we've never wanted or tried to leave each other. And it's why things didn't work out with Bill, and every other guy I ever dated.

A buzzing in my pocket interrupted my thoughts. I pulled out my phone and checked the screen.

"Hi, Patrick! How are you?"

"I'm good, Nate. Hey, we, umm, we miss you. Ken and I are going dancing tonight and it wouldn't be the same without you."

"That sounds fun, Pat, but I've been working so much lately that I want to spend tonight with Jake."

As soon as I said it, I realized that I sounded like a broken record.

"Oh, right." I heard him take a breath. "Well, why don't you bring him? I know things didn't go so well when you brought Jake out the last time. And, umm, then the next time I saw him, there was that incident at the bar when he was working. But..."

"Third time's a charm?"

Patrick laughed and sounded relieved as he continued.

"So what do you say? Will you come dancing tonight? It'll give us a chance to get to know Jake and make up for last time."

"That sounds great, Pat. I'll talk to Jake. Are you going to Vida?"

"Yup. We'll be there around nine. See you tonight, then?"

"Count on it. If it's an issue, I'll call you back."

I called Jake to check in with him about going out with my friends again. I thought he might be hesitant because of how things had gone last time, the things he'd heard Patrick say. But he seemed genuinely happy.

"I like your friends, Nate. Besides, that night at the bar was six months ago. I'm over it. I never gave a shit about what Patrick said anyway. The only thing that mattered to me was whether *you* believed it."

And there it was. Typical Jake. He is one of those rare people who genuinely doesn't care about what anyone thinks. He never has. Even when the rest of us were going through insecure adolescent years where we wanted to fit in with everyone else and impress our friends, Jake just did his thing. Of course, that made people admire him even more. That incredible self-confidence had always drawn people to him.

I got home at six that night. I figured that gave us enough time to eat dinner, catch up, get ready, and meet my friends by nine. As soon as I walked in the door, I smelled something homey and delicious.

Jake walked out of the kitchen wearing old, faded jeans with holes in the knees. They were hanging on his hips and he had a towel tucked into his waistband and no shirt. I could see every ripped muscle in his chest and stomach. My eyes lingered on the narrow cut of muscle at his hip. I raised my gaze to his face and looked at his deep green eyes. He hadn't gotten a haircut in a while, so his hair was a bit shaggy and, at that time of day, he had a noticeable shadow on his face.

My body immediately reacted to the sight of him. To me, Jake was the epitome of masculinity and strength, which was a major turn-on. I walked over and wrapped my arms around him, locked my hands behind his neck, and licked him from the bottom of his neck up to his cheek. He laughed.

"I made tuna casserole. It'll probably taste better than my face."

"I doubt that," I mumbled into his neck. "The only thing that tastes better than your face is your dick."

He cracked up as I pulled the towel off his waist and tried to unbutton his jeans while he fought me off.

"Dinner, Nathaniel, dinner!"

I was hungry, and that casserole smelled delicious, so I stopped attacking him and got some plates out of the cabinet.

"It smells great, Jake. Thanks for cooking."

We sat down and ate the casserole and a Caesar salad that Jake had also made.

"So what's the plan for tonight, Nate? Are we going to hang out with Patrick and Ken at that same bar?"

My mouth was full, so I waited until I finished chewing and took a drink of water.

"No, not that bar. We're going dancing at a place called Vida."

He looked surprised.

"Dancing?"

Now, let me explain the thing with dancing. Where we were raised, folks did some line dancing, some country dancing, and a few folks even did traditional ballroom dancing. But there was no place in town where people danced like, well, like they dance at a gay dance club in New York.

When we first moved to the city, I was probably just as excited to meet other gay guys as I was to start my science program. I know, that sounds pathetic, but hey, I was eighteen, horny, and frankly, I was ready not to be the only one. Since I was too young to get into bars, and I hadn't figured out the whole fake ID thing yet, I started going dancing.

There were clubs that had eighteen-and-over nights and some that had wristbands so people under twenty-one could get in just to dance. I met some friends there, other gay guys my age. It was great not to have everyone talk about whatever girl had just walked into the room. I loved it.

I'd never been a sports guy, so I'd assumed that anything involving coordination wasn't going to be my strength. But the thing about dancing at those clubs was that you didn't need to be big or athletic. The guys who got the most attention were the ones who danced dirty. And, as it turned out, I could grind with the best of them. And I did. Before I got comfortable going home with guys, I used to enjoy the physical closeness on the safety of the dance floor. It was public and anonymous, so I knew I didn't have to actually do anything with them...unless that was what I wanted. And I loved the attention. So I'd put everything into those dances and, I'm proud to say, every dance partner I had was hard by the time we were done.

Of course, Jake didn't know any of that. We'd always spent a lot of time together, but he had his friends, and I had mine. So, on the nights I went dancing, he'd go out with his football buddies or have sex with some girl. We'd always end up home together, and while I told him about my friends, I didn't mention the one-step-removed-from-actual-fucking type of dancing that filled my nights. There are just some things you don't talk about with your straight friends.

After we cleaned up the dishes and the kitchen, Jake and I took a long shower. We kissed and touched each other softly, enjoyed each other's company. He lathered my body and washed my hair. It was something he did whenever we showered together, which was most showers, and I really enjoyed it. I was once again struck by how incredibly tender he could be.

We got out of the shower, dried off, and Jake threw on a pair of brown canvas pants and a plain white T-shirt.

"I'm going to watch the end of the game, okay? We can take off as soon as you're ready."

The sleeves on the shirt were a little short, so his bulging biceps were noticeable. Because his shirt was tucked in, I couldn't help but admire the V shape of his broad shoulders leading down to a narrow waist. And I could easily make out the shape and outline of his back muscles under that white shirt. He walked into the living room, combing his fingers through his hair. I don't think it took two minutes for him to get ready. How the guy can always look drop-dead gorgeous without giving it any thought or even looking in a mirror is beyond me.

It'd been a long time since I'd gone out dancing. Since before Jake and I got together. And, actually, even a couple of months before then, because I'd been so busy at work in the months leading up to our vacation. I went through my closet and settled on a pair of tight, black low-rise pants and an even tighter black shirt. I combed my hair and put some shaping wax in it, ruffling it a bit as I walked out of the room. Jake was glued to the television until I cleared my throat. His jaw dropped open as he looked me up and down. My stomach did a little flip of joy that he found me attractive.

He swallowed hard when his eyes took in my packed crotch in the tight pants.

"You, ehm." His voice caught in his throat, so he cleared it. "You're wearing that?"

His face seemed to be turning a little pale as he spoke. I decided to keep him on edge, so I walked over and stood right in front of him with my dick in direct line with his eyes.

"Ah-huh. Ready to go?"

He swallowed hard and nodded. Then he stood and we walked toward the door, with me following him. He opened the door and held it open for me. As I walked past him, I heard what sounded like a strangled cry and I turned to see Jake raise his eyes from my ass as he shook his head. Then he mumbled to himself.

"It's a good fucking thing I carry a gun."

CHAPTER TWENTY-THREE

Jake

I **WAS** looking forward to spending the evening with Patrick and Ken. Things hadn't gone so well the previous time I'd seen them, but I realized they weren't at fault. They just cared about Nate and had been trying to warn him when they thought he was wasting his time with me. They were completely fucking wrong, of course, but hey, they did it because they cared about Nate. How could I possibly be mad about that?

We got to the club and looked around for Patrick and Ken. We didn't see them, so we headed over to the bar and got our drinks. Nate was on his second vodka and cranberry, sporting a happy buzz, when Patrick walked up. He looked Nate up and down and gave him a long, tight hug. He was trying to talk quietly, but he was pretty drunk and didn't realize how much his voice carried.

"You look hot tonight, Nate."

My stomach tightened and I clenched my fist. Gotta love jealousy. Well, Nate did look hot. He was one hundred percent off limits to Patrick and every other guy checking him out in that place, but yeah, he was fucking hot. Patrick pulled himself off Nate and extended his hand to me. I tried to smile.

"It's, umm, nice to see you again, Jake. I'm glad you two could come out tonight." He looked a bit nervous as I shook his hand. Then he turned back to Nate. "Ken is already on the floor. Come on, let's join him."

Patrick took Nate's hand and began pulling him through the crowd. I had my arm around Nate's waist and I didn't let go. It made it a bit difficult to navigate through all the people, but I wasn't fucking letting go.

When we made it to the dance floor, we saw Ken dancing with a really young-looking guy. Neither of them was wearing a shirt. Patrick shouted so we could hear him over the music.

"Come on! Let's get out there."

I looked around, taking in the scene. There were guys in various states of undress all over the dance floor. Some were in pairs, others in groups of three and sometimes more. They were touching themselves and each other, grinding together. It was hot as hell, but I'd never danced with anyone like they were dancing. Other than with Nate, I'd never even had sex with anyone like they were dancing. Nate turned to me.

"Are you ready to dance, Jake?"

I shook my head.

"You go ahead. I'll just stay here and watch."

Nate looked worried. He put his arms around my neck and gazed into my eyes.

"Are you sure? Is everything okay?"

I didn't want to keep him from having fun. Besides,

if anyone got too close to him I'd blow his fucking head off. Okay, this was why people shouldn't carry guns in bars. I calmed myself down and smiled at him.

"I'm fine, baby. Really. I just want to watch you dance."

Nate kissed my cheek, then joined his friends on the dance floor. As soon as he got out there, it was like the music surged through him. He moved his body around to the sound of the music, gyrating his hips, and putting his hands behind his head. Then he swayed from side to side, moving his body all the way to the ground and back up again. As he squatted down, he ran his hands over his chest and down his stomach. Then when he came back up, his hips still swaying, he ran his hands up his thighs, letting his thumbs slide on top of his cock. When his hands reached the bottom of his shirt, they'd sometimes pull the shirt up, revealing his smooth sculpted chest. And he'd intersperse all of that with a bump and grind motion. I was mesmerized.

After about forty-five minutes of dancing—with Patrick, Ken, and their new, half-naked friend accidentally brushing up against Nate more times than I cared to count—Nate walked over to me. He was a bit out of breath, his shirt was damp with sweat, and his blond hair was all disheveled. He looked so damn beautiful. My chest tightened from the intense feelings I had for him. I wrapped my arms around his waist and pulled him against me.

"Did you have fun dancing?"
"Yes. Did you have fun watching?"

I didn't know why he was asking me that. My hard dick pushing against him should've given him the answer.

"It was the hottest fucking thing I've ever seen. If I hadn't been so busy trying to keep myself from beating the crap out of every guy lusting after you—and there were endless numbers, believe me—I think I would've come in my pants just from watching you."

"Awww, Jake, you say the sweetest things. If you liked that, you'll really enjoy the X-rated version. Buy me a drink and I'll show you when we get home."

I wasn't sure what he meant, so I raised my eyebrows. He took my hand and walked toward the bar, giving me a view of the world's best ass.

"The clothes come off in the X-rated version."

My dick pulsed and my breath hitched in reaction to that thought.

"Oh shit."

When we got to the bar, Nate was in front of me. He leaned down on the bar, which caused his ass to stick out and up. I was standing behind him, imagining him in that same position, without the clothes, and with me sliding into him. I started to lose my breath. Nothing and no one had ever come close to turning me on the way Nate did. My physical reaction to him was so strong that it almost overwhelmed me.

Nate got our drinks and we sat down at a table. My pants were stretched across my crotch and there was no way to hide my hard cock snaking down my thigh. Nate looked down at my lap and smiled.

"Is that for me?"

He reached his hand into my lap and stroked my cock.

"Jesus, Nate. You're killing me here."

My hands were shaking as I picked up my beer and gulped it down. Nate stood and reached his hand down to me.

"Come on."

"Where are we going?"

"Trust me."

I took his hand and, like always, enjoyed the feeling of his warm touch, his smooth skin. Nate led us to the bathroom and pulled me into a stall, closing the door behind us. He pressed his body against mine, grinding our dicks together as he kissed me. I sucked on his tongue and whimpered into his mouth. Then I felt him unbuckling my belt and unbuttoning my pants.

"Nate? What are you doing?"

He pressed his mouth to my ear and answered as he pulled my pants and briefs down in one stroke.

"I'm taking what's mine."

He was on his knees with my cock down his throat before I could react or respond. I threw my head back against the stall wall and moaned. He moved his head up and down on my shaft, sucking softly. Then he pulled up so only my crown was in his mouth. He squeezed my balls and pulled on my sack as he firmly sucked my glans.

"Oh fuck, Nate! You're so good at that."

I looked down and met his eyes as he licked the length of my cock and then moved his tongue up and down in swirls. Finally, he put my cock into his mouth and just held it, looking at me wantonly. I knew exactly what he wanted me to do. I put my hand on the back of his head and gently thrust in and out of his mouth. Nate loved having me pump into his mouth that way, and his body reacted with a loud moan I felt vibrating on my cock.

I moved my other hand into my mouth to absorb the sounds I knew were coming. Two thrusts later I was grasping Nate's head and shooting into his mouth as he moaned.

"Oh fuck. Oh fuck. Oh fuck."

I'd had countless blow jobs from countless women over the years, but not one of them had ever been anything like what I experienced with Nate. The way he used his mouth, his tongue, and his throat; the sounds he made; the way I felt about him…. It all added up to an incredibly erotic, sensuous experience. I hoped I could make him feel at least something close to what he made me feel. I wondered if my lack of experience with men disappointed him.

My head was back against the wall and my eyes were closed. I could feel Nate lifting up my briefs and pants, tucking my softening cock and balls back inside, and buttoning and buckling me up again. Then he nuzzled into my neck.

"Thanks for that. You're delicious. Ready to go back out there? Patrick and Ken are probably wondering where we are."

"Holy shit, Nate. I'm not sure I can walk right now.

How the fuck do you do that to me?"

I reached my hand down and palmed his cock. He entwined his fingers with mine and took my hand to his mouth, kissing it.

"Not right now. This was for you. Just you. Come on."

He opened the stall door and we walked out to find Patrick standing in the bathroom.

"Oh, there you are. I, or umm, we were just wondering where you went."

He was looking down at the ground, moving his foot nervously. Nate kissed me on the cheek and turned to him.

"Sorry about that, Pat. More dancing?"

"Yeah. That sounds good. I'll see you out there. I just need to use the bathroom."

Nate and I walked out of the bathroom and I let go of his hand.

"You go ahead. I'll wait for Patrick and then we'll come find you."

He seemed surprised, but I think he was happy I was getting along with his friend, so he nodded and walked toward the dance floor. I turned and walked back into the bathroom. Patrick was standing at the sink.

"So how long have you been in love with him?" He froze and looked at me in the mirror. I'm good at getting people to talk, even when that's the last thing they want to do, and even when it's a bad fucking idea for them to open their mouths. So I used all my patience and training to speak calmly, not letting my feelings show. "It's okay.

If anyone understands how amazing he is, it's me."

He hesitated, and then turned to me.

"Yeah. He's great. But I'm not in love with him. I just always thought he was someone I *could* love, you know? But there's always been a wall around him and no one could ever get it down. God knows I tried. He's different when you're around. Even before you two got together. When you were there, he was more open, talkative, physical...no wall."

"Does he know how you feel about him?"

Patrick snickered.

"Oh, I don't know. I came on to him once, years ago. He asked me whether I was interested in a fuck or a relationship. I've got to tell you, with a guy like Nate, I thought relationship was the right answer. I didn't even mean it at the time. I just wanted to get into his pants, but..."

He stopped and looked at me, suddenly realizing who he was talking to. I pushed the bile down and just smiled and nodded, so he continued.

"He told me things wouldn't work out. That he could share his dick but not his heart because his heart wasn't his. He said it never had been. I thought he was just being dramatic, you know? Until that night he brought you to the bar. The way he looked at you when you left, I realized for the first time that what he felt for you wasn't just an infatuation or some dumb crush. And the way you looked at him, I knew the feelings were mutual."

I sighed. It's impossible to put into words what Nate and I share, what we'd always shared, but it sure as fuck wasn't infatuation or a crush. Even before we'd started acting on our feelings physically, those feelings were the driving force of my life. And I realized that the same was true for Nate. Being able to share our bodies with each other, well, it was the most amazing gift that I could imagine, but it wasn't the basis for our relationship.

Patrick's voice interrupted my thoughts.

"So, umm, you're really gay?"

Seriously? Why was that so fucking hard for people to believe?

"Looks that way."

Patrick walked over to me and lightly moved his fingertips up and down my chest.

"Maybe the three of us could…"

"No fucking chance, Patrick."

He started to walk toward the door.

"That's about what I thought. Just be grateful you got to him first."

I grasped his shoulder hard enough to leave a bruise. "I am grateful. Every fucking minute of every fucking day. And I know you're his friend, which is great. But just so we're clear, whatever he told you back in the day, about being able to share his dick, is no longer true. Same goes for every other body part. Keep that in mind from now on. And keep your hands to yourself."

He swallowed hard and nodded. I looked into his eyes and was happy to see fear. Yeah, I know, I'm not a very nice guy. So the fuck what? I put my arm around his shoulder and walked him out the door.

"I'm glad we understand each other, Patrick."

CHAPTER TWENTY-FOUR

Nate

JAKE AND Patrick came walking up to the dance floor. Patrick's face was pale and he seemed very nervous, maybe even scared. I looked into Jake's face and he met my eyes. I walked over to them and put my hand on Patrick's arm. Just as I expected, he pulled away and stuttered.

"I...I, um, I'm going to dance with Ken." He smiled weakly and walked away.

"So. I'm guessing you staked your claim, or something, in the bathroom."

I was looking at Jake, trying to keep myself from smiling. He looked down at the ground.

"Shit. I'm sorry, Nate. I shouldn't have done that. I'll...I'll apologize to him. I know that he's your friend and I don't want to come across like some territorial asshole."

He looked ashamed and sad. I couldn't do that to him. I had to let him off the hook. I put my hand on his cheek and stroked it gently, until he looked into my eyes.

"Jake, I...well, it's okay. I don't mind. When it comes to you, I find territorial to be an unbelievable turn-on."

He raised his eyebrows in surprise and his eyes dilated. I lowered my hand from his cheek, stroked his chest, and rested my palm on his crotch.

"Let's go home."

My voice was husky and low. Thinking of Jake wanting me enough to tell off other guys was making me hot. My hard dick was uncomfortable in those tight pants, and I felt like my asshole was twitching with need.

We somehow made it back to our apartment with our clothes on. That was a major accomplishment, considering the fact that I was practically in Jake's lap in the cab. I started kissing him as soon as we got in and I only broke the kiss long enough for Jake to give the cabbie our address. By the time we made it to our door, I had his belt off and his pants unbuttoned. He managed to unlock the door and lead me into the apartment, while constantly sucking on my tongue.

"Let's go to the bedroom," he whispered to me.

"No time," I replied as I stripped off my shirt and kicked off my shoes. Jake looked at my chest and made a sound that could best be described as a growl. Then he unbuttoned and unzipped my pants and pushed them, along with my briefs, down to my ankles. I stepped out of them as Jake plunged down on my cock, taking me into his throat.

I leaned back against the wall and moaned.

"Ahhhh. Jake, that feels so good. But I need to feel you inside me."

He pulled back a little but continued sucking.

"Ohh, Jake. I won't last. Please, come up here. I

need you!"

He stood and I pushed his pants and briefs down. His cock slapped up on his stomach and our eyes met. Jake's eyes seemed almost wild. He kissed me deeply as he wrapped his arms around me and grasped my ass. Then he lifted me up. I put my arms over his shoulders and clasped my hands behind his neck, wrapped my legs around him and locked my ankles. I felt his cock pressing against my ass. He moved slowly, trying to find my entrance. I moaned into his mouth when he brushed against my pucker.

Jake pulled his mouth back and looked into my eyes as he simultaneously thrust upward and lowered me down onto his cock. It was a hard, fast movement. I gasped at the stretching, slightly burning intrusion. It felt incredible and my cock reacted by twitching and dripping.

"Ungh!"

I lost the power of speech. I could only grunt and moan. Jake had me pressed against the wall. His arms were under my legs, holding me up and he had his hands pressed against the wall to brace himself. His biceps were flexing, sweat was dripping from his forehead, and he was pushing himself up and down, using the strong muscles in his legs while moving me up and down by raising and lowering his arms.

I could feel my cock rubbing against his stomach. I could smell his skin, his sweat. The sound of us both moaning and grunting filled the room. The whole experience was primal and erotic.

The friction of his cock plunging into my ass without lube caused an incredible combination of extreme pleasure with just a hint of pain. I was really getting off on it. Jake was kissing me and thrusting up into me when I felt his body tense.

He pulled his face back and looked into my eyes. I was so close, I needed to trip. I was gasping for air, banging my head back against the wall in frustration. Jake seemed to know exactly what I needed—he bent his head down and bit the spot where my neck meets my shoulder.

"Ahhhhhhh!"

I screamed as I released all over our chests and Jake responded by shooting deep inside me.

After a few moments, he turned around while still holding me up. He pressed his back against the wall and slowly slid down, lowering us to the ground so he was sitting on the floor with me straddling his lap. He gazed into my eyes.

I was struck by how comfortable, how safe I was with him. His look held the knowledge of every hope, every failure, every achievement, every dream, every disappointment, every success, every humiliation, every joy I'd ever experienced.

"Was...was that okay? Did I give you what you needed, baby?"

He was looking at me intently. I nodded and nuzzled into his neck, licking his skin, sucking gently. As I regained the power of thought, I realized that his voice sounded different. It sounded...unsure. I picked my head up and looked at him. He brushed my hair back and ran his fingers through it. I searched his eyes.

"Jake? Is everything okay?"

He sighed and then tightened his grasp on me.

"I just...I want to make you feel as good as you make me feel. I want to give you everything." He hesitated. "But, I don't have the experience of those guys tonight. I could never move like they were moving." He leaned his forehead on mine and continued.

"And they were all looking at you, wanting you. Man! You looked fucking amazing tonight, Nate. You always look so fucking amazing. You're beautiful. So beautiful. And you're such a good lover. The things you do with your body...the things you do to my body. You make me feel a way that I never even imagined. And you're sooo fucking smart. I mean, that guy Bill is an ass, but he's right. You could be with someone so much smarter than me."

I opened my mouth to stop him, but then he finished in a whisper so low, I wouldn't have heard him if I'd made any sound, or if we weren't so close together, sharing the same air.

"Am I enough for you? I want so much to be enough for you."

I couldn't believe what I was hearing. I had never known Jake to be insecure. And he was way out of my league—how did he not see that?

"Oh, Jake. Enough for me? You're everything to me. I lose my breath when I look at you. Do you realize that you could be on the cover of a magazine? You are so gorgeous, without even trying. And don't say that you aren't smart, Jake! You know that isn't true. I'm good with numbers, books. So what? I never have the right words. I don't understand people. Hell, I barely even understand myself. But you do. You always have. You can walk into a room and somehow understand what every person there is doing and feeling. Do you have any idea how much I admire you?"

I realized that I was crying when I felt Jake's hand brush the tears off my cheeks.

"I'm not that great, Jake. Trust me on that. Or ask any guy I've ever been with. None of them would be singing my praises in bed. The way I am with you, it's...it's different. It's because of you, because of the things you make me feel, because of how much I love you, because I know how much you love me."

I sniffled. My face was damp with tears. Jake was still wearing his shirt. The front was wet and sticky from my cum, but the sleeves were dry. He reached down and took off his shirt. Then he found the dry areas and used them to wipe my tears and the rest of my face. I laughed.

"What? Why are you laughing?"

"You just...you just made love to me to within an inch of my life, Jake. I can still feel you in my ass. You have the most incredible body I've ever seen." I slid my hand down his perfectly sculpted, chiseled chest. "And you took the shirt off your back and used it to wipe my nose. So, yes, I think it's safe to say you're enough for me."

JAKE STAYED at my parents' house whenever we went to Bryerville after his parents died, even though he never sold their old house. My parents had found folks to rent the place over the years, and they made sure it was kept in good shape; not too difficult, since they still lived next door.

"Top or bottom, Jake?"

We'd just gotten home for a long overdue visit, and Jake set our bags down in my old room. He pulled me close to him for a kiss.

"Are you talking about the bunk beds, Nate, or..."

My folks had bought bunk beds for my room when we started high school. I guess they figured we were too big to keep sharing a bed on the weekends when Jake slept over. We were standing in front of the beds, and I frowned with the thought that I wouldn't get to feel Jake's body against mine at night. I had gotten used to that feeling and I wasn't sure that I could handle sleeping apart from him, even only a few feet apart. Jake seemed to read my mind.

"The beds aren't staying that way. I'm pretty sure those can be separated and used as regular twin beds. I just need to push them together and we'll have plenty of space." He had walked over to the beds and was lifting the upper bunk. "Give me a hand and we'll get this settled so we can get out there for dinner. Smells like Mama C is making her famous jambalaya."

I walked over to the other side of the bed, and ten minutes later, we had the bunks separated and pressed against each other in the corner of the room. That didn't leave a lot of space for walking around, but I knew we wouldn't be spending too much time there anyway.

"Are you boys ready for—"

My mom was standing at the door, wiping her hands on her apron and looking at the new bed arrangement. Her eyes moved from the joined beds to the two of us. She smiled and finished her sentence.

"Dinner? It's just about done. Nathaniel, I think your dad could use your help with the salad. You know how hopeless he is with anything involving the kitchen."

I nodded and started walking toward the door, with Jake close behind me. My mom gently took his arm.

"I see you boys still need to unpack. Jacob, I can help you with that while Nathaniel works on the salad."

Jake stayed with my mother and I walked into the kitchen to see my dad butchering a tomato. I opened the knife drawer, took out a serrated knife, and handed it to him.

"Try this knife, Dad. Serrated is better for tomatoes."

"Oh, right. Thank you, Nathaniel."

I walked over to the fridge and took out some lettuce and a cucumber, rinsed them in the sink, and started cutting. My dad and I chatted for a while. He filled me in on work, what everyone in the family was doing, and the latest town gossip.

"All right, son. It looks like we're done with this salad. How about getting a couple of beers out of the fridge and joining your old man out on the porch? I bet you don't get to see the stars like this in New York."

I'm not usually a beer drinker, but I wasn't going to spoil the father-son moment. So, I took the beers out of the fridge and followed my dad outside. I looked up at the night sky. It really was beautiful. I sighed wistfully as I handed my dad his beer and took a long pull of mine. We sat on the two rockers that'd been on that porch for years and enjoyed the night sky and each other's company.

"I'm sorry it's been so long since our last visit, Dad. Things are always so busy with work that it's hard to get away. It's really fast-paced over there. Time just flies by."

He reached over and patted my hand with his. Then he left it there and gave me a squeeze. I wondered whether he could sense my growing frustration with my job and life in the big city.

"Don't be sorry, Nathaniel. We understand. We just miss you. Both of you. Your mother keeps hoping that you'll decide to move back home." He took another drink and started peeling the label off his bottle. "And, so do I."

Had my father said those words to me at any other time in my life, I probably would've shrugged them off. I'd never wanted to stay in Bryerville. But at that moment—sitting with him on the porch, looking at the stars, hearing the crickets—I couldn't think of anywhere else I'd rather be. But it wasn't that easy.

"I miss you too, Dad. You know that. But I just

don't think we can have a life here. I mean, it's still the South, and I'm still gay."

My father shook his head. I could tell he was frustrated, but he kept his voice even.

"If you don't want to live here, Nathaniel, then you don't want to live here. But don't use being gay as an excuse. I know this isn't New York, but this is your home. Your mother and I were both born in this town and so were Jacob's parents. You have uncles, cousins, and any number of distant relatives here. You're part of this town, both of you, and you're loved and accepted here.

"Sure, it might be different for an outsider. I'm not saying people don't have their closed-minded opinions. Maybe it would've even been different if you'd tried to bring another man home. But you didn't. It's just you and Jacob. You're part of this town and you've never been treated badly here, Nathaniel. You boys are family to everyone here. I don't think it's fair for you to assume the worst of people who have always cared about you. About both of you."

I knew he was right. I'd heard lots of horror stories from my gay friends over the years. Stories about angry parents, friends who wouldn't have anything to do with them when they came out. Some had been taunted or even beaten by classmates. But that hadn't ever happened to me. None of it.

I guess that was the thing about a small town, at least when you were as deeply entrenched in it as our families. It was easy to hate a nameless, faceless person, but in Bryerville everyone had known us since birth—

same with our parents, and their parents. They probably wouldn't be out fighting for gay rights, but if Jake and I moved back, they'd welcome us with open arms.

"I'm sorry, Dad. You're right. Everyone here has always been good to me. I guess I just never thought I'd want to move back here. Neither of us did. I'll talk to Jake. See what he thinks. I do miss this place. And it really would be nice to be closer to you and Mom."

He nodded and we sat silently for a few more minutes and finished our beers. Eventually, my father patted my knee and got up.

"I'm going to set the table, Nathaniel. Please, go get your mother and Jacob and tell them that I'm too old to eat dinner this late."

I laughed as I walked inside and headed toward my bedroom. Just as I was walking up, the door opened and I saw my mom walking out. Her eyes were red and puffy. I could tell she'd been crying, which could only mean one thing—she and Jake had been talking about his parents.

I quickly walked into the bedroom to check on Jake and saw him sitting on the bed. He looked sad and tired. I wanted so much to make it better, but I couldn't bring his parents back. So I just wrapped my arms around him and held him tight as he mumbled into my chest.

"I miss them so much, Nate."

"I know you do."

I held him and told him how much I loved him, that he wasn't alone. He calmed down and pulled back a little, looking into my eyes.

"I'm sorry about that, Nate. Coming back here just brings up a lot of memories, you know?"

I understood how hard it must've been for him to come back to Bryerville and not have his parents there. How could I ask him to move back when every day would be filled with that loss?

"No apology necessary. I understand. Come on, let's get some dinner. I need to make sure you've got lots of energy for tonight. I seem to remember promises of fulfilling our childhood fantasies."

He laughed.

"And I plan to honor those promises after dinner, Nate. Come on, let's get out there."

He gave me a sweet, gentle kiss and took my hand as we walked out of the room.

CHAPTER TWENTY-FIVE

Jake

NATE AND I were back in Bryerville for a long overdue visit. We'd just set up the beds in his old room so that we could sleep together when his mother walked in.

"Are you boys ready for dinner? It's just about done."

She was smiling as she looked at the rearranged beds.

"Nathaniel, I think your dad could use your help with the salad. You know how hopeless he is with anything involving the kitchen."

Hmmm. Sounded like she was trying to get Nate out of the room. He walked toward the door, and I followed, knowing she'd ask me to stay.

"I see you boys still need to unpack. Jacob, I can help you with that while Nathaniel works on the salad."

I laughed to myself and turned back into the room.

"So you want some alone time with me, Mama C?" I gave her a hug.

"Am I really that transparent, honey?"

I put the suitcases on the bed and started

unpacking. "I'm pretty sure you weren't going for discreet. Is everything okay?"

She opened the closet door, pulled out some hangers, and helped me put our clothes away.

"Everything is fine, Jacob. Better than fine. I just want to tell you that Ted and I are thrilled about, ehm, things between you and Nathaniel." She stopped working on the clothes and turned to me. I could see tears in her eyes. "I can't tell you what it means to me to know that you boys have each other."

I was taken aback and confused about where this rush of emotion was coming from and where it was going. Then she grasped my arm.

"You know, I've been with Nathaniel's father since I was sixteen years old. He is the only man I've ever loved. And your mother was my best friend my entire life. We were inseparable, until she died. I never had a sister, but I do have my brothers, and we've always been very close. I guess that's what comes from growing up in the same house, having a shared background. I always knew that you and Nathaniel loved each other, but I was never quite sure what kind of love it was—whether it was the way I felt toward my brothers, toward your mother, or toward Ted."

She was peering at me with tears in her eyes, still clutching my arm. I knew she was holding something back, but I wasn't sure what it was. Did she want me to explain how I felt about Nate? Did she need to be sure that I wouldn't hurt him?

"I, umm, I don't know how to respond to that,

Mama C, because I don't have another frame of reference. Nate is the only person that has ever fit any of those roles for me." I gathered my thoughts and tried to put what I felt for Nate into words. "I guess what I'm saying is that I do love him like the closest thing to a sibling I've ever had, like my best friend all of my life, and like the only person I've ever been in love with. So, yes, it's all of those things. But it's also none of them.

"Somehow the intensity of having all of that love, all of those feelings, those desires wrapped up in one person...there just aren't words to explain what I feel for him, what he means to me. But I can promise you that I won't hurt him. He's my whole world. I'll always take care of him. You don't have to worry."

Tears were running down her face as I spoke, but she gave a small chuckle at my last comment.

"Is that what you think, Jacob? That I'm worried about you hurting Nathaniel?"

I wasn't sure how to respond, so I just held her hand and waited for her to continue.

"I know you'll never hurt him, Jacob. I may not be able to completely understand what the two of you share, but I have no doubt that you'll take care of him. Just like you always have."

She got up and hung some more clothes in the closet. After a few minutes she cleared her throat, her back still to me.

"I know about the accident, Jacob. I had a friend who worked at the hospital pull your parents' medical records. We went through them over and over again. I know they weren't killed on impact. And I know Nathaniel wasn't brought to the hospital by ambulance; you carried him in."

I jumped up from the bed and closed the door. I didn't want to take a chance that Nate would hear any of this.

"I know it wasn't my place, but when you insisted on taking a settlement right away from that trucking company even when the lawyers said you could get so much more by going to trial, or at least dragging things out a bit, going through discovery...I thought you were holding something back. I, umm, I'm ashamed to admit this, but I thought maybe your father had been drinking. That you were trying to protect him and keep that hidden."

She sat down on the bed, trembling. Shit. I tugged my fingers through my hair and tried to think of how to respond.

"My dad hadn't been drinking, Mama C. It wasn't his fault. That truck driver really did fall asleep and cross into our lane. He came out of nowhere." I hesitated a bit, not wanting to lie to her, but knowing that I had no other choice. "And they died on impact. That's all I'll ever say and that's all that Nate should ever hear. He can never see those records or hear about whatever else you suspect."

My voice had been soft to that point, but then I raised it a bit and finished speaking with a very firm tone, so she understood that I was serious.

"He can't handle that kind of guilt. And I won't let him be burdened with it."

She was wringing her hands in her lap. "And you can handle the guilt, Jacob? You can carry that burden all by yourself?"

I didn't hesitate. My voice was strong, firm, and cold.

"I can and I have. For the past nine years. And that's what I'll continue to do."

I suddenly felt very tired. Thinking about that night, about my parents' death, about how close I came to losing Nate, was still painful. I felt my defenses slipping away as I sat next to the woman who'd been a second mother to me my entire life and put my arm around her.

"Please? I don't want to talk about this anymore. Not now, not ever. He was unconscious the entire time. It was my choice, Mama C." I looked directly into her eyes. "And it's not a choice I've ever regretted. Not once."

She wiped her face with her apron and put her hand on my cheek.

"All right, honey. I understand. And I'll never say anything to Nathaniel. You have my word. I'm grateful for what you did for my son, Jacob. That night and all the other times that I know you've protected him."

She got up, but kept looking into my eyes.

"You have her eyes, you know, and her strength. She would've been so proud of the man you've become."

She turned and opened the door just as Nate was walking up. He looked at his mom's red eyes and my face and hurried over to the bed, wrapping me in his arms. I leaned into him, rested my head against his chest, and let the tears flow.

"I miss them so much, Nate."

"I know you do."

He held me and stroked the back of my head and my neck, whispering soothing words into my ear. I felt so incredibly lucky to have him in my life. After a few minutes, I got myself under control and sat up.

"I'm sorry about that, Nate. Coming back here just brings up a lot of memories, you know?"

A look ran across his face—disappointment, understanding, maybe both.

"No apology necessary. I understand. Come on, let's get some dinner. I need to make sure you've got lots of energy for tonight. I seem to remember promises of fulfilling our childhood fantasies."

That made me laugh. It also made my dick plump up a little.

"And I plan to honor those promises after dinner, Nate. Come on, let's get out there."

We walked downstairs and joined his parents, who were already sitting at the table. Dinner was delicious. I wasn't sure whether it was the meal, the company, or the fact that I'd eaten that jambalaya so many times in my life that it was comfort food for me. Whatever it was, I felt glad to be home. After we were all finished eating, Nate's mother got up to start clearing the plates.

"The three of you made dinner, so I'll take care of the dishes. You sit and relax, Mama C."

"Thank you, Jacob. I really appreciate that."

I took the plates into the kitchen and started washing them at the sink. I was standing in front of the window and I could see the clear sky above and the lights twinkling from the houses around us. I'd been in every one of those houses at some point in my life. For a barbecue, a birthday party, a family dinner, something. It was different in New York. We didn't really know our neighbors. We had friends there and coworkers, but it wasn't the same.

"I'll help you dry."

Nate had walked in and placed his arms around me. I leaned back against his chest and brushed my cheek against his. He sighed and kissed my neck before removing his arms and getting a towel out of the drawer. After a few more minutes, we had the dishes washed, dried, and put away. I walked over to Nate, clutched his waist and pulled him until he was settled between my spread legs, pressed up against me.

"Okay, so here's what I propose. We share our fantasies, then we go upstairs and start acting them out. You go first."

I could feel him hardening against my thigh. He was rubbing my back and speaking quietly.

"Well, I guess the first time I fantasized about us, it was pretty innocent. I used to imagine that on one of the nights you slept over, I'd walk into my room after getting out of the shower and catch you beating off."

We were standing in the kitchen, pressed together, when Nate's father walked in.

"Thanks for, ehm"—he looked down at the ground—"cleaning up the dishes and the kitchen, boys."

I kissed Nate on the cheek and pulled away.

"No problem, Ted. I'm beat after that trip, so if it's okay with you and Mama C, I'm going to take a shower and hit the sack."

I gave Nate's father a hug and he squeezed me tightly.

"Of course, son, of course. We'll catch up tomorrow. I want to hear all about your latest cases and your promotion."

Nate's grandfather had been the town sheriff, so his dad had grown up around law enforcement. He always loved to hear about my job.

"Sounds like a plan. Good night, Ted."

I winked at Nate as I walked out of the kitchen. Then I said good night to Mama C, took a shower, and got into bed. I crawled under the sheets and thought about all the fun times I'd spent in that room.

When we were kids, Nate and I used to stay up all night, hiding under the covers with flashlights and telling each other stories. We had a game where one of us would start a story and tell a bit and then the other would pick up the story and continue it. We'd do that back and forth until we fell asleep.

Looking back, I knew that I'd loved him even then. In fact, I couldn't remember a time when I hadn't loved him. I couldn't even think of a memory from any point in my life that didn't center on him in some way. I wasn't exaggerating when I'd told Mama C that Nate was my whole world.

I heard the water running in the hallway shower, so I knew Nate would be coming into the room soon.

The lights were off, but the curtains were open, and light streamed in from the full moon outside. I moved the covers off my body, so I'd be exposed, and I started stroking my cock. I'd gotten myself good and hard by the time I heard the water turn off and Nate's hand on the doorknob.

I closed my eyes, leaned my head back on the headboard, and continued stroking myself.

"Mmm. Ungh," I moaned as he walked in.

Nate gasped and I heard him close the door, but I didn't open my eyes. I just continued stroking my cock. I rubbed my thumb over the wet tip and spread my precum down my shaft, using it as lube.

After a couple of minutes, I felt Nate sit next to me on the bed. I opened my eyes and looked at him. He was naked and still a little wet from the shower. His pupils were dilated, his mouth hung open, and he was as hard as a rock.

"God, that is so hot, Jake. You look so hot doing that."

I sat up, so we were facing each other. I spread my legs around him, so he was sitting between them. He did the same thing, draping his legs over mine. Our torsos weren't touching but we were very close together. I could hear his ragged breathing and feel the warmth of his skin as I continued stroking my cock.

"You want to join me, Nate? Or is this a one-man show?"

As I spoke, I reached underneath the pillow, where I'd stashed a small bottle of lube. I squeezed some onto my hands and then continued stroking myself with one hand as I reached my other hand into Nate's lap and caressed his cock. He moaned and tilted his head back. He was incredibly hard and leaking, moaning.

I almost shot my load just from looking at the pleasure in his face, so I slowed down the strokes on my cock. But I kept up the pace on Nate, hard and fast, up and down. He was grasping my back, digging his nails into me, moaning loudly, and repeating my name, over and over again. I was glad that his parents had a big house and that they were on the other side.

"Oh, Jake. I'm so close. Jake, Jake, oh Jake."

I increased the pace of my own strokes, knowing it wouldn't take long now for either of us. We were both looking down at each other's cock, and then we released. I wasn't sure who went first, but suddenly, we were both pulsing and shooting. Our chests were covered with cum and I noticed some on Nate's chin. Mine, his, ours? I didn't know, didn't care. I flattened my tongue and ran it from the bottom of his neck and up his chin, scooping the ejaculate onto my tongue. Then I kept licking upward until I was pressing my tongue into his mouth. He groaned and let me in, sucking on my tongue, sharing our seed. We kept kissing, rolling our tongues together, until I could feel Nate shivering.

"Hang on, baby. Let me dry you off and then we can get under the blanket."

I reached onto the floor and picked up the towel Nate had discarded when he'd gotten into bed. I wiped the wetness off his chest and stomach, did the same to my own body, and dropped the towel back on the floor. I wrapped my arms around Nate and pulled him on top of me as I lay down. He tugged the blanket over us and kissed my neck.

"That was incredible, Jake." He sighed. "I love you so much. You know that?"

I did know. I could feel his love throughout my entire body.

"Mmm-hmm. I know. I love you too."

We cuddled together and I was just falling asleep when I felt Nate raise his head off my chest.

"Jake?"

I opened my eyes and saw him looking intently at me.

"Yeah?"

"Do you, umm, do you ever do that at home?"

"Do what? Masturbate, you mean?"

He nodded.

"I guess so. Not too much because you leave me pretty dry. But sometimes, when you're working late or when you leave early. Why? Do you want me to set up a video camera for the show?" I laughed. "I usually do it in the shower so I don't think that'd work."

Nate looked a little uncomfortable. He was biting his lower lip and I could tell he wanted to ask me something, but he was hesitating. Finally he spoke, quietly, his head lowered but he raised his eyes to meet mine.

"I want you to stop. I mean, when I'm not there, I, umm, I don't want you to touch yourself when I'm not there." My face must have shown my confusion because he explained further. "I want to be responsible for your orgasms, Jake. I want you to associate those feelings with me, only me. And I want the same from you, so I promise that I won't touch myself without you, either."

I wasn't sure why, but that was incredibly arousing to me. My heart felt like it was beating out of my chest, I hardened right away, and I was losing my breath.

"Shit, Nate. That is so...so...so fucking kinky and possessive."

I bucked up against him so he'd feel my hard dick and understand that I meant those words as a compliment, and I pulled his face toward mine and kissed him. The kiss was deep, penetrating, and needy.

"I promise, Nate. Unless it involves taking a piss, I won't go near my dick without your permission. I belong to you."

Of course, I'd always belonged to him. And he'd always belonged to me. But at that moment, lying in bed in his childhood home, we both finally embraced it completely.

CHAPTER TWENTY-SIX

Jake

I **WOKE** up to Nate's bright blue eyes inches away from my face, gazing at me.

"Morning," I whispered hoarsely.

We were both lying on our sides, facing each other. Our legs were intertwined, my arm was draped around his waist, and his arm was resting on my back. It was a great way to start the day.

"Morning," he whispered back as he reached over and brushed my hair off my face. "How'd you sleep?"

I rolled onto my back and took his arm with me so that it was resting on my chest as I stroked it.

"Not too bad, considering the gap in between these two mattresses. I thought maybe I'd miss the traffic noise and random, late-night conversations that drift up to our apartment from the street, but it turns out that a cricket serenade is really all I need to zonk out."

He laughed and nuzzled into my neck.

"Yeah. It's nice, isn't it? I never thought I'd miss the quiet." He hesitated and then continued, "But I do."

"Me too." I kissed his forehead. "So what do we

have on deck for today? I know there's the barbecue with all the uncles and their clans, but I was hoping to go visit Coach Westenbrook. Do you think Mama C and Ted would mind if I made myself scarce for a little while?"

"Nope, I don't think it'll be an issue. I noticed big bowls of egg salad, potato salad, tomato salad, and ambrosia in the fridge last night. I don't think we'll have much to do today other than fire up the grill. Besides, my mom is so excited about having everyone over that I'm sure she's been up for hours getting things ready. If we try to jump in now, we'll probably just get in her way."

Nate and I got out of bed, showered, and then I headed out to meet my old football coach for an early lunch. I walked into the local greasy spoon and felt a sense of comfort when I saw that nothing had changed. The place had looked exactly the same my whole life. I saw Coach Harold Westenbrook sitting in a booth. Another man, whose back was to me, was sitting across from him. I walked over, and Coach smiled broadly when he saw me.

"Jacob! It's great to see you, son. How's Nathaniel Richardson doing?"

I shook Coach's hand and squeezed his shoulder as I laughed to myself. He didn't really know Nate. Of course, it was a small town, so he knew the family, and Nate had come to all my football games when I was in high school and even some of the practices, but Coach Westenbrook wasn't really a talkative guy and he certainly wasn't one to chat with students, unless they were on his team. Nope, he didn't know Nate. But he'd been asking me about Nate ever since the time I'd visited Coach during my senior year in college.

WE WERE home for winter break, and Coach Westenbrook had called and asked me to come by the school and say hello. I was happy to stop by. I would've done it even if he hadn't called. Coach was great and he'd been really good to me all through high school. He'd even kept in touch when I went to college and called me a few times to check how I was doing after my parents died.

I got to the high school gym and walked into Coach's office. I think he said hello and gave me a pat on the shoulder, but right after that he launched into me.

"So I got a call from your coach, Jake. What's this bullshit about you refusing to enter the draft?"

Leave it to Coach Westenbrook to cut right to the chase. The man was always a straight shooter. It was one of the things I admired about him.

"Call from my coach? Have you finally reached senility, old man? You're my coach!"

He didn't even break a smile.

"Cut the crap, Jacob. I'm too old to find it cute. I haven't been your coach in four years. I'm talking about Coach Fields."

Of course, I knew exactly what he was talking about. So my college coach had called my high school coach when he couldn't get me to go into the professional football draft.

"There's nothing to tell, Coach. I've had a good run, but I'm done with football after this year."

He practically growled at me as he pounded his fist on his desk.

"What the fuck do you mean, you've had a good run? Jacob, you have the opportunity to play professional football! Do you have any idea how many guys would jump at that chance? Why on earth are you walking away from this?"

I sat in the chair across from his desk and spoke quietly, hoping that would calm him down. The man was only one or two pounds away from a heart attack.

"Look, they can't guarantee what team will draft me. And the reality is that I wouldn't get to stay in New York."

He sat in the chair behind his desk and I could see he was trying to calm down, but it wasn't in his nature. He exploded again.

"So what if you can't stay in New York? What the hell does it matter what team you join? You'd get to travel anyway, so you could see all parts of the country, and you'd be playing football, making more money than any of us could imagine."

Nothing other than spelling it out for him was going to work, so I went with the honest approach.

"Coach, staying in New York matters because Nate has two more years of medical school left. He can't just pick up and move. And after that, he'll have his residency for another few years, so we'll have to go wherever that is. I'm just not in a position to move around right now, and by the time he's done with all that, I'll be too far removed to play football."

I paused a bit to make sure he understood, and then tried to change the subject.

"So, how is Mrs. Westenbrook? I heard that your youngest daughter had another baby, so I'm sure that her days are filled taking care of—"

I didn't get to finish my sentence.

"So you're telling me that you're passing up the chance to play professional football because you can't move away from your friend, who is in school in New York?"

I nodded, relieved that he'd finally gotten it, and hopeful that we could move on. No such luck, though. He cleared his throat and looked uncomfortable. I could see the gears moving in his head.

"Ehm. So your friend—Nathaniel Richardson, right? I, umm, remember him, of course, and umm, I think that people said that he was, ehm, gay, back when you kids were in school."

I immediately got my guard up. Was he going to try to belittle Nate somehow? I really liked Coach and he was too old to punch. So I tried to get control of my rising anger.

"Yeah, he was and he still is. What's your point, Coach?" I spoke between gritted teeth.

"I guess what I'm asking, Jacob, is...I mean, it doesn't make any sense for you to give up your life just to stay in the same city as a friend, so... Fuck, Jacob, are you sleeping with this guy?"

His face was red; he was clearly embarrassed to be having that conversation. The whole thing just struck me as fucking hilarious, so I started laughing. My stomach hurt from the deep laughter and tears were running down my face.

"No, Coach, unfortunately, I'm not sleeping with him. But you sure as fuck better believe that I'd love to. Not the sleeping so much, though that would be nice, but I'm guessing that you're not really asking about sleep."

I winked at him, still laughing under my breath.

"Jacob Owens, I am serious here. This is your life we're talking about. You cannot just give it up because your friend, or whatever he is, happens to be in school in New York."

Okay, this was going nowhere. He wasn't going to understand, and I was bored of trying to explain it to him.

"Look, Coach, that's where you're wrong. Football isn't my life. *Nate* is my life. And I'm not going to give him up just to play football. Not even for a couple of years. I'm sorry to disappoint you, I really am. But, like you said, it's my life, so that means it's my choice. Now, I've only got a few more minutes before I have to take off, so let's move on."

I thought he still didn't understand, but that he couldn't think of anything else to say. He was quiet, and he nodded in response to a few questions I asked about his family and last year's season, and then I said goodbye and left.

I went back to visit Coach whenever we came

home over the years and I could always tell that he was happy to see me. He never asked about football again, but he made it a point to ask me about Nate every time I saw him, so I realized that he'd understood after all.

"NATE'S GREAT, Coach. Really great. He's been working in medical research. It's amazing what that man can think up." I turned to the guy across from Coach and held out my hand. "I'm Jake Owens. I don't think we've met."

He scooted out of the booth and stood in front of me as he took my hand and shook it. He was a few inches shorter than me, about forty-five or fifty years old, and his whole demeanor and look just screamed "law enforcement."

"Hello, Jake. I'm Martin. I hope you don't mind that Harold invited me to join you for lunch."

No last name—interesting. I slid into the booth next to Coach, though there was barely enough room. He was a large man and he seemed to get larger every year.

"I don't mind at all, Martin. It's always nice to meet a fellow officer. So how long have you been on the job?"

He laughed, a deep loud, laugh, as he shook his head and sat back down.

"Well, shit. Either you're as good as they say, son, or I've been a cop way too long. How'd you know? I'm not wearing my uniform and I don't even have my service weapon."

He seemed like a good guy. When he smiled, it was genuine, and his eyes crinkled.

"I'm as good as they say, Martin. And damn proud of it." No one ever said I was modest. In fact, "arrogant asshole" was the more frequent description. I took a drink from one of the water glasses on the table. "And from the way you were favoring your right foot as you stood up, Martin, I'm guessing that you have a .22 in your ankle holster, service weapon or not. You might want to consider a Beretta. It's easier to conceal, if that's your goal."

He raised his eyebrows and his jaw dropped open. I laughed. He had clearly been hugging a desk for a long time. There was no way a guy that openly expressive could interview suspects or work on the streets. I thought an explanation was in order.

"I've been doing undercover work for the past five years, Martin. Trust me when I tell you that knowing how to spot a weapon is a matter of survival. It's probably just as important as knowing how to hide one."

I decided not to share my thoughts about what he'd probably been doing for the past five years. Desk jockey or not, he was a cop, and no cop wants to hear that he's lost his edge. Or maybe that he never had it.

Just then, the waitress came over and took our orders. By the time we were done, Martin seemed to have a handle on himself and Coach Westenbrook was grinning like the cat that ate the canary.

"Jacob, I've known Martin here for over twenty years. His wife, Nicole, went to school with Gloria, and they've kept in touch all this time. Martin and Nicole have visited us over the years and they fell in love with Bryerville. So when Sheriff Johnson was getting ready to retire, I called Martin. He had enough years under his belt in one of the police departments in Massachusetts for partial retirement, so he and Nicole packed up and moved here."

So this was Sheriff Wells. There wasn't lots of serious crime in that area, and having a guy with that open, friendly personality probably put folks at ease. That would be important, considering the fact that he wasn't local. I couldn't remember a sheriff who hadn't been born and bred in the area.

"You must be one hell of a cop, Martin. Folks around here aren't usually too fond of outsiders." I took another drink and smiled at him. "Or Yankees."

He gave me that same surprised look and, again, shook his head.

"No, no, they're not, Jake. That's actually one of the reasons I wanted to join you and Harold for lunch."

Well, that was unexpected. And interesting.

"Is that right? And here I thought it was just to have the best chicken-fried steak in a four-county radius. That and my charming personality, of course."

Coach jumped in with his usual straightforward style.

"Let's cut to the chase, Jacob. Martin here needs a deputy sheriff. You interested in the job?"

Now it was my turn to laugh. I turned to Coach.

"Why can't every fucking person I meet be like

you, Coach? It'd make things a hell of a lot easier to figure out."

Martin spoke to me from across the table.

"Oh, I don't know about that, Jake. From what I heard about you and from what I've seen here today, you don't have too much trouble figuring people out, even when they're not so, ehm, forthright. Let me explain what I need, Jake, and why I think you're the right man for the job."

He told me about his staff—a couple of young guys, some support personnel, and another officer who'd been in the office for years but wasn't too thrilled when he was passed over for the sheriff's job. They were good, honest men, but they were all trained there in town and they didn't have a lot of street experience or, from what Martin said, street smarts.

"Our jurisdiction and responsibilities have expanded, Jake. We're not just taking care of Bryerville anymore. That means more work and more serious crime, though nothing as serious as what you're used to, of course. But we could still use a man with more skill. Truth is, I've been in management for the past fifteen years, so I'm a bit rusty myself."

I nodded in appreciation of his honesty and self-awareness. Not a lot of cops would admit to being rusty. I'd probably enjoy working for him. Our personalities and skills were just different enough to complement each other well. The waitress brought our food over and all three of us dug in as Martin continued talking.

"I'm sure I could find a guy with some good

experience and lure him over here...."

I helped him finish.

"But you want a local guy. Bringing in another stranger won't make your current team or the community happy."

I was looking at him as I spoke and he nodded, with that same honest smile on his face.

"And if you bring in another Yankee, Martin, you're completely fucked."

He laughed.

"That's exactly right, Jake. Finding a man with your police experience, who folks know and trust, well, there really isn't anyone that matches that description, except for you."

He picked up his fork and moved the food around on his plate. Incredibly, Coach had finished eating his entire meal. The man could really pack it in. Coach Westenbrook pushed his plate away and turned to me.

"What do you say, Jacob? Truth be told, I need an assistant coach at the school. I'm getting too old and tired to run some of the drills with those boys. And, besides, I'll be retiring in a few years and someone needs to take over the program. If Martin can convince you to move home, then I'd love to have you join me on the field."

It sounded great. Coming home, being closer to family, and getting away from the noise and the fast pace of the city. Away from the danger of my job. I hadn't figured out how I could do my job in New York without putting Nate's happiness at risk and leaving him in a constant state of anxiety. Working for the sheriff in

Bryerville would be completely safe, compared to what I'd been doing.

"It sounds great, Coach. I'd love to come home, and, Martin, I'd really enjoy working with you. But I need to talk with Nate before I can give you an answer."

Martin seemed happy with my response.

"That's great, Jake. I'd really love to have you. Now, who is this Nate?"

Did he seriously not hear me telling Coach about Nate as soon as I'd arrived? The hairs on the back of my neck prickled.

"Nate is my partner, Martin."

"Oh, of course. I had some great partners over the years. Those guys have your back. You get to trust them like family."

I didn't know what kind of game Martin was playing but I didn't like it. I glared at him across the table.

"Not that kind of partner, Martin. Nate isn't a cop. He's a doctor and he won't be able to do the kind of work that he does in New York if we move here. Besides, he was the one who wanted to leave town right after high school, and I'm not sure he'll want to come back. Do you really expect me to believe that Coach Westenbrook brought you here to talk with me about moving back to town and he didn't mention Nate?"

Not fucking likely, considering the last time Coach had talked with me about moving away from Nate. I was sure Coach could see my entire body clenching, because he jumped in.

"Listen, Jacob, last time we talked about Nathaniel

Richardson, you said he was a friend. It's not like I really knew—"

Martin interrupted him with a calm, steady tone. "That's all right, Harold, you don't need to run interference for me. Yes, I know about Nate. In fact, I've spent a lot of time talking with his father. Ted Richardson is very well-respected around here and he has a lot of historical knowledge about the office because of all the years his father spent as sheriff. Ted told me about your relationship with his son. He's very proud of both of you. I just wanted to know what you'd say about it, Jake. I'm looking for an honest man. A cop with big secrets in his personal life leaves himself open to compromising situations."

I didn't appreciate his assumption that I'd try to keep my relationship with Nate a secret, but I also realized that Nate had had the same belief several months earlier, so I tried to relax. I wasn't sure I succeeded but, hey, I was trying.

"I have no interest in keeping Nate or our relationship a secret, if that's what you're implying, Martin. The two of us have been a matched set since birth. Everyone around here knows that. And the fact that our relationship has gotten deeper, stronger, and *much* more physical over time isn't a cause for secrecy. In my book, it's a cause for celebration."

Martin nodded and pulled a business card out of his pocket.

"You're just what I need, Jake. Just what our office and this town needs. Here's my number, cell is on the back. Call me after you talk with your partner. I'd love to make this work."

We said our goodbyes and I headed home. I thought about how much Nate had wanted to move away as soon as we were done with high school. At the time, he'd said that he never wanted to come back. That he didn't want to live in that little town. I'd always loved Bryerville, so I was sad to leave, but I loved him more, of course, so that was that. But I had some hope that maybe things had changed. Nate seemed truly happy to be home.

I was trying to think of a way to ask him about it without pushing him. As I got to the house, I decided that I'd just talk to him. Holding our feelings back from each other had caused us enough confusion over the years. I wasn't going to make that mistake again. Nope. When we got back to New York, I'd raise it with Nate so we could talk it through and decide the best place for us to live. The bottom line was that as much as I wanted to move back to Bryerville, I could be happy living anywhere, as long as I was with Nate.

CHAPTER TWENTY-SEVEN

Nate

JAKE WAS out with his old football coach and my parents were out running some last-minute errands when I heard a knock at the door. All eleven of our uncles, their wives and children, and their children's spouses and kids would be joining us that afternoon, but I wasn't expecting anyone until then.

I opened the door to see my cousin Aaron standing in front of me with a big smile and tired eyes. I pulled him into my arms for a hug and kissed his cheek.

"Hey, Air Bear! How's my favorite cousin? I didn't expect to see you here. I thought you were away at school."

He squeezed me tightly and then rested his head on my shoulder.

"It's so good to see you, Nate. I've missed you. And e-mails and phone calls don't feel this warm."

I rubbed his back and then guided him inside. "Let me get you a drink. Do you want sweet tea or lemonade?"

"Sweet tea would be great, Nate. But you don't have to serve me. I'll come with you to the kitchen."

When we had our drinks poured, I sat with Aaron at our kitchen table and rubbed my hand over his arm.

"You look tired, Aaron. Tell me the truth, how are you?"

He gave me a weak, half-hearted smile. "I'm good, Nate. Really. I'm just tired because I haven't gotten much sleep. Yesterday was the anniversary of Michael's death, and I knew his mom would want me here, but I had tests all week, so I had to drive through the night to get here and now I have to drive back to get ready for more exams."

He took a drink of his sweet tea.

"That's why I can't stay for the get-together this afternoon. I'm sorry. I was hoping to see you and Jake, since I'm in town for another..." He looked at his watch and then finished his sentence with a laugh. "Fifteen minutes. Where is the big guy?"

Aaron was almost as big as Jake, so I laughed.

"Jake is going to be so sorry that he missed you, Aaron. He's out with Coach Westenbrook this morning."

Aaron's smile looked genuine.

"Oh yeah? That's great. Coach must be thrilled. He never stopped talking about the great Jacob Owens." He paused and then looked at me with another smile, this one wistful. "I'm really happy for both of you guys. It's great that you have each other." He took another drink of his tea and then continued in a quiet voice. "I envy that. Sometimes, I'm just so tired of being alone."

My heart ached for Aaron. He was such a great guy and incredibly generous. Aaron was several years younger than us, but we'd always been close. When he was thirteen, Aaron had called to talk to me and told me that he was gay. Just like that. No questioning, no wavering. Just that he was gay and he wanted my advice on the best way to tell his parents. I was in college at the time, and I didn't really feel like I had any answers. But we stayed on the phone for hours and talked it through and everything seemed to have turned out fine, because there was never any family drama. That was typical for Aaron. He'd always been incredibly calm, even-tempered, and mature beyond his years.

Jake and I were already living in New York by then, so I didn't have the chance to see Aaron often, but we'd stayed in touch. When he was in high school, Aaron started dating a guy. I admired his bravery. And then, when I found out more about his boyfriend, I admired Aaron even more.

Michael was his name. The poor kid had leukemia and was going through all sorts of treatments. Eventually, they thought he was heading into remission, but he still couldn't go far from home. So Aaron turned down some great college offers to study locally and remain close to Michael. In the end, the disease came back, and Michael lost his battle.

Aaron had graduated with honors and he was attending veterinary school. I kept hoping that being away and meeting new people would help him move on. But as far as I knew, Aaron hadn't dated anyone else after Michael. I squeezed his hand.

"You don't have to be alone, you know. It's okay

for you to try to meet someone. You're a great guy, Aaron. Smart, kind, hot as hell." I said the last one with a smile. "Seriously, I'm sure there are lots of guys trying to get your attention."

He looked me in the eyes and squeezed my hand.

"Yup. There are lots of guys. But I'm waiting for the right one. I need my heart to be in it. I don't think that a quick roll in the hay is going to make me feel any less lonely. It'd probably just make things worse."

And with an insight that many men twice his age don't have, Aaron quietly finished his tea, put his glass in the dishwasher, and gave me one last hug before leaving for the long drive back to school.

I WAS in the backyard, playing horsey with my cousin Brad's kids, when Jake walked in. He grinned broadly when he saw me crawling on all fours with two little boys straddling my back, yelling, "Ride 'em, Cowboy!" He started to walk over to us but then his uncles caught sight of him, ran over, and covered him with hugs and pats on the back. He smiled at me and shrugged. I nodded in understanding.

I knew we wouldn't get to spend much time together with everyone wanting to catch up with us and hear about our lives. I didn't mind. I missed my family, and I wanted to hear what they'd been doing and spend time with them. I did wonder, however, about how Jake and I would interact in front of our families.

As soon as I'd finally pulled my head out of my ass and realized that the depth of Jake's feelings for me equaled those of mine for him, we'd had a very affectionate relationship. I don't just mean the sex, though our physical attraction to each other was so intense that it was always simmering just beneath the surface. I mean that when we were together, we often held hands, shared light kisses, stroked each other's back, that kind of thing. They were little touches that added up to almost constant physical contact.

But so far, those roles had existed only in New York. Our roles back home were well-established over our lifetimes—we were close friends, more like family really, but other than an occasional wrestling match, pat on the back, or very casual hug, we didn't touch each other. I wondered whether coming back to Bryerville would mean falling back into our old roles.

I was pondering our long-standing family roles and whether we could break out of them as adults and find a way to establish new roles in Bryerville, when I heard a crashing sound followed by crying. I turned toward the sliding glass doors leading into the house and saw my cousin Linda's six-year-old daughter standing in the kitchen, surrounded by broken glass, with blood covering her face.

"Hey, boys, let's take a break, okay? I need to go check on Emily." I removed the protesting boys from my back and hurried into the kitchen.

"Hey, jelly bean. Looks like you made quite a big

noise. Let's take a look at you. Come here, Emily."

I used a calm voice as I spoke with her and hunched down so we were at the same height and I could look at her eye to eye. Emily came over to me, blood still dripping down her chin.

"Oh my God! Emily, honey, are you okay? What happened?" Linda was rushing over to Emily, looking panicked.

"Hey, Linda, can you please get a box of tissues and some wipes for me?"

Linda was shaky, but she nodded and got me the tissues and wipes. I brushed Emily's hair out of her face and then started wiping up the blood, making sure to put the discarded tissues behind my back so she wouldn't see the amount of blood coming from her face. After about a half-dozen wipes, her face was clean and I could see that the blood had been coming from her nose.

"There we go. That's much better. Did you get a bonk on your nose, jelly bean?"

Emily nodded.

"Does it still hurt?"

"Only a little, Uncle Nate. I...I'm sorry for breaking the bowl. I just ran into the counter and it fell from my hands. I was being careful. Really, I was."

"That's okay, sweetheart. Aunty Catherine has way too many bowls anyway. Come on, let's get a little ice on your nose and I'll read you a story."

Linda looked relieved as soon as she realized we were just dealing with a bloody nose.

"Thank you, Nate. It's wonderful to have a doctor

in the family. I wish you'd been here when Cole broke his arm or when Kyle broke his leg. These kids are going to be the death of me."

"No problem, Linda. You go relax and I'll read to Emily for a little while."

Three books later, I could hear all of our male cousins gathering outside for our Wiffle ball game. Ever since we were in middle school, the cousins played Wiffle ball during family gatherings. Our uncles had a similar tradition, except they'd played football. When we became old enough to play, Jake told everyone that he played enough football at school and he wanted our games to be different. I knew the truth, though—I was too small to play football with our cousins, all of whom were much bigger than me back then. By changing the game to Wiffle ball, Jake made sure that I'd be able to join in.

All the guys were splitting into teams. I'd be on Jake's team, like always, so I had a few minutes left before I had to get out there.

"Okay, Emily. Let's take a look at your nose."

She was no longer bleeding and her nose didn't look swollen.

"You look great, jelly bean. All ready to go play."

I held her hand and walked her outside.

"Thanks, Uncle Nate!"

She gave me a hug and then ran off to play with the other kids.

I smiled and walked over to where the guys were gathered. They were all laughing as they separated into two teams. Jake was our team captain, of course. He was wearing old cargo shorts with holes in the legs and a faded T-shirt from his football days. His hair was fairly long and he hadn't shaved that day. The whole look was typical Jake—rugged, a little rough around the edges, and unbelievably gorgeous.

As I walked over to him, I felt an almost uncontrollable urge to touch him. It was like some sort of magnetic force drawing me to him. But I didn't know how our cousins, or even Jake, would react to that.

Don't get me wrong, I suspected that everyone knew about our relationship. I mean, my parents knew, and it's not like my mom to keep that kind of information from the rest of the family. And our families weren't homophobic. They'd always been great to me. But my sexuality had always been theoretical. I hadn't dated anyone when I lived in Bryerville, and I sure as hell wasn't ever serious enough with a guy to bring him home with me once I'd moved away.

Understanding something in theory and seeing it right in front of your eyes...well, those were very different things. And that didn't even account for the fact that Jake's family had never had an inkling that he was anything other than completely straight. I mean, *I* hadn't even known he was gay, so how could they?

It turns out that I didn't have to make a decision about how to act around Jake in front of our family, because as soon as I got within reach, Jake put his arm around my waist and pulled me right up against him.

"Okay, Steve. You guys take the outfield first and we'll bat."

His cousin Steve's team ran onto the field and our team stood around in our batting order.

"Did you have fun playing with the kids? They love you, Nate. They all follow you around like you're the Pied Piper."

Jake was gazing into my eyes, stroking my arm. Basically, the same loving Jake I'd gotten used to over the past seven months. Being around our cousins didn't faze him.

"Yeah. It was nice. I love spending time with those kids." I looked down and continued in a whisper. "You know, the only thing I've ever regretted about being gay is that I won't get to have kids."

Jake looked surprised.

"What do you mean? If you want kids, Nate, we'll have kids. We'll find a way to make it work."

I smiled at the "we." Not that it surprised me. I mean, when it came down to it, we'd always been a team. But having children together, that certainly took things to a new level.

We had fun playing, and three strikes later, it was our turn to take the field. My cousin Brad was pitching for the other team, and as he ran off the field, he threw Jake the ball. We'd been playing together for so long, that we knew everyone's favorite positions.

"You pitching today, Jake?"

Jake started to answer when his cousin, Steve, smacked Brad on the shoulder.

"Fuck, Brad, Jake's sex life is none of your business. Where are your manners, man?"

Did Jake's straight cousin just make a gay sex joke…in front of everyone? I could feel my neck starting to get hot. I looked over to Jake, worried about his reaction. He was smiling.

"Yeah, I'm pitching today. I was catching last night and I'm still a little sore. All this country air has turned Nate into a real animal."

He mouthed a silent "owww" as he jogged to the pitcher's spot, rubbing his ass.

Steve and Brad laughed. My face had to be bright red. I walked over to my spot in the outfield and tried to process how it'd been possible for Jake to have gone from being the biggest womanizer around to telling our cousins that he took it up the ass, without making so much as a pit stop in the closet.

The afternoon went by too quickly. We had a great time seeing our family and, for the first time, I realized how much we were missing by living far from home. All the little things in life—new jobs, remodeled kitchens— the things that matter on a daily basis. We didn't know any of those things about the people we'd been closest to all of our lives (other than each other, of course). Almost all of them still lived at home. Aaron and some of our cousins had gone away to school, but almost all of them had come back to Bryerville.

And then there were the kids. It seemed like every time we came home, there was a new baby or someone was pregnant. There were so many kids in the family that it was hard to keep up with them from far away. And the younger ones didn't really remember us. I felt like I was missing out on so much.

There weren't any kids in our lives in New York. That wasn't a surprise, considering that the people I knew were either lab rats or gay men in their twenties or early thirties. Moving away to the big city had seemed so exciting and adventurous when I was eighteen, but now it just felt isolating and lonely.

As we said goodbye to our uncles and their families, I wondered how much we'd miss over the next however many months we'd be gone. I swear, if it wasn't for Jake's pain from the memory of his parents' death, I would've quit my job over the phone and never gone back to the city. Thankfully, I didn't have time to wallow in those feelings, because we had to get showered and then meet our high school friends for a mini-reunion.

JAKE HAD his arm around me as we walked into the Buck and Bull, a favorite watering hole. I don't think we made it through the front door before our friends were all over us and we were separated. Almost everyone we knew had either never left home, or had gone away to school but returned right after. So, the two of us were the ones who'd been gone the longest.

It didn't take Jake long to end up at one end of the bar, talking with his old football buddies. I smiled at how happy he looked as he stood listening to his friends, nodding and drinking his beer. He had changed into his old Levi's and boots before we left, and I was admiring his ass when I heard someone calling my name.

"Nate! Hey there! Welcome home, honey."

I turned to see my friend Amanda running up to me. She had a big smile on her face and she looked exactly like she had in high school, except she was about thirty pounds heavier. Her blonde hair was cut in a shoulder-length bob and her face was round, accented by pretty brown eyes.

"Hi, Amanda." I smiled at her and gave her a hug. "So I hear you have three boys now, right?"

"Yup. Three wonderful boys." She dug through her purse and handed me a small album. "Here's my brag book."

I looked at the pictures and smiled at her.

"Oh, they're beautiful, Mandy. They look like a perfect combination of you and Walt. How's motherhood?"

"It's great. I'm tired—well, we're tired. But I want to try for one more. I really want a little girl."

I laughed and put my arm around her.

"Is that right? Well, what does Walt have to say about that?"

"I say that I learned a long time ago to just nod and go along with whatever the boss wants."

I turned to see Walt behind me, grinning. He put his arm around me for a quick pat on the back.

"How're you doing, Nate? It's been too long."

I stood with Walt and Amanda and caught up on their lives. He was working at his father's hardware store and she was home with the kids for the most part, but did some babysitting and housekeeping for extra money now and then. People came and went from our corner, and every so often I'd look across the room and catch Jake's eye. He'd always smile at me or raise his beer in a silent toast.

After about forty-five minutes, I noticed that I wasn't the only one looking at Jake. Mary Pat was standing not too far from him and talking with a woman I didn't recognize. Their heads were together and they'd talk to each other and then look up at him. I'd seen this before. A lot. They were hatching a plan to come on to Jake.

Over the years, those plans almost always resulted in some girl getting Jake into bed. Being surrounded by all our old classmates sort of made me revert back to those days. I started to walk over to Jake, not really sure what I was going to say or do. Just as I passed Mary Pat, she called my name and hopped over to me.

"Hi, Nate! How are you, darling?"

She gave me a tight hug. We were never really friends, so I realized this was just an attempt to get to Jake.

"Hello, Mary Pat. I'm good. How have you been?"

She didn't even bother answering. She just pulled me close to her and her friend, who she didn't introduce.

"So, Nate, is Jake seeing anyone or is he still single?"

I thought about the best way to respond. I couldn't very well "out" Jake. That wasn't my place. So I just went with an honest but evasive approach.

"He's not single, Mary Pat."

She pouted and made a "hmph" noise. Then she crossed her arms and turned to her friend.

"Well, I don't see a ring on his finger. And she isn't here, so he obviously isn't serious enough about her to bring her home. I'd say that means he's still available."

Her friend nodded. I should've just walked away. It wasn't like I thought Jake would respond to her advances. And I didn't really care whether she'd get embarrassed by throwing herself at him. Still, though, I didn't like that she felt so comfortable going after him, and that she so easily dismissed the possibility that he did have someone important in his life. I turned to her.

"He's not available, trust me. And he is serious enough about *him* to bring him home. Or, more accurately, we came home together."

I quickly realized what I'd said and was just starting to regret it when Mary Pat started laughing.

"Yeah, right, Nate. Good one."

I immediately went from regretful to frustrated.

"I'm not kidding, Mary Pat. We're together."

"Whatever, Nate. A boy can dream. I get it." She turned to her friend. "I'm going over there. How does my hair look?"

At that point, I was angry, more angry than I should've been. So what if Mary Pat wanted to flirt with Jake? I should've been used to it, and it had never bothered me too much before. Of course, back then I'd never thought I had a chance with Jake. Things were different now, and I hated that anyone could think that he was available, that we weren't together. And it probably didn't help that we'd been out in the sun most of the day and I'd already had a few drinks at the bar. The bottom line was, I lost control and spoke more loudly than I should have.

"Damn it, Mary Pat. I'm not joking and I'm not dreaming. Jake's mine! What do I have to do to prove it to you?"

Jake and his friends stopped their conversation and looked over at us. I realized that I had basically just outed Jake to our entire high school class, and while we were out at a bar, with everyone drinking. I was mortified and could feel tears prickling in my eyes. I looked up and saw Jake walking over to me. I was frozen on the spot, my eyes locked with his, and then he was right in front of me.

"How are you planning on proving it to her, Nathaniel? I have some ideas, but I think we might violate a few indecent exposure laws if we try them here."

He wrapped his hand around my neck and pulled me to him for a kiss. When our lips met, I could feel his tongue seeking entry into my mouth. I forgot that we were standing in a room full of our old friends. I was only aware of Jake, of his smell, his taste, the feel of his skin.

By the time the kiss was over, my knees were weak, and I knew there could be no doubt in anyone's mind about the nature of our relationship. Jake pulled back and softly bit my lower lip before we separated. His eyes were twinkling and he was smiling. I was in shock, staring at him, when I felt a hand on my shoulder. I turned to see Jake's friend, Dwayne.

"I can't thank you enough for getting this guy off the market, Nate. Whenever y'all came home, we'd worry about our wives throwing themselves at him. Do you have any idea how embarrassing it is to have your wife go after another man right in front of you? Hell, I think Tanya was six months pregnant last time y'all were here, and that didn't stop her! It's a good thing you have him on a short leash."

I still hadn't regained the power of speech so I didn't respond. But Jake was fine.

"Trust me, Dwayne, Nate's leash isn't short."

Jake waggled his eyebrows and Dwayne laughed as he walked over to the bar. I felt like I was in the Twilight Zone.

Jake took my arm and walked me over to a chair. I sat down and he pulled up a chair right in front of me. Our knees were touching and he leaned close to me. I could tell that he was waiting for me to say something.

"Umm. What just happened here, Jake? I...I shouldn't have said that to Mary Pat but...why is everyone acting so, so...normal? It's like they're not even surprised."

"Well, I'd guess it's because they're not surprised. I trade e-mails with a bunch of these guys every few weeks. I told them about us when we got back from our trip, and they probably told their wives. And all these folks see each other all the time, so I'm sure word got around. I think Mary Pat just didn't know because no one's talked to her since she cheated on Rod with that older married guy."

"When we got back from our trip? I don't think I told you I loved you until after we'd been home for over a month. And you'd already told all of your friends that you were dating a guy?"

He put his hand on my knee and squeezed gently.

"Not just any guy and not just dating. I told them that I was in love with you." He lowered his voice and his eyes. "When are you going to realize that I am *never* going to try to hide what we have between us?"

Dwayne's booming voice interrupted us. "Hey, Jake! You can talk to lover boy anytime. Now get over here and let me kick your ass in darts."

Jake laughed and got up. He bent down and spoke softly into my ear just as he walked away.

"And I knew that you loved me, Nate, even when you were too scared to say it. But it sure is nice hearing it."

CHAPTER TWENTY-EIGHT

Nate

JAKE AND I boarded the plane for our flight back to New York. I was moving pretty slowly. It'd been a busy three days and we'd had to get up at four in the morning in order to catch our crack-of-dawn flight, after having been out until after one with our high school friends.

We settled into our seats and I wanted to cuddle up on Jake and close my eyes. I realized that there was a man we didn't know in the seat next to me, and three people in the row parallel to ours who could also see us.

I thought back on the past three days, and how Jake had been so open and affectionate with me in our hometown, in front of our family and friends. I also thought about his comment to me the previous night: *"When are you going to realize that I am never going to try to hide what we have between us?"*

Now—I realize it now. Yeah, I'm a little slow on the uptake. Okay, I'm really slow. But I did *finally* realize it. I sighed and kissed his neck. Then I settled my head on his chest and relaxed. He turned his head toward me and kissed the top of my head as he took my hand in his.

"Get some sleep, baby."

As I was drifting off, I thought about the rest of that night. I'd overreacted when Mary Pat was planning to flirt with Jake. Intellectually, I realized Jake had no interest in her or, for that matter, any other woman. And, so far, men had never been an issue. Jake comes across as scarier than hell—like he could kill you with his bare hands if you did anything to piss him off. That was a pretty big deterrent to any man taking a chance coming on to him. But now that we were so openly together, men were bound to realize he was gay. He was so incredibly good-looking and charismatic that, once the fear of him being a homophobe who'd beat them up for trying anything was gone, men would likely go after Jake too.

So, on an emotional level, I was paranoid about everyone. And there was no way for me to follow him around everywhere and tell those interested people that he was mine, which was probably a good thing, because that'd be downright pathetic. Besides, since we'd gotten together, he'd never given me any reason to be jealous or believe that he'd be interested in any other person. But I knew there'd always be someone who'd come on to him.

I tightened my grip around Jake as I thought about the other thing he'd told me at the bar: *"I knew that you loved me, Nate, even when you were too scared to say it. But it sure is nice hearing it."*

By the time we finally got back to the apartment that evening, I felt like I was coming apart at the seams. I wanted to show Jake how much I loved him, and I *needed* a tangible, physical reminder that I was the one for him, and not Mary Pat or anyone else. Jake was standing in the bathroom, putting away our toiletries when he caught my eye in the mirror and grinned.

"You're bouncing like a little kid that needs to use the bathroom."

He turned to me and leaned back on the counter, crossed his feet at his ankles and his arms across his chest. I stood there, trying to process what I was feeling, and hoping that I could somehow rein in my out-of-control hormones.

"The toilet is right there, bud. Are you gonna whip it out and go for it or are you pee-shy all of a sudden?"

I could feel myself blushing. I wanted to whip it out, but it wasn't so I could use the toilet. I didn't think that would have been possible anyway, given how hard I was. Jake pushed himself off the counter and walked over to me, putting each of his hands on my arms, and slowly walking me backward as he whispered into my ear.

"You know, we haven't had a chance to fool around since yesterday morning."

He kissed my neck.

"We were busy all day, and then we stayed out so late last night and had to get up so early this morning."

He licked behind my ear and sucked on my earlobe.

"I thought about taking you into the bathroom on the airplane, but there just isn't enough room in there."

He moved his tongue to my mouth and sucked on my bottom lip before pressing it into my mouth and kissing me so deeply that I moaned.

"Fuck, Nate. Those noises you make get me so worked up."

The back of my knees hit the bed and I sat down. Jake peeled off my shirt and unbuttoned my pants. I lifted my ass off the bed and he pulled my pants and briefs to my ankles. Then he kneeled in front of me and removed my shoes, socks, pants, and briefs. He remained on the floor and looked up at me.

"Tell me what you want, Nate."

His voice was deep and rich, thick with lust. His eyes were full of desire. I knew what I wanted and I knew that it sounded silly, like something out of a bad movie. But I had to answer him.

"I want you to make me yours. Show me that I'm yours, Jake."

His eyes sparkled as he bent down and kissed the top of my cock. He darted his tongue out and gave short, fast licks to the head before he took it in his hand, pushed his tongue into the piss slit, and ran it around. My head fell back and I moaned. Jake put his whole mouth over just the head of my cock and sucked on it, while letting his saliva drip down the shaft.

After a couple of minutes, he removed his mouth and lifted my legs onto his shoulders. He straightened, but remained on his knees. That movement forced my upper body back onto the bed, but I supported myself with my elbows and forearms and looked into his eyes. He buried his nose into my scrotum. I knew that Jake enjoyed smelling me as much as I enjoyed smelling him.

I could feel his tongue licking my balls as he moved his hand up and down my dick, which was still wet with his saliva.

I put my hands on his head and brushed my fingers through his dark hair as I moaned in appreciation. When I neared the edge, Jake took his hand off my dick and propped my legs higher on his shoulders, which raised my ass as a result and put it right in front of him. He softly moved his fingers through the crease and then spread me apart, with each of his hands holding one cheek. I could feel the air blowing on me and shuddered.

Then Jake got serious. He started at my perineum and worked his tongue down my entire crack. After a few swipes, I was pretty wet and then he began licking at my asshole. The licks were firm and forceful. He was demanding entry.

I fell back on the bed and relaxed all of my muscles to let him in. He rotated his hands so they were still pulling my ass cheeks apart, keeping me open, but now his fingers were next to his tongue, pushing at my hole. And then they were suddenly inside me. A finger from each hand, pressing into me and moving slowly around until they were pulling me open on the inside, just like his hands were doing on the outside, and his soft, wet tongue between those fingers, not darting but licking around the perimeter and into me in a swirling motion.

It was like he was trying to taste the walls of my cavity. There was rimming and then there was eating ass. This definitely fell into the latter category, and it felt amazing, but eventually, I needed more.

"Jake."

I panted, trying to catch my breath and noticing that my voice was hitching. He understood and knew what I wanted. He pulled himself out of my ass and gave a few swipes to my balls before he stood up and lifted me under my arms, pushing me back onto the bed until I was flat on my back and he was on top of me.

My body was completely relaxed and my eyes were glazed over as I looked up at him. He raised his body and took off his shirt. Then he unbuttoned and unzipped his pants and pushed them down. He held himself above me in a push-up position as he used his foot to toe off one shoe and then the other. At that point, I raised my knee and used it to push his pants and briefs down to his ankles, finishing the job with my foot.

Once we were both naked, I wrapped my legs around his waist, locked my ankles, and looked into his eyes expectantly. My ass was still very wet with his saliva as he pushed his dick against me. He moved it slowly around my pucker, and then leaned down and whispered in my ear as he pushed into me.

"You're mine, Nate."

I moaned as he slowly moved his dick inside my passage. When he was fully seated, he said it again.

"You're mine, Nate. Can you feel that, baby? Can you feel that you belong to me, just like I belong to you?"

He pulled out and then pushed himself back in, over and over, at a slow pace. And he whispered into my ear the whole time.

"No one else can have you. Not anymore. Only I

get to do this, Nate. Only I get to touch you and taste you. Only I get to lick you and eat you. Only my dick gets to be inside you."

I was crying from the emotion I felt as I answered him.

"Yes, yes, yes. I can feel it. I'm yours."

I pushed back to meet him and I was lost in the feelings. Eventually, I knew that I wouldn't be able to hold off my orgasm much longer. I pressed my fingers into his back to urge him on. He quickened his pace and pushed deeper and harder into me, grunting as he continued to chant softly in my ear between each thrust.

"You're mine. You're mine. You're mine."

When I felt myself reaching the edge, I pushed my fingers into his hair and pulled his head back so I could see his eyes.

"I...need...to...taste...you."

He didn't understand what I meant, so he leaned down and kissed me. I couldn't stop thrusting up against him, meeting his pounding. It was a physical reaction. But that wasn't what I wanted right at that moment. I mumbled against his mouth, "Jake. Ungh. Jake, I need to taste your seed."

His eyes were wide and their green color looked even deeper. He leaned down into my neck and sucked hard for several long seconds as he pummeled so hard and fast into me that the bed was shaking, the mattress was squeaking, and I was whimpering. Then he pulled out, kneeled above me, and pointed his cock at my face.

"Oh, yes." I gasped, and then opened my mouth in

anticipation.

Jake's eyes never left mine as he stroked his cock once or twice and then exploded. My mouth was open and my tongue was out. I caught most of his cum in my mouth, but some landed on my face. By the time he was done, my face and neck were covered with Jake's release and my stomach and chest were covered in my own. We were clinging to each other, both of us breathing heavily, and Jake was gently caressing my head, combing his fingers through my hair.

I could never be like that with anyone else. I could never let myself be so exposed, so vulnerable, so raw. But with him, I was so safe, so secure with the knowledge that he would respect and love me no matter what, that when we were in bed together and the passion was running high, my mind could shut down completely and I could operate entirely on base instincts. That allowed all of my desires to come to the surface. And Jake fulfilled every desire, every time.

I'm not great at saying how I feel, at putting my emotions into words. Jake was constantly telling me that he loved me: when I woke up, as we left for work, before we went to sleep, and other times in between. And I loved hearing it.

As we lay together in our bed and I enjoyed the warmth of his body pressing against me and the taste of him in my mouth, I knew how to make sure he had a constant reminder of how I felt about him, how much I loved him. And to simultaneously make sure that all those men and women who wanted him would realize he was off-limits.

The next morning, I went into work even earlier than usual so I could take a break midday to go see my friend Edward. I was excited all morning, so it was hard to concentrate. Finally, at around noon, I walked into his shop and looked around while he finished helping a couple of other people. Then he came up to me and gave me a hug.

"Nate Richardson. I've got to tell you, I was surprised when I got your call. But I'm really happy for you. So, tell me what you have in mind and we'll make it happen."

Edward was a jewelry designer. He kept hoping to make it big, but satisfied himself with a pretty good Internet business in the meantime. I sat down with him and showed him the drawing I'd made.

"I don't want anything fancy, Edward. I just want a thick, flat platinum band. And I want you to etch this all around the perimeter."

He looked at the paper.

"That won't be a problem, Nate. I can get it done in a couple of days. So what's the deal with the number eight? Is it significant to you for some reason?"

I laughed.

"It's not the number eight. It's the infinity symbol."

WHEN WE were in high school, I spent hours helping

Jake with his homework. It was always fun to spend time with him, even when he complained. But there was one Saturday afternoon that stuck out in my mind.

We were sitting at his kitchen table, studying algebra. I started to explain the concept of infinity to him and I drew the symbol as I was working through a problem. I'd been talking about the details, wanting to make sure he understood. He was being really quiet. I figured that he'd stopped paying attention, so I looked up at him, ready to give him a hard time, but I froze when I met his eyes.

He had a look that reached into me and made me lose my breath. Our eyes were locked together across the table for several long minutes. Then he spoke very, very quietly.

"I understand, Nate. I get the concept of infinity. It's like the two of us, like our friendship. No end, no limit. We're forever. That's infinity, right?"

My heart raced but I couldn't speak. So I just nodded quietly, and after a few more minutes, we got back to work.

Thinking back to that day, I'm not sure how I didn't realize that Jake was just as in love with me as I was with him. But hindsight is always twenty-twenty, and at that time in my life, I just couldn't fathom the idea that Jake could ever be interested in me, or any other guy. Guess I'd always been slow on the uptake.

CHAPTER TWENTY-NINE

Jake

IT'D BEEN a rough Monday. I hadn't had a moment to sit and think all day because we were in the midst of dealing with a drug-trafficking ring. After we were done for the day, I made my way back to the precinct to fill out paperwork, and I thought about what it would be like to work back home in Bryerville. I knew that I wouldn't have the same challenges or excitement, but I would still enjoy it. I'd be helping people that I'd known my whole life, and Nate and I would be close to our family and friends.

I walked upstairs and sat down at my desk to fill out the paperwork. Just then I heard a familiar voice.

"Detective Owens. I've been waiting to see you."

I looked up and smiled when I saw the handsome young man standing before me. Well, handsome was probably an understatement. He really was stunning. He wasn't a big guy—about five foot ten, with a slender but clearly muscular body. He had a strong jawline, thick, black hair, and innocent eyes, which was remarkable considering what he had been doing the first time I'd met him.

"Jonathan! How are you, man? And how's Sam?"

I stood up and opened my arms as he walked over. Jonathan stepped into my embrace and squeezed me tightly. I could feel his erection pressing against me, and I was reminded that his equipment was a nice size.

"I'm good, Detective Owens. And so is Sam. I just came by to thank you and to say goodbye. We're moving."

I pulled a chair over for Jonathan and sat down at my desk.

"Is that right? I thought you liked it here. What brought this on?"

I'd first met Jonathan a few years earlier. He had been working with some guys who were filming and distributing gay porn. There was no law-enforcement issue there, but our unit got involved when we heard that there were some illegal drugs making their way through the organization. It turned out that a couple of the gay-for-pay guys were selling drugs on the side.

We slowly walked into the place where the company was filming. We needed to be quiet so we could get an idea of how many people were in the space and make sure we had them all covered before they realized we were in there. As we moved around, we could see and hear the guys filming. That was when I saw Jonathan.

He was in a sling with one guy fucking his ass and another guy fucking his face. They were talking dirty to him: *"Take it, bottom boy. That's right. You like my big cock in your ass, don't you?"*

Three other guys were standing around, and from the number of used condoms on the floor and the amount of cum on Jonathan's face, hair, and back, it was pretty clear that they'd already taken at least one turn and were waiting for round two. They were egging on the guys at bat: *"Oh yeah. Fuck his cum hole. Give it to him hard and make him nice and loose for me."*

I winced and felt my stomach clench. I really couldn't comprehend how anyone could take part in a gang bang like that. When we announced ourselves and Jonathan got out of the sling, I was shocked to see he had an erection. That probably would've been the end of my interaction with Jonathan, except that one of the young cops decided to play Mister Macho and started making rude comments and calling him names.

I stepped in to intervene, and for the first time, looked closely at Jonathan's face and realized how young he was. I pulled him aside and led him to a bathroom.

"Go clean up."

I left to find him something to wear. It turned out that all the guys had stripped in one area so I scooped up all the clothes and walked back to the bathroom. Jonathan was standing by the sink, his hair, face, and body looking wet and free of semen. I dropped the pile of clothes on the floor.

"Get dressed and then we can talk. What's your name, bud?"

He looked at me with fear in his eyes.

"Will Dragon?"

Yeah, right. Saying your name in the form of a question doesn't exactly instill confidence in the veracity of the answer. Plus, Will Dragon?

"Give me a break. I want your real name."

He sighed and slumped his shoulders.

"Jonathan. My name is Jonathan Doyle."

I put my arm around his shoulder.

"Nice to meet you, Jonathan. I'm Detective Owens. Get dressed and I'm going to buy you lunch as an apology for that asshole's behavior."

He looked surprised.

"Cops aren't the bad guys, bud. I'll wait for you out here."

When I walked out of the room, I gave a fierce look to the rookie who'd harassed Jonathan. Then I asked a more seasoned officer to take the lead on the paperwork.

When Jonathan and I got to a diner down the street, I asked him for his identification. He looked so young that I wanted to find out whether we were dealing with an underage kid doing porn. Turned out he was legal. Barely.

There was something about Jonathan that got to me, and we ended up talking for a long time. Once he started telling me his story, he didn't stop. The kid had a lot on his mind, and I think he appreciated talking to someone who would listen. Turned out he had a baby on the way—don't ask me how that happened, because he was as gay as the day is long and he made absolutely no effort to hide it. Anyway, the how didn't matter. What mattered was what he was going to do about it.

The next time I saw Jonathan was a few months later. He came to see me at work, holding a baby.

"Detective Owens. Do you remember me? I'm

Jonathan. We met..."

I smiled at him and patted his shoulder.

"Of course I remember you, Jonathan. So it looks like you decided to take on the challenge of being a father. I'm really glad, bud."

It turned out that Jonathan was going to raise his baby on his own, and he'd swallowed his pride and come in to ask me for help. The day we'd met, I'd made him a promise that I'd do what I could to help him, and I was glad he hadn't forgotten.

I made some calls and I was able to help Jonathan find a cheap place to live in return for him doing odd jobs around the building. And I knew he'd found work waiting tables and tending bar. I really believed he was done with the porn job. From what he told me, he hadn't been into it all that long anyway.

That was a few years earlier. And now it seemed that Jonathan was done with New York and moving away with his kid. I told him I was happy for him and wished him well. I was a little surprised when he jumped into my arms and squeezed me tightly.

"You're a good guy, Detective. A great guy. You saved my life and Sam's life. I hope you know that. I'll never forget you."

He squeezed me even harder and I could feel something else hard pressing against me. What was it with that guy? Did he have a constant erection?

"Damn, I wish you were gay—I could make you a very happy man, Detective. And you'd really make my day. Even though you're not him..." His voice trailed off.

I had a strict rule never to talk about my personal life at work. I'd already blown that with Suzie, because I'd been spending so much time with her and her daughter. Still, I'd heard stories of other cops' families being targeted in order to get to them, so I didn't say anything to correct Jonathan. Besides, it wouldn't have mattered. I was committed to Nate completely. No matter how gorgeous this guy was.

"Good luck with everything, Jonathan. I'm really proud of you. And whoever you end up with is going to be one hell of a lucky guy."

He smiled and nodded, a wistful look in his sparkling, silver eyes.

"I'll make sure of it, if I ever find him."

AS I was going home that night, I felt sad about the fact that I couldn't share anything about myself all day, in order to protect Nate's safety. That wouldn't be the case in Bryerville. Everyone knew me there, and it'd actually add to my effectiveness on the job. Hell, it was one of the reasons Sheriff Wells had offered me the position. I had to discuss this with Nate. I had to see if he'd be willing to move back.

When Nate got back from work that night, we talked for a long time, and we decided to move back to Bryerville. I was thrilled. We still had some loose ends to tie up in New York and Nate needed to figure out where he could work in Bryerville, but once we got those things straightened out, we'd return.

One thing I had to do was to figure out how to get Suzie and Alexis into a better situation. I was worried that once I left, they wouldn't be able to get along. I don't think Suzie ever even bought food for them. So after spending countless hours looking into programs for Suzie, I went to her apartment with a bag of groceries and a stack of papers in my hands. I felt like I'd found enough things she'd qualify for to allow her to get off the street and make a better life for herself and her daughter. It'd take hard work and a commitment to stop using drugs and turning tricks, but if she really wanted a clean life, I'd found programs for her.

I had barely touched the door when she swung it open.

"Hi, Detective. I was really glad when I got your call. I've been wanting to talk to you."

She stepped aside and let me in. Alexis was lying on the floor, playing with a plastic cup. At least it looked clean, but that baby could really use some toys. I made a mental note to buy her some as I walked into the kitchen area and unloaded the groceries.

I'd been concerned that Suzie wouldn't be interested in any of the programs because she wouldn't want to change her lifestyle, but she was actually dressed, and she wasn't coming on to me, which gave me hope. I decided to talk about whatever she wanted and then approach her about the changes I thought she needed to make in her life, if not for her own well-being, then for

Alexis.

"What do you want to talk about, Suzie Q?"

"A couple weeks back you said that you're gay."

I didn't see that one coming. And I usually see everything coming.

"Yes, I did."

"And you said that you have a boyfriend."

My rule about not sharing information about my personal life was ringing in my head. Had I somehow put Nate in danger? Why was she asking me this? Her tone wasn't threatening, but she did seem nervous, which was unusual for Suzie.

"Cut to the chase, Suzie. What do you want?"

My curt tone seemed to break whatever hesitation she had and she snapped back at me.

"I want you to take Alexis. You and your boyfriend. I know she'll be safe with you. I mean, you're clearly not into girls and you said that your boyfriend has never even kissed a girl. So I know she'll be safe with you."

I had no idea what she was talking about. "Take Alexis? What do you mean? Are you going somewhere overnight and you need a babysitter? I guess we could do that. I'll need to talk to Nate. When are you leaving?"

She walked over to the bed and sat down. "No, not a babysitter. And I'm not leaving."

I sat down next to her and looked at her determined face. "Suzie, you're not making any sense. Start over."

She sighed and rubbed her eyes with the balls of her hands.

"Look, Detective, we both know I'm not winning

mother of the year here. I didn't want a baby. I want to live my own life, and that's impossible when I have to take care of Alexis. But there was no fucking way I was going to give her up because then I wouldn't be able to protect her from whatever asshole got to take her home. But with you, it's different. You're gay, so she's safe with you. And if you take her, then I don't have to do this anymore."

She was waving her arm toward Alexis as she spoke. I was in shock. Suzie was actually asking me to take her daughter. And every instinct in my body told me to agree. I really cared about that baby and I knew she had almost no chance of a decent life with Suzie. But I didn't want to separate mother and daughter, not if there was any way for me to help Suzie make things work.

"Suzie, I understand. You're just a kid yourself, so this is hard. But I've been looking into this and I found some programs that I think you'll qualify for. I mean, you'll have to make some changes with your...job and your... lifestyle. But you can get some help finding a different job and you can get into a substance abuse program. Then you can keep Alexis."

I handed her the papers and she flipped through them quietly. After a few minutes, she set them down on the bed and looked back at me.

"I don't want to keep Alexis. I know how that sounds to you—like I'm a horrible person. What sort of girl doesn't want to keep her own baby? Well, my mother kept me, and believe me, Detective, I'd have given anything to have grown up with a parent like you.

Someone who would take care of me, bring food home like you've been doing..."

Her voice trailed off, but then she continued.

"She'd be happier with you. She'd have a chance for a better life—a chance I never had. And maybe I'd have the chance to start over with a clean slate. What do you say, Detective? Can you help us? Will you adopt Alexis?"

I GOT home to find Nate in the kitchen. I walked up behind him, wrapped my arms around his waist, and kissed his neck.

"I'm surprised you're home. It's only six. And it smells like you made eggplant parmigiana."

He turned around, staying in my embrace, and kissed me softly.

"That's right. I know it's your favorite. And we're moving back to Bryerville, so I'm quitting anyway—I may as well leave at a decent hour. Besides, I have some good news. I spoke with Doc Hamilton today. I told him that we want to come home, and he said I can work with him. He's been wanting to reduce his hours, spend some time traveling, and then retire in a few years. So, eventually, I can take over the practice."

Nate was smiling as he spoke. His voice sounded excited. Then he looked at me more closely and stopped talking. He stroked my cheek.

"What's going on? You have a strange look on your face."

I took his hand and led him to the couch. Then I squatted in front of him and took his hand in mine.

"Nate, did you mean it back home when you said that you want to have kids?" He nodded quietly, his eyes never leaving mine. "I saw Suzie today. She's doesn't want to be a mother. She wants us to take Alexis, Nate. She wants us to adopt her."

I looked into Nate's eyes, trying to read his reaction. He didn't say anything for several long minutes. Then he stood up and walked toward the door.

"Come on, Jake. Let's go get our daughter."

CHAPTER THIRTY

Nate

WHEN I came back from work Monday night, Jake was lying on the bed, flat on his back, with his arms stretched out. I crawled over him and settled my body on top of his, with my head pressed into his neck.

"How was your day?"

He rubbed the back of my neck, his big hand caressing me and making me feel warm.

"My day was...fine. The usual. So, Nate, did you enjoy our trip home?"

I wanted to tell him how much I'd enjoyed being in Bryerville and that I wanted us to move back, where we could be with our family and friends, where I could have a job with normal hours, and where he could have a job that didn't terrify me. But I couldn't do that, not with the memory of his parents casting a shadow over him whenever we went back there. So I licked his neck from the bottom up to his chin and answered, trying to temper my voice.

"I did. It was really nice seeing everyone." I sighed involuntarily and hoped he hadn't noticed. "How about you? Did you have fun?"

He combed his fingers through my hair and remained quiet for several minutes. I assumed he was thinking about his parents. Then he raised his body and took me with him. I leaned back and looked at his face.

"Nate, I, umm, I know that when we left home, you said you didn't want to live in a small town. But we were kids then, and I guess I'm wondering whether you still feel that way. I mean, it seemed like you were happy on this visit, and I know how much you loved seeing the kids and the rest of the family. Do you...do you think you could be happy living there?"

He was looking into my face intently, trying to read my expression. I wasn't sure what to say or do. Of course, I'd be happy living there. But what about him? Jake would move in a heartbeat if he thought I wanted to go back, even if it meant daily pain for him. There was no way I was going to put him through that. I was frozen, trying to figure out what to say. Jake stroked my cheek.

"Hey, Nate?"

"Yeah?"

"Just tell me what you're thinking, okay? I can see that you're worried about something. Talk to me. It's always better when you talk to me, right?"

It *was* always better when I talked to him. I scooted off his body and sat cross-legged on the bed, looking at him.

"Yes, I was happy being back there. And, yes, I could be happy living there. But I know how hard it is for you and that's not something I'd ever ask you to do."

He looked genuinely confused.

"What are you talking about, Nate? It's not hard for me being in Bryerville. I love it there, the weather, the people, the pace, all of it. What makes you think it's hard for me?"

His voice was sincere. I felt as confused as he looked.

"But you were crying. When my mom was talking to you in my room, you were crying. And you said that being back there brings up all those memories of your parents."

He nodded and took my hands into his. "It does bring back memories. But that's not a bad thing. I mean, yeah, it's hard sometimes. Especially when I think about the night they died. But, Nate, there are also all the memories of the years they were alive.

"Remember how my mom would stand outside and complain whenever my dad hung up the Christmas lights? He'd climb on that rickety old ladder and she'd go crazy talking about how he needed to go buy a new one. Or the parades on the Fourth of July, when my dad drove the fire truck and the guys stood on top and sprayed everyone down with the hoses? Or all the times we took bike rides through the neighborhood as a family? There are so many happy memories."

I did remember those things, and so many other happy times. He was right; the good times by far outweighed the bad. And when I really thought about it, I realized he probably felt closer to his parents there, because of the fact that their presence was everywhere.

That was actually a good thing. I squeezed his hands.

"Jake, I'm happy here. I mean, we have our friends and our jobs. But I'm tired. I'm so tired of the noise and the hustle. I don't know how much longer I can handle the eighty-hour weeks at work, and I don't see it getting any better. And your job... I'm proud of you. You know that. And I know it's selfish of me, but I can't stop worrying and wishing that you did something else."

I wasn't sure exactly what to say, so I was babbling nervously. Jake somehow understood, though, and he took charge.

"I want to move back too, Nate." He kissed me softly. "Let's go home."

Jake and I leaned against each other on the bed for several long minutes. I enjoyed the steady thumping of his heart, the feel of the heat radiating from his body, the sound of him breathing. Eventually, we removed each other's clothes and got under the blanket.

We made love slowly that night. Our bodies connected in a way that was more gentle than I ever remember. For a long time, we weren't on the road to a destination; we were just enjoying the journey. Skin on skin, lips together, hands rubbing backs, and Jake deep inside me.

Instead of the usual moans we shared, there were softly spoken words: "My lover. My friend. I love you. I need you. You're beautiful. You're mine." But, eventually, the friction and the motion, the love and the feelings, all met together in long, powerful orgasms.

We cleaned up and held each other, neither of us

ready to sleep. So, instead, we talked about the move. Jake told me that he'd gotten a job offer from Sheriff Wells, and I was so relieved. I don't think I remember any sort of major crime back when we lived at home. That meant he could still be a police officer there but he wouldn't be in constant danger—the best of both worlds.

That just left my job. Obviously, I couldn't keep doing research once we moved. But, actually, that wasn't disappointing. I was tired of that path and the idea of treating real patients sounded nice. I decided to call our old family doctor that week to talk to him about things, get his advice. Once I figured out what to do about work, Jake and I could tell our families about our plan and put the wheels in motion to leave New York and go back home.

With the decision to move back to Bryerville, a huge weight was lifted off my shoulders. Actually, it felt like multiple weights were lifted—I finally had the necessary push to find a job I could enjoy, which would also have somewhat reasonable hours. We'd be close to my parents, which I knew they'd been wanting since the day we'd moved away. We'd be away from the noise, the grime, and the unbearably fast pace of the city, and Jake would have a much safer job. The only downside was moving away from the friends we'd made in the ten years we'd lived in New York. But, then again, by moving back home, we'd get to reconnect with all our friends from Bryerville, the ones who we'd grown up with.

Between work and my attempts to connect with some folks in Bryerville who I thought could help me decide what to do when we moved back, I had a really busy couple of days. So busy that I *almost* didn't have time to think about the ring. Then, on Thursday, everything came together.

Our old family doctor, Doc Hamilton, returned my call. I didn't even have a chance to ask him for ideas of what I could do because as soon as I told him that we'd be returning to Bryerville, Doc jumped in and offered me a job. Well, a partnership was more like it. Turned out he'd been wanting to slow down for years, but his patients needed him, so he was stuck. With retirement a few years away, he'd been trying to figure out how to transition. That left a perfect spot for me. I could work side by side with Doc for a few years and then take over. That would give Doc a chance to slow down right away but still keep seeing some patients for a little while; it'd be a gradual shift for the patients and for Doc. It sounded perfect. I'd be able to get to know my patients, see them over a lifetime, and really make a difference in their lives.

Not long after I hung up with Doc, I got a call from Edward. The ring was ready. By that point I was almost shaking with anticipation to get our future started. I decided to leave work early, pick up the ring, and make a romantic dinner for Jake. I planned to tell him about the offer from Doc Hamilton so he'd know the last piece of the puzzle was in place for our move, and, most importantly, give him the ring.

After stopping by Edward's store and picking up ingredients for Jake's favorite meal at the market, I got back to our apartment and cleaned up a little. We were both pretty neat, so things never got that dirty, but I wanted everything to be perfect that night. I'd just taken the eggplant out of the oven and started cutting vegetables for the salad, when Jake walked in. He stood behind me, wrapped his arms around me, and pulled me back against him as he ran his lips over my neck.

"I'm surprised you're home. It's only six. And it smells like you made eggplant parmigiana."

His deep voice made my skin tingle and my cock harden. I turned to face him and gave him a gentle kiss. It always amazed me how Jake could be so soft and tender with me sometimes, and other times, when we were in bed and when he recognized that I needed him to be more firm, even rough, well, he could do that too.

I told Jake the good news about Doc Hamilton, but I could tell that he had something on his mind. His eyes were sparkling, but he wasn't smiling. He looked happy, yet anxious. I rubbed my hand on his face to calm him down.

"What's going on? You have a strange look on your face."

Jake sighed and then led me to the couch.

"Nate, did you mean it back home when you said that you want to have kids?"

My heart immediately started racing. I was suddenly filled with the overwhelming realization that our lives were about to change forever. I think I managed to operate my body enough to nod.

"I saw Suzie today. She doesn't want to be a mother. She wants us to take Alexis, Nate. She wants us to adopt her."

A baby. We were being given the opportunity to have a baby. I'm normally a planner. I think things through. I organize. I strategize. I make pro and con lists. And I'd never had a decision as important as this one to make. But, this wasn't a list moment. This was our future and I could feel in my gut that it was right. We were going to have a family.

I got up from the couch and walked toward the door.

"Come on, Jake. Let's go get our daughter."

We went to Suzie's apartment and picked up Alexis. I was horrified at their living conditions, but I didn't say anything. I just thanked Suzie for trusting us with her daughter. Jake told Suzie that he'd talk to an attorney to figure out what we needed to do to formalize the adoption and then he'd let her know. Alexis had very few clothes and no toys so we just put everything in a plastic shopping bag, picked Alexis up, and headed out. I knew we didn't have time to get everything she needed that night, but we stopped at the market downstairs to buy some baby shampoo and formula.

The next morning, Jake called his captain and told him that he was taking a leave of absence. Everything after that was a whirlwind. We hired a lawyer, who suggested that we stay in New York until the adoption became final. It delayed our move home, but it allowed both of us to adopt Alexis, something we couldn't do in Bryerville. And, because of some connections Jake had through work, staying in New York helped make the process take less time. We bought toys, clothes, and baby gear. We took parenting classes, went to baby gyms, and found the family-friendly parks and restaurants in our neighborhood. In the blink of an eye, our lives had completely changed. And, though I would have thought it impossible, I loved Jake even more when I saw him taking care of our baby girl.

Jake accepted the job with the sheriff's office back home and he told Sheriff Wells that he'd start in three months. I did the same thing with Doc Hamilton. And we both told our current jobs that we'd be leaving in a few months. The delay in the move was necessitated by the adoption, but it also gave my mom time to remodel Jake's parents' house so that when we were able to move home, the place would be modernized and ready for our new family. My parents were beside themselves with joy— not only were Jake and I coming home, but they were getting a grandchild.

With everything that was happening in our lives, I never did find the time for the romantic proposal I had planned. I had kept the ring hidden in a file box holding some of my old medical school notes. And then, before I knew it, we were coming to the end of our time in New York. Our adoption of Alexis was finalized, our household items, Lexi's things, and most of our clothes were packed, and I was on my way back to the apartment after a goodbye party with the guys from the lab.

I walked into the apartment and saw Jake, asleep on the couch with Alexis sleeping on his stomach. He was holding her tightly and she looked so peaceful and happy in her daddy's arms. My heart ached with the love I felt for both of them. I walked over to them and kissed Jake's forehead. His eyes fluttered open and he smiled at me.

"Hi, beautiful. Did you have a nice time?"

I smiled at him and picked Alexis up, holding her tight against my chest.

"Yeah, I had fun. I'll put Lexi in her crib and meet you in bed."

I walked into Jake's old bedroom, which we'd been using as Lexi's room, and settled the baby into her crib. Then I found the file box where I had hidden the ring and got it out. I didn't have a candlelight dinner ready, but it would have to be enough. I couldn't wait any longer. I took a few minutes to calm myself down, and then walked back to our bedroom with my hands behind my back, clutching the ring box.

As soon as I opened the door to our bedroom, a warm glow and a calming scent surrounded me. Every surface in the room, most of which were boxes ready for our move, was lined with candles and jars holding flowers. And in one of the few empty areas of floor space was Jake. He was kneeling on one knee. He waited for me to meet his eyes and then he started talking, his voice full of emotion.

"Nate, I have loved you for as long as I can remember. I admire your kindness, your integrity, your intelligence. You make me smile. You make me think. You challenge me. You inspire me to be a better person. I cherish you, Nate. And I'm always going to be here with you. We'll laugh together and cry together. We'll keep growing and changing, Nate. And like everything else we've done in our lives, we'll do it together."

He swallowed, caught his breath and then continued.

"When my parents died, I didn't hold on to much. Mostly just pictures and letters. But I insisted on keeping this."

He held his hand out and showed me a gold ring.

"It was my dad's wedding ring. He inherited it from his grandfather. And I'm not sure how far back before that it went. When I asked for the ring, one of my uncles said he was glad that I was holding onto it so that I could wear it once I got married. Even then I knew, Nate. I knew that I wasn't keeping this ring for myself. I was keeping it with the hope that, one day, you'd love me the way I've always loved you. And then I could give you the ring so you'd always know what you are to me. And that's everything, Nate. You are my everything."

I had tears streaming down my face as I fell to my knees, before Jake. I moved my shaking hands from behind my back, opened the box, and showed him the ring I'd had Edward make. He looked at the ring with the infinity symbols and then back at me with moisture in his eyes. I knew he was remembering that day all those years ago, doing homework at the kitchen table.

Jake took my left hand into his and slipped his dad's ring onto my finger.

"No end, no limit."

We kissed deeply. Then we each pulled back slightly and I gazed into Jake's green eyes. The first eyes I ever remember seeing. The eyes I looked into to calm me down on the first day of kindergarten. The eyes I'd met across the stage to give me courage when we had our elementary school winter play. The eyes I'd looked into before I fell asleep during so many nights growing up and then dreamt about all night. The eyes that had been full of relief and anguish when I woke up in the hospital after the accident that took his parents. The eyes I'd looked into for strength when I needed to talk through any concern that I'd ever had—about school, a job, a guy, anything. And the eyes I knew I'd be looking into for the rest of my life. There, in those green eyes that had carried me through my past, I saw my future.

I picked up his left hand and raised it to my lips, kissing his palm and then the back of his hand, before I slid the ring onto his finger.

"You're my everything too, Jake. We're forever."

THE END

(But wait…there's more—bonus chapter ahead.)

BONUS CHAPTER

When the U.S. Supreme Court released their historic marriage decision, I wanted to celebrate so I wrote a bonus chapter with Nate and Jake's reaction to the wonderful news. I hope you enjoy it. –CC

Jake

SIX YEARS after Nate and I moved back home to Bryerville, it felt like we'd never left. It took no time for us to reconnect with old friends and catch up on all the little details in our family's lives. And though some things about us were different—we had a daughter and we'd added the role of partners to our already multilayered relationship—for the most part, we were still the same guys we'd been all our lives.

Nate was still the smartest person in town, still a nice guy who always had a smile for everyone. I still spent time on the high school football field, as the coach now, and went out for the occasional beer with my old buddies. We lived in the house I grew up in, which was right next door to Nate's parents' house. Our evenings were spent enjoying family barbeques, school plays, and walks under the country sky. To our old friends in New

York, that sounded dull and miserable. To Nate and me, it was a slice of heaven on earth.

I pulled up to our house after practice one evening and caught sight of Nate and Alexis through the front window. He was wearing a pair of jeans that fit his ass just right and a blue T-shirt that I knew made his already gorgeous eyes pop. Our daughter was wearing one of her dozen pink nightgowns and her hair was damp, like she'd just gotten out of the shower. And the two of them were jumping and wiggling and dancing all around the room, occasionally holding imaginary microphones up to their mouths.

When we were kids, Nate and I used to dance with my folks just the same way in that very room. On the nights he slept over, we'd eat supper, get into our sleeping clothes, and then have some family time with my parents. Sometimes it was board games, sometimes we'd watch a movie, and sometimes my mom would turn the stereo up loud and start dancing. She'd always try to get us to join her. My father used to sit on the sofa and smile at her fondly, but he almost never got up. Nate and I usually refused at first, but after a song or two, she'd talk us onto our feet, and then three of us would spin around and sing like mad.

Going on three decades later, my Nate was carrying on that family tradition with our little girl. My heart felt full when I climbed out of my car and walked into our home through the kitchen door.

Normally, I call out to Nate and Alexis when I get home, but with as loud as that music was playing, I knew they wouldn't hear me. Didn't matter. As soon as I approached the living room, Nate knew I was there. He came skipping over and held his arm out to me.

I chuckled as I took his hand and yanked him up against my chest. "You're skipping now, are you?"

He dropped a kiss on my lips. "I sure am. Alexis says skipping is *way* more fun than walking." He looked back over his shoulder and increased his volume so he could be heard over the loud music when he said, "Isn't that right, jelly bean?"

"Yes! Skip over here, Papa, you'll see."

"You heard the boss," Nate said with a wink. "We're skipping."

If anyone walked by our house and looked in our window at that precise moment, they'd have pissed themselves laughing at the sight of a six-foot-four-inch, two hundred fifty pound man skipping across the room. Even Nate was having a hard time keeping it together. His lips were pursed tight and he was shaking. I stuck my tongue out at him and then focused on our daughter.

Alexis was singing and dancing full tilt. I tried to catch up, but I'd never been a great dancer. Nate, on the other hand, looked gorgeous when he moved to music. I looked over at him.

He shimmied over to me and leaned up so his mouth was close to my ear. "If our daughter wasn't here, you'd be in sooo much trouble right now."

I gripped his hips and we swayed. "Is that right? Goofy dancing does it for you now, baby?"

He rose up on the balls of his feet and gave me a

quick peck on the lips. "It does when you're the one doing the dancing, Jake." Then he shook his ass as he backed away and threw his arms up in the air, waving them from side to side in concert with his hips.

I watched Nate as we danced. His blond hair was damp with sweat, his cheeks were flushed, and he was rolling his hips in a way that made my mouth go dry and my dick get hard. Our eyes connected, and he dragged his gaze down my body, lingering at my crotch.

I assumed he could see my need because suddenly he stopped dancing and said, "It's dinnertime." Then he walked over to the iPod and turned off the music. "Let's go wash up."

TWO HOURS later, dinner had been eaten, the dishes were washed, and Alexis was asleep in her bed after two stories. I was sitting on our bed, taking off my shoes and socks, when Nate walked into our room. He closed and locked the door and then leaned back against it.

"So," he said.

I raised my eyebrows in a silent question.

"I figure you'll want a shower." He stripped his shirt off over his head and tossed it in the direction of the laundry basket.

"You figure right." I pulled my shirt off too. And my throw landed inside the basket.

He unbuttoned and unzipped his jeans. "From

the way you were looking at me when we were dancin', I figure you want to fool around too." He hooked his thumbs though his briefs and jeans and shoved them down to his ankles. Then he raised each bare foot, stepped out of his clothes, and kicked them toward the basket.

"You're two for two, Nate," I said. I stood up, pushed my track pants and jock down, and used my foot to flip them in the air. I caught them with one hand, tossed them into the basket, and then crossed my arms over my chest and met Nate's eyes.

He raked his gaze from my face to my feet and back up again. "Which..." His voice broke on the word, and he swallowed hard. "Which one do you want to do first?"

I lowered my eyes to Nate's groin. His pink, smooth cock was standing tall and proud in a nest of blond curls. As I continued to look at him, his breathing quickened and his dick rose even higher. I licked my lips and, seemingly in reaction, a bead of moisture dripped from his slit and slid down his shaft.

I slowly lifted my gaze, and when our eyes met again, I hoarsely said, "Why do we have to choose?"

He shuddered, his skin flushed, and his pupils dilated. I decided there was way too much distance between us, so I walked toward him until our bodies were touching from knee to chest and every place in between. Then I pushed his hair off his face and leaned down, letting my hot breath ghost over his mouth, his jaw, and finally his ear.

"Let me tell you what's going to happen." I

wrapped my hand around his dick, and he whimpered. "We're going to get in the shower, and I'm going to do you up against those little green tiles." I gave his shaft a couple of pumps. "Then I'm going to wash you up real thoroughly all over." He thrust forward and cried out. I cupped his balls with my free hand and squeezed them gently. "After that, I'm taking you to bed, and if you're still conscious, I'm going to fuck you through the mattress."

"I want you so bad, Jake," he rasped.

"Me too, baby." I bit down on his earlobe. "I want you every fucking second of every fucking day." I slammed my mouth against his, licking and sucking and tasting. "Let me show you how much."

I took Nate's hand and pulled him behind me, through the doorway of our bathroom and into our shower. Then I turned on the water and followed through on my promise by gently pushing him up against the wall. He planted his palms on the tile, widened his stance, and tipped his ass up, giving me better access.

As hot as we were for each other, I didn't bother with any foreplay. I just reached for the bottle of lube, coated my shaft, and lined up with Nate's hole. Then I kissed his shoulders and nape as I slid into his hot, tight body.

"Jake," he said with a sigh.

"Right here, baby." I held onto his hips, pulled out until just my crown was inside his channel, and then slammed back into him again. "Right fucking here."

"Ah!" he cried out. "Ah! Ah! Ah!"

I didn't slow down, didn't let up; I just pumped

in and out of his body relentlessly until I knew I couldn't hold out any longer. Then I curled my arm around his hip, grasped his dick, and stroked him in time with my last couple of thrusts.

The sound of Nate calling out my name at the apex of his pleasure, along with feeling his release dripping over my hand, sent me over the edge. "Nate!" I yelled one last time as I shoved in as hard as I could and then stilled, pulsing deep inside his welcoming body. When I was drained and breathless, I dropped my forehead on his shoulder and kissed his damp skin. "Nate," I whispered and squeezed him tightly.

He covered my hand with his and made a happy, contented sound. We stayed in that position for a few minutes, happy to be together again after a day apart.

"I'm beat," Nate said with a deep sigh. "Let's finish up and go to bed, okay?"

"Yup." I planted one last kiss on his nape and then reached for the shampoo. "I'll get you washed and we can get out."

I poured the liquid into my hand and then lathered his hair, taking a few seconds to massage his scalp. Then I washed his body, paying extra special attention to his fine ass.

"Jesus, Jake, are you playing with me or cleaning me?" he asked when I crooked my finger inside his hole and tapped his gland.

"A little of both," I answered. Then I stepped back and said, "Go ahead and rinse off, baby."

I soaped myself up quickly, finger-combed

shampoo through my hair, and took my turn under the water. Then we were off to bed.

I WAS lying on my back with my head propped up on a bunch of pillows. Nate was on his belly with his head resting on my chest.

"Aaron called before you got home tonight," he said as he traced my nipples with his long fingers. "He and Zach are coming in this weekend."

I ran my fingers through his soft hair and looked at him. The years had been damn kind to my Nate. He had filled out a little, so though he was still thin, he looked stronger. And he had a few lines next to his eyes when he laughed now, which made him even sexier. Plus he was always happy, always flashing that knee-buckling smile. I was a very lucky man.

"They staying with us?" I asked.

"Yeah." He chuckled. "You know how Zach gets all twitchy when he spends too much time at Uncle Fred and Aunt Mimi's house."

I smiled at the memory of their last visit. "Remember how he freaked out about the plates?"

"I do," Nate said. "And you have to admit it's odd how Aunt Mimi keeps the table set all the time with plates she won't let people use."

"I know. Why have plates if you can't eat off them?"

"Who knows?" Nate shrugged. "They also have

that formal living room where nobody's allowed to sit on the furniture."

"Right. Poor Zach. I don't know how he held it together when Mimi told him those weren't sitting chairs." I shook my head and grinned at the memory. "Did Aaron say why they were coming in? They were just here two weeks ago."

Nate shook his head. "He said they had news to share, but he wanted to do it in person."

Given the recent Supreme Court decision and knowing Aaron, it wasn't hard to guess what that news was going to be. "They getting married?" I asked.

"That's my guess," Nate answered.

"He happy?"

Nate looked up at me and grinned. "Oh yeah. Aaron's crazy about Zach, you know that. And Zach looks at Aaron like he hung the moon."

"Yeah, he does." I chuckled. "I'm glad Aaron finally has someone in his life who feels that way about him. He deserves to be happy."

"He does," Nate agreed.

I stroked his hair gently, and his eyes fluttered shut. We lay in silence for a bit, sharing gentle touches.

"Your mom called me at work today," I said eventually.

Nate opened his eyes and then rolled them. "Let me guess—she tried to talk you into having a big wedding in her backyard."

I grinned, reached for Nate's hand, and twined our fingers together. "Yup. You get the same speech?"

He nodded and said, "What'd you tell her?"

I raised his hand to my mouth and kissed the back of it. "I told her we already got married in New York last summer, and we weren't looking to renew our vows quite yet, but that I'd talk to her at the twenty-five-year mark."

Nate snorted. "I'll just bet that went over really well. She's still fuming that we got married without her and my dad there."

I cupped Nate's cheek with my free hand. "That was just between us, baby, nobody else. I know Mama C and Ted don't understand, but I wouldn't change a thing about that day."

He turned his face and kissed my palm. "I wouldn't either," he whispered. When he looked at me again, his eyes were wet. "I wouldn't change a thing about the past thirty-five years with you, Jake."

THE END

ABOUT THE AUTHOR

Cardeno C.—CC to friends—is a hopeless romantic who wants to add a lot of happiness and a few *awwws* into a reader's day. Writing is a nice break from real life as a corporate type and volunteer work with gay rights organizations. Cardeno's stories range from sweet to intense, contemporary to paranormal, long to short, but they always include strong relationships and walks into the happily-ever-after sunset.

Cardeno's *Home*, *Family*, and *Mates* series have received awards from Love Romances and More Golden Roses, Rainbow Awards, the Goodreads M/M Romance Group, and various reviewers. But even more special to CC are heartfelt reactions from readers, like, "You bring joy and love and make it part of the every day."

Email: cardenoc@gmail.com

Website: www.cardenoc.com

Twitter: @CardenoC

Facebook: http://www.facebook.com/CardenoC

Pinterest: http://www.pinterest.com/cardenoC

Blog: http://caferisque.blogspot.com

OTHER BOOKS BY CARDENO C.

SIPHON
Johnnie

HOPE
McFarland's Farm
Jesse's Diner

PACK
Blue Mountain
Red River

HOME
He Completes Me
Home Again
Just What the Truth Is
Love at First Sight
The One Who Saves Me
Where He Ends and I Begin
Walk With Me

FAMILY
The Half of Us
Something in the Way He Needs
Strong Enough
More Than Everything

MATES
In Your Eyes
Until Forever Comes
Wake Me Up Inside

NOVELS
Strange Bedfellows
Perfect Imperfections
Control *(with Mary Calmes)*

NOVELLAS
A Shot at Forgiveness
All of Me
Places in Time
In Another Life & Eight Days
Jumping In

AVAILABLE NOW

He Completes Me
(2nd Edition)

Not even his mother's funeral can convince self-proclaimed party boy Zach Johnson to tone down his snark or think about settling down. He is who he is, and he refuses to change for anyone. When straight-laced, compassionate Aaron Paulson claims he's falling for him, Zach is certain Aaron sees him as another project, one more lost soul for the idealistic Aaron to save. But Zach doesn't need to be fixed and he refuses to be with someone who sees him as broken.

Patience is one of Aaron's many virtues. He has waited years for a man who can share his heart and complete his life and he insists Zach is the one. Pride, fear, and old hurts wither in the wake of Aaron's adoring loyalty, and as Zach reevaluates his perceptions of love and family, he finds himself tempted to believe in the impossible: a happily-ever-after.

Home Again
(2nd Edition)

Imposing, temperamental Noah Forman wakes up in a hospital and can't remember how he got there. He holds it together, taking comfort in the fact that the man he has loved since childhood is on the way. But when his one and only finally arrives, Noah is horrified to discover that he doesn't remember anything from the past three years.

Loyal, serious Clark Lehman built a life around the person who insisted from their first meeting that they were meant to be together. Now, years later, two men whose love has never faltered must relive their most treasured and most painful moments in order to recover lost memories and secure their future.

Just What the Truth Is
(2nd Edition)

People-pleaser Ben Forman has been in the closet so long he has almost convinced himself he is straight, but his denial train gets derailed when hotshot lawyer Micah Trains walks into his life. Micah is brilliant, funny, driven... and he assumes Ben is gay and starts dating him. Finding himself truly happy for the first time, Ben doesn't have the willpower to resist Micah's affection.

When his relationship with Micah heats up, Ben realizes has a problem: his parents won't tolerate a gay son and self-confident Micah isn't the type to hide. If Ben wants to maintain his hold on his happiness, he'll have to decide what's important and own up to the truth of who he is. The trouble is figuring out just what that truth is.

Love at First Sight
(2nd Edition)

The moment naïve, optimistic Jonathan Doyle glimpses a gorgeous blue-eyed stranger from afar, he believes in love at first sight. Unfortunately, he loses sight of the man before they meet and then spends years desperately trying to find him. Just as he is about to give up, Jonathan gets a break and finally encounters David Miller face to face.

Successful, confident David turns Jonathan's previously lonely life into a fairy tale, giving him more than he ever imagined. But the years spent searching were hard on Jonathan, and he's terrified his young son and scandalous past will destroy his blossoming relationship. For David and Jonathan to build a future together, they'll both have to dig deep: David for the courage to share himself in a way he's never considered and Jonathan for the strength to tell the truth.

The One Who Saves Me
(2nd Edition)

At fourteen, Andrew Thompson and Caleb Lakes become best friends. As the years pass, they stand by each other through family trauma, school, and the start of their careers. They share their first sexual experiences, learning and experimenting, and they talk each other through countless dates and breakups.

Decades of trust and loyalty build a deep and abiding friendship, one that surpasses any relationship in their lives. But when the parameters of their unique friendship change, neither man knows how to break out of their established roles to build something new. After all, boyfriends come and go, but best friends are forever.

Walk With Me
(2nd Edition)

When Eli Block steps into his parents' living room and sees his childhood crush sitting on the couch, he starts a shameless campaign to seduce the young rabbi. Unfortunately, Seth Cohen barely remembers Eli and he resolutely shuts down all his advances. As a tenuous and then binding friendship forms between the two men, Eli must find a way to move past his unrequited love while still keeping his best friend in his life. Not an easy feat when the same person occupies both roles.

Professional, proper Seth is shocked by Eli's brashness, overt sexuality, and easy defiance of societal norms. But he's also drawn to the happy, funny, light-filled man. As their friendship deepens over the years, Seth watches Eli mature into a man he admires and respects. When Seth finds himself longing for what Eli had so easily offered, he has to decide whether he's willing to veer from his safe life-plan to build a future with Eli.